Dusters and Dreams

Dusters and Dreams

Hannah Buckland

Ambassador International
Greenville, South Carolina & Belfast, Northern Ireland

www.ambassador-international.com

Dusters and Dreams

ISBN: 978-1-62020-832-8
eISBN: 978-1-62020-838-0

Scripture quotations taken from The Authorized Version.

Cover Design and Page Layout by Hannah Nichols
eBook Conversion by Anna Riebe Raats

AMBASSADOR INTERNATIONAL
Emerald House
411 University Ridge Suite B14
Greenville, SC 29601, USA
www.ambassador-international.com

AMBASSADOR BOOKS
The Mount
2 Woodstock Link
Belfast, BT6 8DD, Northern Ireland, UK
www.ambassadormedia.co.uk

The colophon is a trademark of Ambassador, a Christian publishing company.

ACKNOWLEDGMENTS

I would like to thank my husband for his interest in and support of my writing. Also our sons - our own version of Tom and Dan.

CHAPTER 1

WALKING HOME FROM THE VILLAGE bakery with the sun on her back, Rebecca resisted the urge to skip. Ignoring all grim sayings about the month of March and the wintery conditions it can bring, she was as confident as the roadside primroses that winter was almost behind them. Soon lambs would be playing in the meadows, and the woodland would be carpeted in bluebells. Skipping seemed an appropriate response to the coming of spring, but in the eyes of the good women of the parish, it may have been deemed inappropriate conduct for a vicar's wife. Many of the formidable matriarchs had welcomed her with wholehearted, even motherly, interest into her new role in village life. But Rebecca was well aware that the churchwarden's wife and not a few of the charity knitting group could never quite forget how shamefully slow she was at knitting . . . or the fact that she had been a domestic servant.

Soon Rebecca's journey took her out of the village, away from twitching curtains and along quiet country lanes to the little cottage she shared with her husband, Jack. When Jack was appointed as relief clergyman to Capford, the powers that be had struggled to find suitable accommodation in the village and so had rented a small property in a neighbouring hamlet. Here he and his capable mother had set up camp, here Rebecca had come to pay a courtesy visit, from here she and Jack had courted, and now here they lived in marital bliss. With characteristic wisdom, Jack's mother had insisted the newlyweds should start married life alone together and had moved out to live with her daughter Elizabeth. Jack's sudden posting to Capford was due to the austere Rev. Sidney Brinkhill, the regular rector, having had a serious fall and fracturing his thigh bone. This injury had confined him to bed and resulted in the arch-deacon sending in Reverend Jack Hayworth. This was a two-fold blessing: the congregation, who for many years had suffered spiritual starvation under Rev. Sidney Brinkhill's dry, dogmatic ministry, benefited from Jack's evangelical, Christ-centred preaching; and, even more amazingly in Rebecca's eyes, as a result of Rev. Brinkhill's accident, she had met her husband. At the time when she was contemplating leaving her post as a housekeeper at a manor in the parish and wondering what to do with her solitary life, Jack had arrived and completely swept her off her feet (despite a twisted ankle).

Rev. Sidney Brinkhill's recovery was slow. He had been able to drag himself off his sick-bed to conduct Jack and Rebecca's wedding service, but his ashen face and frail frame made everyone fear that the next big village occasion would be his funeral service. The church officers had firmly persuaded him back into further convalescence, and Jack continued filling the post *pro tem*. Now the Hayworths had been married for five happy months, and still there was no mention of Rev. Sidney Brinkhill's return.

As Rebecca walked along the quiet, muddy lane to their cottage, she once again rejoiced in the poor state of the road. Unlike many clergymen's, Jack's evenings were seldom disturbed. Members of the congregation would think twice before sending for pastoral assistance after dark. The inconvenience of wading through mud or saddling their horse put their spiritual need into perspective, and they often decided to wait until morning. Thus, the Hayworths' little cottage was their private nest and cocoon. During the winter months Rebecca had replaced the old, shabby curtains with ones of her own choice and making. After three years of being a domestic servant, subject to the will and whim of her employers, Rebecca was now the mistress of her own home and delighted in her new role. Baking, cooking, ironing, and cleaning for one's own husband—and an appreciative husband at that—was a privilege, not a chore. After years of loneliness, Rebecca blossomed in the sunshine of Jack's love, laughter, and company.

The potatoes had roasted to fragrant perfection when Rebecca heard Jack's feet at the back door. Her heart swelled with joy as she anticipated another cosy evening together by the roaring fire. After rubbing her greasy hands on her apron, she went to greet her husband, but one look at his face told Rebecca that all was not well, and his absent-minded kiss confirmed her suspicions.

"What is wrong?" she asked, suddenly feeling anxious.

"I'll explain over dinner" was his un-reassuring response.

The quicker Rebecca tried get the food on the table, the longer she took. The gravy refused to boil and the Yorkshire puddings to go crisp, but finally they sat down, said grace, and started eating. However, until she knew what had upset Jack so badly, the food would be tasteless in Rebecca's mouth.

"So, what happened today?" she asked, unable to bear the suspense a moment longer.

Jack put down his knife and fork and lifted his gaze to meet hers.

"The Rev. Sidney Brinkhill is retiring to Dorset, and I am to parson the parish on a permanent basis."

Relief flooded over Rebecca.

"And what is so bad about that?" she asked.

"We are to move into the vicarage" came the unexpected reply.

Rebecca's relief ebbed away rapidly. "Not that dark, dreary house . . ." Rebecca moaned.

"Yes."

"Surrounded by overgrown elm trees . . . "

"And old, sunken graves."

They munched the delicious food in sober silence. When Jack had emptied his plate (his appetite seemingly unimpaired by the news), he leaned back in his chair and put his hands behind his head.

"The problem is that I still won't actually be the vicar. Brinkhill has the freehold of the vicarage and technically remains the vicar until he dies. He will just continue to pay me as his curate."

"So, this isn't a promotion?"

"No, thanks to obscure ecclesiastical legalities."

"So why do we have to move?"

"The church wardens and Brinkhill want us to be 'more accessible.' They obviously have not considered how difficult it will be to run that huge vicarage on a curate's income."

They sat silently, mulling over the difficulties, until Rebecca asked, "What happens when Brinkhill dies?"

"I'm not sure, but I suppose we will be offered the freehold."

If packing boxes and gradually watching their little cottage grow bare and empty was joyless, much more so was the task of unpacking at the cavernous vicarage. Jack and Rebecca had dutifully waved the Brinkhill family off the premises. Rev. Brinkhill departed with the air of a last prophet leaving the country, Mrs. Brinkhill barely acknowledged the young couple as she fussed around her invalid husband, and Miss Brinkhill's farewell look at Jack was a mixture of haute disapproval and condescending pity, which stated loudly, "You could have done so much better." If Miss Brinkhill could have shaken the dust of Capford off her feet, Rebecca felt sure she would have delighted in doing so, but it being March there was no dust to shake—only mud. Having watched the trio disappear out of sight ("Just to make sure they have really gone," whispered Jack), the daunted couple went inside to see how the men were progressing with furniture moving.

Their much-loved furniture, which had snugly filled the cottage, now stood sad and small in the vast, forbidding rooms. The whistles and banter of the workmen seemed as incongruous here as it would be in a church.

Will I ever manage to laugh or joke here? Rebecca asked herself.

The workmen soon finished their task, leaving the Hayworths in the silence and dusk, surrounded by boxes and odd assortments of household paraphernalia. Rebecca wanted to sit down and cry, but instead she stoked the range and put the kettle on for tea.

They had yet to decide which reception rooms would be best suited to the function of a study, dining room, or sitting room, but both strongly agreed that Rev. Brinkhill's former chamber should not be the marital bedroom. It was by far the stateliest room upstairs, but as Jack put it, "If we were to attempt a chaste kiss, I would feel the ire of the Brinkhills resting upon me."

Rebecca laughed. "How can we get rid of their lingering presence?"

"How does one exorcise Brinkhills?" replied Jack.

"If anyone hears us talking like this," Rebecca said in playful warning, "we will be forcibly removed from house and parish for heresy before we have even unpacked."

So, with various outrageous suggestions of methods of exorcism and more giggling than the old vicarage had heard in a decade, the couple finished their tea and went to bed.

The architecture of the Capford vicarage showed great lack of imagination. At the front was a grand door which led into a long, overly wide hall ending with a back door. Off the hall on the left side were three doors, two being reception rooms, and the one nearest the back door being the kitchen. Off the hall on the right side were three doors: a reception room, a study, and a pantry. Thus, no rooms interlinked. The stone-floored central area had no windows except three prison-cell ones above each door, which barely allowed in any light. What the hall did allow in though, were drafts. On windy days (and especially nights), these drafts moaned and howled their way under the doors as if they were the dis-embodied occupants of the surrounding graves. When alone for an evening, Rebecca had to steel herself to keep robustly sensible and not let her lively imagination turn unbiblical. One of her first sewing projects was to make draft-excluders for both ends of the corridor, thus eliminating the moaning intrusions on all but the wildest nights. But although the drafts could be somewhat conquered, nothing could be done about the icy coldness of the stone-tile floor. For storing milk and meat, it would have been ideal, but fearing the raised eyebrows of lady visitors, Rebecca ignored her husband's suggestion of thus utilizing the coolness, and kept their provisions hidden in the pantry like normal, regulated families do.

If the hall was chilling, the curate and his wife were warmed by the practical kindness of the villagers during the first few days of moving upheaval. Warm pots of steaming casseroles, dishes of meat pudding, and jars of milk were offered at the door, along with good wishes and expressions of appreciation that Jack had been given the role of vicar. As Rebecca gratefully received a meat pie from one little girl, the child confided, "Don't eat that corner, cos the cat ate a bit."

On inspection, Rebecca could see some pastry was missing.

"Thank you for the warning," she said with a chuckle, mentally deciding to cut off the corner.

"Me muver said you 'ave te be 'onest with vicars and the likes."

"Is that so?" Rebecca said.

"Yep, cos otherwise they'll pray against ya."

"How extraordinary!" Rebecca exclaimed, then bending down to her level, she told the child, "I can assure you Reverend Hayworth never 'prays against' anyone."

"Well, that's alright then, ain't it?" replied the girl, turning around to go. Looking back over her shoulder, she added, "But I told the troof anyway, didn't I?"

As they ate the (trimmed) pie that evening, Rebecca rehearsed the incident to her husband.

"Who do they think I am?" he asked, aghast. "Some sort of papal priest cum witch doctor?"

"Casting magic spells," Rebecca added.

"You're the only one who casts spells," Jack declared with a laugh. "I've been under one ever since I met you. Anyway, I believe the girl is in your Sunday school class, so maybe you can correct her erroneous theology."

"And I believe her mother is in your congregation, so maybe you can enlighten her."

CHAPTER 2

THAT EVENING, HALF A MILE down the road at Biggenden Manor, Edward bade his visitors good night and closed the front door. Slamming it shut would have been very satisfying, but good manners prevailed, and he resisted the temptation. He reluctantly crossed the hallway to the drawing room where Sophia was sure to be waiting, keen for a verbal dissection of the evening's entertainment. But to his relief, his wife has already retired to bed.

Kicking off his shoes, Edward drew a chair to the fire and slumped into it. There he sat, motionlessly staring at the flickering flames. How irritated he was with his hideous guests! And how utterly irritated he was with himself! After eating far too much rich food and drinking far too much wine, his wealthy neighbours and so-called friends had sat around grumbling about their staff and farmhands. They had mocked their ignorance and stubbornness at not embracing change and agricultural inventions. Over Edward's best port, they had exchanged swelling threats of how they would deal with any labourer who resisted the introduction of threshing machines and the likes. Their eyes glinted with malice as they boasted of high-handed mastery and gossiped about newspaper stories of labourers sabotaging new equipment. And all the time Edward sat, sipping in silence. How he now wished he had spoken up! With some satisfaction, he imagined swiping their glasses from their pudgy hands and the startled look on their fat, ruddy faces as he ordered them out the door. But the satisfaction was short-lived as he contemplated the hard lot of the labouring class. Over the last decade or so, life had changed more for them than it had for centuries—and not for the better. Amazing new inventions like the threshing machine and mechanical weaving machines had put many people out of work. Country folks desperate for jobs were being uprooted from the village communities their families had been part of for generations and moved to anonymous, crowded, inhospitable towns seeking work. Their once much-valued rural skills, passed on from father to son and learned with pain and diligence, were now outdated and redundant.

Edward thought of his own staff. Even at this time of night, various maids were busy in the kitchen and scullery washing the dirty dishes of his visitors, and out in the frosty meadow, Mr. Brookes, his faithful shepherd, would be tending the lambing ewes.

This thought galvanised Edward into action. He left his comfortable armchair and, drawing back a curtain, looked out into the night until he spotted what he was searching for. There in the distance was the wobbling lamp light—just as he had predicted, Mr. Brookes was still at work. Hardly knowing what he was doing, even less why, Edward crept upstairs, changed into the thick, old trousers that Sophia had threatened to throw away, and having dressed warmly, he stole out of the house toward the sheep pens. Rex, his dog, noticing Edward's departure, appeared from the warm kennel and stretched, hoping for a nocturnal walk.

"Sorry, old boy," whispered Edward, "but you would scare the ewes."

The frosty night air dispelled any remaining sense of tiredness from overindulgence, and Edward felt reinvigorated as his boots crunched the frozen grass. Within the cosy protection of the sheep hurdles, most of the flock were quietly slumbering, undisturbed by their shepherd's familiar presence. But in one corner, Mr. Brookes had a ewe on her side and was half kneeling on her to keep her still. With his big, weather-beaten hands, he was gently easing the ewe's teat into her reluctant lamb's mouth. Edward crept forward, not wanting to disturb the process, but curious to see the lamb's reaction. The lamb refused to suck, but Mr. Brookes patiently repeated the process, squirting some milk into the lamb's mouth, which he deftly opened with his thumb and forefinger. Finally, the penny dropped and the lamb sucked vigorously on the swollen teat. Mr. Brookes did not relax his hold of the ewe or the lamb but now could acknowledge the arrival of his employer with a nod. Edward watched the newborn lamb as it sucked steadily and occasionally wagged its tail. Eventually the ewe's patience ran out, and she gave a disgruntled kick, dislodging her lamb from the teat.

"Okay, ol' gal," said the shepherd as he let her go. Mr. Brookes slowly stood up and stretched. "It don't 'alf give ye pins and needles in ya legs, sittin' like that," he said with a laugh, jiggling from one foot to the other. "And what brings you 'ere, sir?"

"I saw your lamp light still moving around and wondered how things were."

"Ahh, thank ye. 'Tis a normal night—the action starts once the ewes relax in the darkness."

"So, you are busy?"

"Yep, and Joe too. Look over there. One has just started, and the other side, one's 'aving 'er second."

"Can I help, please?" asked Edward, suddenly longing to do something useful.

"Well, I reckon ye can. Just roll up that sleeve of yorn and pull out 'er second one—'tis easier than the first—while I see to the tuther."

Edward cautiously approached the ewe and was relieved that she didn't attempt to stand up or run away. With one knee gently anchoring the sheep to the ground, as he had seen Mr. Brookes do, he gently pulled the two slippery hoofs.

"Just ease them out, one at a time," instructed the shepherd, keeping a watchful eye while dealing with another ewe.

Edward pulled, and as he did, a little head appeared, nose first.

"Gently ease it out, pulling back and down."

With hardly any effort, the whole body slipped out, and the new lamb thrashed about, steaming warm in the cold night air.

"Clear 'is mouth and get 'im to 'is mother."

Edward did as he was bidden, then looked in wonder as the contented new mother licked her lamb lovingly and answered its first call with low, reassuring bleats. Within minutes the wobbly wet lamb was trying out its oversized limbs and staggering unsteadily. The mother hauled herself up and followed her wayward offspring. Hunger must have kicked in, for soon the lamb was sniffing out the udder and making erratic lunges toward the teats.

"It don't take 'em long," Mr. Brookes said with a chuckle.

"It is wonderful," agreed Edward.

CHAPTER 3

THE VICARAGE GRADUALLY BECAME MORE ship-shape, but despite Rebecca and Jack's best efforts, it did not become cosy or homely. They did their best to ignore the vast middle room. The Brinkhills had left a large mahogany table and matching chairs, and their presence stubbornly lingered. The kitchen was big enough to comfortably hold the Hayworth's dining table, so they decided to eat there, designating the dining room for high days and holy days—or so they ignorantly thought. The members of numerous church and village committees knew otherwise: this room was pivotal in parish life and the meeting place for all local groups. Not only was the room commandeered into action, but so were the newlyweds. Without so much as a "by your leave," Jack found himself on every committee from the Church Bell Restoration Committee to the Prince Albert Memorial Fund. Rebecca found herself on every ladies' committee, of which there was an abundant number.

The Ladies' Committee for Charitable Endeavours was made up of all the notable matriarchs in the village, including the church warden's wife and many of the knitting group. It was undoubtedly the most illustrious women's committee in the village. Rebecca felt her membership of it had been allowed somewhat grudgingly and that she would have to prove her worth. But she was prepared for the first meeting: the dining room fire was lit early to warm the room thoroughly, she had baked tea loaves and scones to go with a cup of tea, and the house was clean and tidy.

At three o'clock in the afternoon, the ladies started arriving. Some were more successful than others at concealing their curiosity over the couple's possessions and the changes they had made to the interior of the vicarage.

Trying to appear more confident than she felt in committee meeting matters, Rebecca breezily suggested they start "with a nice cup of tea and piece of cake." A sharp intake of breath was audible.

The sidesman's wife tutted. "That is not how Mrs. Brinkhill would start the meeting."

"We normally attend to the business first," said another.

"Then after that she served the meal."

The meal! Rebecca's knees went weak. The Committee of Charitable Endeavours had to endeavour to be charitable to Rebecca as she apologetically explained her ignorance of the normal meeting ritual. They graciously allowed Rebecca to serve tea and cake. Mrs. Collins, the church warden's wife, presided over the meeting and soon engineered to manage the teapot too. A hard stare from her accompanied by a delicate head tilt toward the pot saw Rebecca hurrying to the kitchen to refill it. On one such visit, she not only took the teapot but also whisked off the almost empty cake plate, determined that Jack would have at least the final slice of her tea loaf.

Rebecca had wrongly assumed that the charitable endeavours of the committee were village-based but quickly learned that, for them, charity did not begin at home. Most of their fundraising effort was for overseas missions. This did not prevent a thorough discussion of village life, for "we need to keep abreast with local news to ascertain where there is need for our own private alms giving and prayers," explained Mrs. Collins in case anyone suspected the women of gossip.

The Sunday school teachers' meetings were of a very different nature, although they were in the same room and around the same table. Tea and cake was a welcome innovation, as previously nothing had been served. The Sunday school superintendent, Mr. Grey, opened with reading and prayer and conducted the whole meeting in a very business-like manner, while still allowing for relevant discussion. Each term the teachers would decide on a biblical theme to teach and how best to get the salient points across to each age group. Some teachers emphasised moralizing the children, and some emphasised evangelism. Some thought the children ought to be catechized and learn by rote, while others preferred dramatic, lively storytelling. Mr. Grey veered toward the catechizing camp but diplomatically left it to each teacher to run his or her class as they saw fit and as their talent allowed. Rebecca had the infant class and was definitely of the lively story telling school of thought. After every meeting Mr. Grey politely but sincerely thanked her for allowing them to use the dining room "and for the delicious sustenance so kindly provided," whereas Mrs. Collins gave the impression Rebecca should be humbly grateful that the good ladies of Capford had graced her with their company.

If Rebecca did not look forward to committee meetings with unmitigated joy, one thing that gave her great satisfaction in her role of vicar's wife was visiting the sick or needy. She knew what was expected of her from her mother's example. A good vicar's wife must have a discreet ear to the ground at all times to discover who is ill, in need, bereaved, or has recently given birth, and be one of the first to visit, armed with a suitable gift and a relevant Scripture reading. During her employment at Biggenden, she had gained experience in these visitations as Mr. Thorpe had wiggled out of his landlord duty of visiting his ill tenants by calling it ladies' work and delegating it to Rebecca, his housekeeper. It was a rather uncomfortable arrangement, for she often felt she had no right to intrude into people's lives at a crisis point and felt like a bit of a fraud playing Lady Bountiful at her employer's expense. But the tenants were usually grateful for the visit, and Rebecca built up several strong friendships. Now she was the vicar's wife, no one doubted her suitability to visit, and her work was made easier by the fact that she already knew many of the villagers from her previous role.

Back in their little cottage, Jack and Rebecca had prayed for guidance regarding where they should serve the Lord and had felt ready to go anywhere for Him and His cause. An inner-city parish, a rough sea-side church—they were willing to go anywhere for His name's sake. It had taken them a while to get over the disappointment of realising that instead of asking them to up sticks and move some great distance for Him, the Lord wanted them to move a mile and a half down the road, to the dreary Capford vicarage and continue His work there. Their attitude was rather like Naaman's when he was told to dip himself in the River Jordan. The Lord had to rebuke them, like Naaman's servant did, and point out that as they would have willingly done a big thing for Him, they should be just as willing to do something seemingly small and unheroic. With touching sincerity, they looked deep within themselves and realised maybe pride had made them want to do something amazing, not purely a desire to work for their Saviour.

But once this problem was dealt with, they both privately committed themselves to Capford and wholeheartedly set to work, with the text "Whatsoever thine hand findeth to do, do it with all thy might" ringing in their ears. And what their hand did not find to do, they could be sure some villager's hand would find it and deftly delegate it to the vicarage pair!

Thus, they were busy week in and week out. Instead of running an organised household like most women, Rebecca often had to abandon her regulated plans for a laundry Monday, baking Friday, etc. and just do chores when she could fit them in—often working late into the evening. She had prided herself on being methodical in her work after a few years in domestic service and having been rigorously trained to Mrs. Milton's exacting standards, but now she was pathetically relieved if she had managed to press and starch her husband's Sunday shirt before Saturday evening.

One evening as the exhausted Rebecca was heating her pressing irons on the kitchen range, Jack appeared from his study.

"This has to stop," he insisted. "You are no longer a domestic skivvy; you are my wife, and I am not going to stand by and watch you work yourself to the bone."

Rebecca looked up, surprised at this outburst. "So says the man who works in his study every night."

"Not anymore," he replied. "From now on I will plan some uninterrupted time in my study each week, freeing up some evening hours to spend at my own fireside with my wife."

They looked at each other, both suspecting this plan might fail but sincerely hoping it would succeed.

"And as for you, my dear," he continued, "you need to hire a daily maid."

"That would be an expense!" Rebecca argued.

"An expense well worth paying for if you can relax in the knowledge that the household chores are taken care of."

Rebecca gave Jack a big hug. "That sounds a lovely idea—how kind of you to think of it!"

"Good. Now I will shut my concordance. Take those pressing irons off the heat and put the kettle on instead. Tonight we will pretend to be in our dear old cottage."

The following afternoon Rebecca purposefully left the vicarage with two missions. One involved Mrs. Kemp and the other, Mrs. Brookes. Mrs. Kemp had been the former cook at Biggenden while Rebecca was employed there. She was a kind, motherly sort and now lived with her rapidly aging husband in her daughter's family cottage in the village. Mrs. Kemp lived a very stationary life, moving from her armchair next to the kitchen stove only when strictly necessary. This was due to rheumatism. But that kitchen was the heart of the house, where her daughter toiled and her grandchildren played, so Mrs. Kemp was perfectly satisfied. Rebecca knew she would receive a warm welcome and was not disappointed. The children were at school, leaving the kitchen comparatively calm. Mr. Kemp was in a rocking chair in the corner of the room, fast asleep with a blanket over his knees, and there he remained for the duration of Rebecca's visit. After exchanging news over a cup of tea, she explained her mission.

"Mrs. Kemp, I need your help."

"I ain't no 'elp to no one these days."

"You like knitting, don't you?" Rebecca persevered.

"Well, ya right, tha' is somefing I can do."

"Every week, or so it seems, I have to pay a visit to women with newborn babies. It is all very nice, but I feel some sort of knitted garment is expected of me for the new little one, and there is no keeping up with it. Do you remember how slow I am?"

"So ya want me ta make bonnets, blankets, and the likes?"

"If you don't mind."

"*If I don't mind!* Why ya know I am no 'appier than when I've got a pair of knitting needles clicking away!"

"So, would you?"

"Of cou'se, my dear."

"I can supply the wool."

"I'm 'oping soon ta be knitting for you."

Rebecca ignored this comment and changed the subject. After a little more chat, she left to go on her next mission.

As Rebecca neared Mrs. Brookes' house, she reflected on the motherly woman's kindness to her. Her daughter Agnes had been a housemaid at Biggenden, and through her, Rebecca had met this lovely, large-hearted woman. It was Mrs. Brookes who insisted Rebecca spend Christmas with them when it was discovered she would be alone, despite having a house full of family already. It was Mrs. Brookes who gently put Rebecca to bed, as if she was a child, when she fell and twisted her ankle. It was Mrs. Brookes who, along with her now mother-in-law, enthusiastically organised Jack and Rebecca's wedding breakfast, and it was from the Brookes' residence that Rebecca left for their marriage service. To sum it all up, Rebecca felt greatly indebted to this capable lady. And now yet again she needed her wisdom and advice as she sought a suitable maid.

Rebecca was relieved to find Mrs. Brookes at home, for she was frequently out helping her daughters with their big families. Over yet another cup of tea, they chatted animatedly about recent events. The older lady laughed heartily at Rebecca's mistake with the Charitable Endeavours group, and Rebecca wondered aloud why Mrs. Brookes was on no committees.

"Me on a committee? Not likely!" Mrs. Brookes roared with laughter at the idea. "I couldn't stand the meetings and anyway, if all those rich ladies on the committee dug a bit deeper into their silken pockets for their 'charitable endeavours,' there would be no need trying to wheedle the money out of the poor by organising bazaars and the like."

Rebecca laughed heartily.

"Moreover," she continued, fully warmed to her theme, "I maintain that most committees are established because something needs doing or paying for, and all the members want it done but are unwilling to do it or pay for it themselves."

"I think you have it in a nutshell," Rebecca said with a smile. "I must remember that summary to tell Jack tonight."

Mrs. Brookes listened quietly as Rebecca explained their domestic situation, a smile playing on her lips.

"Well, that is what I call providential!" she exclaimed.

"Why providential?"

"Well . . . " Mrs. Brookes rose to close the back door, as if scared of being overheard. "It's about our Violet."

Violet was the Brookes' youngest daughter. When they had been extra busy at Biggenden Manor due to guests or dinner parties, Violet was often conscripted to do the duty of a scullery maid. After Rebecca had left, Violet was given a permanent role as kitchen maid and as far as Rebecca was aware, all was going well.

"A week ago, a cousin of Mrs. Thorpe, Christopher, came to stay. As far as I can make out, 'e is a 'andsome young man who has never done a day's work in 'is life, but spends 'is time either socialising or shooting, all at 'is doting parents' expense. Well, as you know, our Violet isn't bad looking, and she is such a dreamy romantic, filling her silly 'ead with ridiculous love stories from Mrs. Thorpe's discarded copies of *Englishwoman's Domestic Magazine.*

"So, she was a sitting duck for this Mr. Christopher's advances, flattery, and vows of undying love. Somehow, through lying and deception, he engineered a meeting in the stables. I dread to think what would 'ave 'appened 'ad not they been disturbed by the farrier, who just 'appened to be calling in. He knows my 'usband well, so was quite shocked and angered at seeing Violet thus compromised. He immediately stalked off to find Mr. Thorpe, who was unfortunately not at 'ome. The situation was dealt with by Mrs. Thorpe."

"What did she do?" Rebecca asked, agog.

"Yes, that is it. Violet was instantly dismissed, and apparently, Mr. Christopher was gently admonished over a friendly cup of tea."

Rebecca seethed with the injustice of the situation.

"When Violet came 'ome in tears, I wanted to go straight to Mr. Christopher and give 'im a piece of my mind. Give him a few 'ome truths like he probably has never 'eard in all his pampered life. But Mr. Brookes stopped me, reminding me that Mrs. Thorpe had the power to dismiss him from his shepherding job and kick us out this 'ouse."

"Could no one speak quietly to Mr. Thorpe about it?"

"Rebecca, really! As if 'e would go against 'is wife? And wiv apologies offering Violet 'er job back? And send Christopher off the premises? Not likely!" They sat in silence, mulling over the incident.

"So that is why your coming is so providential," explained Mrs. Brookes. "Violet needs a new position. She is 'ere, moping about like only fifteen year olds can. You need a maid, and as you know, when she sets 'er mind to it, Violet can work 'ard. She would be in safe 'ands wiv you at the vicarage."

Rebecca nodded. Yes, it did appear to be a good solution. She had worked with Violet and knew she was honest and hard-working. It would suit her and please Mrs. Brookes.

"But what would Violet think?"

"Think? I know what she *should* think! She should be grateful for a second chance."

"So, you will ask her for me tonight?"

"Ask 'er? No, I will *tell* 'er tonight, and she will be wiv ya first thing tomorrow morning."

On returning home, Rebecca couldn't stop herself from bursting in upon Jack in his study to triumphantly inform him about her two solved problems. Jack had clearly been miles away in thought so took a little while to register the news, and Rebecca immediately felt guilty for disturbing his spiritual musings.

After his wife apologized, Jack chuckled guiltily. "Oh no, I wasn't considering elevated matters. I was trying to work out how many seed potatoes to order."

They discussed the employment of Violet further over supper. Jack had been suitably shocked at her treatment at Biggenden and was pleased they could help out the Brookes family, who were loyal and undemanding church members. Rebecca went to bed happy with the day's outcome and was just about to fall asleep when Jack said, "I hope we are not breaching some kind of domestic diplomacy, taking on a neighbour's dismissed servant." Then rolling onto his side, he fell into a peaceful slumber, whereas Rebecca, now fully awake, wondering what she would do if Mrs. Thorpe—or even Mr. Thorpe—called to complain about her conduct. She also began wondering how far the story of Violet's impropriety had spread. Her fellow maidservants Molly and Clara would probably be unable to resist spreading such a juicy bit of scandal in the quiet rural village where the last big excitement was a roving ram breaking into a neighbouring farmer's flock of ewes. Was Rebecca about to incur the united wrath of the various committees she sat on?

CHAPTER 4

IN THE PALE LIGHT OF the weak early morning sun, Violet hurried down the lane from the shepherd's cottage on her way to the vicarage. There was a shortcut across the fields, and she was tempted to take it, but the heavy dew would wet her hem, and anyway, she wanted to show the gossipy villagers that she was not ashamed to show her face.

Violet had mixed feelings about working for the vicar and his wife. She admitted the need to work but resented her mother organising her life once again. If she had been left alone to sort out her next job, she would have found something in a big town. Admittedly she didn't have a clue where to start looking, or even if she could get a position without a reference, but she would have done her utmost. But of course, all that would have been too slow for Ma.

All Ma cared about was usefulness. Everything and everyone had to be *useful*. That is why their garden boasted of more vegetables and fewer flowers than any other in the village. That is why Violet was always dressed in practical, frill-less frocks when she was young. She shuddered when she thought of the awfully plain, hand-me-down dresses she had had to wear to school. Being the youngest meant she never, ever got new clothes.

Usefulness was the reason half of Violet's evenings were spent helping her older siblings with their offspring. Mrs. Brookes generously offered Violet's services as a babysitter or "an extra pair of hands" willy-nilly, far and wide, totally disregarding her daughter's own plans. Any expression of reluctance on her part was considered disloyal and selfish. Violet loved every one of her runny-nosed, squawking nephews and nieces, but wished her siblings produced more manageable-sized broods.

The new Mrs. Hayworth (or Spinster Stubbs, as Violet used to secretly call her) was not bad, as far as superiors go. She had always been a kind and fair housekeeper at Biggenden Manor, providing the maids with ample hand balm, acknowledging a job well done, and being reasonable about gossiping in the kitchen; yet now it would be different. Stubbs had married a vicar, so she was sure to have changed—to have become pious and pernickety or, even worse, ask searching questions about Violet's spiritual well-being.

Of course, Violet was grateful she had a job. The whole world had turned against her after the Mr. Christopher incident. What a ridiculous fuss they had all made! Especially her mother. *She ought to have been pleased,* Violet thought with a smile, *'cos it was useful . . . in giving the village gossips something to wag their jaws about.* In this boring backwater village, the last excitement was a runaway dog who had attacked the sheep and had to be shot. Ahh, the gossips loved being totally shocked by the incident: tutting about the dog's irresponsible owner, the poor ewes, whether they might miscarry their lambs due to the trauma. They chewed over the details as if it were an old bit of mutton. *And now it's me they have their teeth into.* And what is so shocking about a kiss? (And a very good kiss it was too!)

Looking around at the boring old villagers in church last Sunday, she'd guessed hardly a kiss had been exchanged in Capford for years. The thought of some of the sour, grim-faced couples expressing affection was more than the imagination could stretch to. In church, to give them their due, no one is looking their affectionate best—everyone is either attentively listening or looking drowsy. But the way they sat, with a pew of offspring or at least a wide space between them, hardly made them seem lovey-dovey. Courting couples sat shoulder to shoulder even if the rest of the pew was empty, but none of the married folk sat so close. A delightful tingle ran down Violet's spine as she imagined sitting shoulder to shoulder, leg to leg with Christopher. Why, she would have no complaints if the sermon was an hour, or a five-pointer instead of a three!

Now, as she made her way to the vicarage, she decided that the village gossips were actually jealous. Who wouldn't want to be kissed by a young, handsome, rich man? Most of the local women lived such mundane, insular lives. Anyone with any ambition would have left Capford long ago, even if only moving a few miles along the road to a town like Tunbridge or Tunbridge Wells. That would show a bit of imagination and aspiration. But some Capford women wouldn't even venture there on market day. Violet shrugged. They fully deserved their dreary little lives and petty chin-wagging.

And I bet the vicarage couple will want to put in their penny-worth too, thought Violet woefully, bracing herself for another earful as she knocked on the vicarage door with an air of defiance and determination.

The "vicarage couple," still eating porridge at the kitchen table, invited Violet to join them. Violet felt strangely disconcerted. *The vicar, in just his shirtsleeves and unshaved to boot, eating porridge at this hour! I thought religious people rose at the crack of dawn.* Yet she sat as bidden and endured the inevitable kindly questions about her parents, siblings, and the lambing season, followed by a Bible reading and prayer. *I don't suppose it's too bad, sitting 'ere listening to 'im read and getting paid for it.*

Violet soon realised that Mrs. Hayworth had no intention of sitting like a fine lady in her front parlour, delicately employed in fine stitch work. Instead, her mistress rolled up her sleeves and worked alongside her new maid in the mornings, helping and supervising the cleaning, meal preparation, laundry, and baking; then after lunch she would change into her fine clothes and reappear as a proper lady, ready for committee work or visiting. Violet felt proud of her new employer, the way she wasn't shy of hard work and perspiration but then could dress up all grand in her best frocks and look as genteel as a duchess. It made her toes curl a bit the way the vicar also seemed to appreciate his wife's fine looks—not to mention the unnecessary number of kisses they exchanged. *Nothing that time and a few babies can't solve,* she thought, unconsciously quoting her mother.

When all was said and done, it wouldn't be bad working for the Hayworths, especially as it was such a temporary arrangement. Violet felt a bit uneasy. Mrs. Hayworth expressed such delight in having a maid to help her, and she was so pleasant to work with, that it seemed almost treachery to keep her in the dark. So, on the third morning of her employment, while kneading bread, Violet blurted out—

"Mrs. Stubbs, er . . . I mean Hayworth, I 'ope you realise I may not be with you for long."

Rebecca looked up at her questioningly.

"I mean," she said looking at Rebecca's perplexed face, "that I will soon be married and leave you."

"Indeed," Mrs. Hayworth replied guardedly. "And on what is your assumption based?"

Violet's eyebrows shot up. "Why, hasn't mother told you about Mr. Christopher?"

"Well, yes, a little." Rebecca thumped her bread, rather harder than necessary.

"Well, any day he could return for me!"

"And then?"

"Why, it is simple! If he has his parents' blessing, he will marry me, and if not, he will elope with me up to Gretna Green and marry me there."

"And live happily ever after?" Rebecca asked, somewhat sarcastically.

"Oh, you are just as bad as the rest of them," moaned Violet, wishing she had not said anything. "I don't suppose you understand much about romance, being married to a clergyman."

"I will ignore your rude comment about romance," Rebecca replied, looking ruffled, "and tell you a little about the ways of the world. What does this Mr. Christopher what's-his-name do to earn money?"

"He was born rich. He doesn't have to work."

"So, it is from his parents?"

"Yes, it is."

"So, they can easily cut off his money if the way he behaves disgraces the family like, say, marrying a kitchen maid against their wishes."

Violet sighed heavily. *Here we go again, more doom and gloom.* If only her mistress, parents, and everyone else knew Christopher, they would realise how different he was, and if he was so nice, surely his parents weren't bad. How misunderstood the poor man was!

Silently the women divided the dough into rolls.

"But it happened in the Bible," protested Violet.

Mrs. Hayworth looked up quizzically. "What happened?"

"Romantic love stories."

"Where?"

"Esther," replied Violet somewhat triumphantly.

Mrs. Hayworth tilted her head. "I do not think being more or less kidnapped from your own home, taken to the king's harem, and forced to marry a man far older than you, who could, at a whim, sentence you to death, could be called exactly romantic."

"What about Ruth then?"

Rebecca had heard some very unromantic explanations of the economic and marital agreement that Boaz and Ruth entered into, and still found the near-kinsman aspect hard to understand, but deep down she hoped it was a beautiful love story and so kept silent. Violet took her silence as wholehearted agreement and smugly continued her chores.

She can't say I didn't warn her.

Now that their domestic situation was under control and the summer was upon them, Jack and Rebecca belatedly turned their attention to the garden. To say that the lawn was flood lit with summer sun, beckoning them to sit outside, would be false on two accounts. Firstly, little sun penetrated the thick canopy of pine and elm branches, and secondly there was little lawn due to the perpetual shadows and the thick carpet of pine-needles and cones that poisoned the soil, rendering it infertile. Jack was all for increasing their log pile by cutting down half a dozen of these overgrown evergreens. But these happy dreams of a sun-filled garden were dashed to pieces by the no-nonsense assessment of Mr. Brookes.

"If ya cut 'em down, the water level'll rise, and yer at risk of them graves flooding."

This sounded grim.

"And ya don't want te run the risk of diphtheria again."

He went on to explain. The vicar prior to Rev. Brinkhill had lived in the vicarage with his wife and family. They drew water from a well in the garden. One year diphtheria struck the young family and, one by one, four of the children aged from one year old to eight became ill and died. The local doctor suggested the illness had seeped out of the graves into their well, which was duly filled in.

As the men continued discussing the garden, Rebecca went to find the graves of these poor little souls. She knelt to read the inscriptions on the lichen covered stones, following the engravings with her finger and imagined the mother's sorrow. A sturdy, playful eight-year-old son, the first born, full of mischief, laughter, and energy, complaining of a sore throat. Instead of getting better, he got worse. Mild anxiety would turn to grave concern as his symptoms worsened, until his distraught parents, despairing of life, urged their son to commit his soul to Christ and begged the Lord to take up their child in His arms as He did whilst here below. No sooner had they buried him than the next child fell ill, and thus four times they had to stand before an open grave, dug within sight of their living room window, and commit the mortal remains of their offspring to the damp, inhospitable soil. The last victim was a tiny infant, only a year old. An age so dependent and needy, so trusting and loving, but already with hints of her character unfolding. An age when she needed the constant presence of her mother to feel safe; yet that tiny soul had to make the momentous journey from this world to the next with neither parent to escort her. Unless one could trustingly commit their fragile offspring into the loving Heavenly Father's hands, this thought would be utterly, crushingly unbearable. The little soul fell asleep in her mother's arms and awoke in the Saviour's.

This obviously had been the comfort of the bereaved parents, for on the tombstone of the children was engraved this verse:

How happy are the infant souls,
That leave this dark abode.
And go to dwell in realms of light,
With their dear Saviour God.

With deep thoughts and a full heart, Rebecca looked at the mother's grave alongside it. It was a testament to human resilience and to God's care that she had lived another thirty years and had borne nine more children. The simple text on her grave stone read, "By grace ye are saved." These two weather-beaten gravestones preached a silent sermon to Rebecca on the brevity of life and the security of believers in Christ for all eternity. She reluctantly turned away to re-join the men and propose a cup of tea.

For almost a year Capford estate, village, and church had enjoyed the absence of its landlord and dictator—Lord Wilson. His ailing mother, the dowager, had been advised by her longsuffering physician to winter in southern France. Whether this was for the dowager's benefit or the physician's remained a moot point, but to France she went, along with her son, his wife, and their two unmarried daughters. Their winter in the sun extended throughout spring right up until the social season opened in London, and from there the family made their way north to their Scottish estate for grouse shooting without once setting foot in Capford.

Lord Wilson had delegated responsibility for his estate to his loyal steward, who capably ensured the home farm ran efficiently, that the tenant farmers paid their rent, and that regular church attendance was faithfully maintained by all employees.

Everyone in the village had grown used to the sight of the superior side pews, which alone could boast of both seat cushions and doors, standing empty from one week to another, so church members were rather taken by surprise when one October Sunday morning those pews were once again filled with the distinguished Wilson family in all their finery. Lord Wilson's pew position ensured his unobstructed view of the pulpit and the reader's lectern straight ahead, and the entire congregation to his left. Entire, that is, except where the gallery pillars obscured the view. These were sought after spots, for whoever occupied them could indulge in a well-deserved snooze secure in the knowledge that they were hidden from their employer's hawk-like eyes. But this prominent position meant he and his family were in full view of the congregation. It was for all to see how restless he became if the minister preached for more than his allotted half hour. Rebecca suspected that, on leaving the church, were you to ask any woman the three sermon points, she might have struggled to reply, but if asked the colour and design of the fine ladies' hats, she wagered you would have received a full and accurate description.

If Jack was surprised or disconcerted at Lord Wilson's presence that October morning, Rebecca saw no sign of it in his preaching. Indeed, he did a fine job of exposition. She hoped Lord Wilson would appreciate the change of minister in his parish as much as his subjects, but his angry scowl and stomping out of church at the end of the service seemed to indicate irritation rather than approval. Lord Wilson's non-attendance at the afternoon service threw no further light on his mood, for despite insisting his employees attend church twice on a Sunday, he rarely did himself.

Jack was always tired on a Monday morning. *A Sunday of preaching is more exhausting than a long day in a carpenter's workshop,* he thought. He had learned through bitter experience not to attempt sermon preparation on a Monday due to a sluggish brain, but to do something non-ministerial instead. He was not in a gardening mood, but really fancied a few hours of carpentry work. He sat at his desk, opened the bottom drawer, and after rummaging a while, pulled out a plan.

This is what he really wanted to make—a baby's cot. The designing phase was complete, all he needed was a word from Rebecca indicating a cot would be required, and he would begin. But month followed month, and no such news came. Jack's heart ached every time Rebecca's pain and tears indicated that no baby was imminent. He longed to be the father of Rebecca's children and felt inadequate as he tried to comfort his grieving wife. The brave face she put on in public made Jack love and feel for her all the more. Only he and the Lord knew her sorrow, and only the Lord could help. Jack was thankful that the cot design was safely hidden away in the drawer again when Rebecca unexpectedly entered the room.

"A letter for you from Lord Wilson's footman."

Jack read the letter and saw his relaxing morning disappear before his mind's eye.

"I am to go and see Lord Wilson."

"Was it an invitation?"

"No, more of a summons."

"When does he want you?"

"Probably about five minutes ago. The carriage is waiting. Here, read it for yourself," snapped Jack, tossing the letter at Rebecca as he left the room to get changed.

Her husband's reaction startled her more than the letter. Why should Lord Wilson cause Jack such consternation?

Jack's heart was pounding as he took his seat in Lord Wilson's spacious study. From the paneled walls hung various guns and pistols and heads of unfortunate prey that had come in said fire-arms' sights. The whole room oozed masculine power and confidence. Jack had little time to admire the surroundings, for his interrogator was too rich and powerful to waste his precious time on pleasantries.

"Why are you living in Capford vicarage, Hayworth?"

"Following Rev. Sidney Brinkhill's unfortunate—"

"Spare me the details. I know all about his confounded leg!"

"Well, he was unable to carry out his duties and finally decided to retire."

"And not before time!"

"He asked me to continue as his curate and to live in the vicarage."

"Well, I hope you are not presuming on a long residence."

"I am not presuming anything, sir," replied Jack, rubbing his clammy hands on his trousers.

"That is just as well, because as you well know, I am the landlord around here, and when your Brinkhill eventually dies, I am the one who chooses the next vicar for Capford."

"I see."

"And I would prefer someone a bit more sophisticated in the post."

"Excuse me, sir. What do you mean by *sophisticated*?"

"I want a more modern free-thinker, like myself. Not some narrow-minded man who takes the whole Bible literally, but one who embraces science and higher criticism."

"And Darwin?"

"Yes, indeed, his theory is most interesting. Doesn't it dent your faith, Hayworth?"

"No, not at all. Anything contrary to the Bible is wrong. Darwin's evolution ideas undermine the Genesis record and all we know about sin, death, and God."

"Then it is time to look again at Jewish legends."

"You mean God's revealed truth!" corrected Jack, no longer awed by his adversary.

"I knew you were narrow-minded, Hayworth."

"The Bible says, 'Let God be true and every man a liar.'"

"Trust a parson to start quoting Scripture when he can't think of his own reply," retorted Lord Wilson. Then, with a dismissive wave of his arm and a "That will do, Hayworth," he picked up a periodical and started to read, making it abundantly clear that the conversation was over and Jack's continued presence in the study would be a source of irritation.

Jack hastily grabbed his hat (he had never been invited to remove his coat) and after bidding the gentleman a good morning (a greeting that was not reciprocated), he left the room with all speed. The carriage used to convey him to the manor was not in evidence, and as no footmen seemed inclined to summon its return, Jack walked home.

Rebecca listened carefully to Jack's report of his interview. Evening after evening they discussed, dissected, and chewed over Lord Wilson and his information, wondering if he was as powerful in the church as he imagined and wished; ruing the unholy interference of secular considerations in ecclesiastical and spiritual matters; questioning why Reverend Brinkhill had not informed Lord Wilson of his retirement; and repeatedly resolving not to let the news affect them in any way, especially not in preaching the gospel, until they jokingly wondered what they had found to talk about before Lord Wilson stirred their nest!

CHAPTER 5

OF COURSE, EDWARD WAS DELIGHTED when Sophia shyly shared with him the hope that she was expecting a baby. The darling little secret that grew in their minds and her body drew them together most tenderly, but once the news had been announced to the world in general and the Harrington family in particular, everything changed. According to Mrs. Harrington's wisdom, there was nothing a woman needed more during this delicate period in her life than her mother's support and guidance. So, following her own mantra, Mrs. Harrington duly descended on Biggenden and made herself comfortable. Edward ruefully asked himself when his mother-in-law would feel they could cope without her and return to Hertfordshire. When the baby turned eighteen?

This afternoon he had won a small victory by spending twenty minutes alone with his wife in the sitting room, drinking tea while his mother-in-law had a nap, but before the teapot was drained, their tête-à-tête was rudely disturbed.

"Why, Sophia!" gasped her mother from the doorway. "You should still be resting in your bed. Think of your poor legs!"

"My poor legs are just fine, Ma," Sophia said gaily. "And I wanted to join Edward for tea."

"Then he should have put your feet up. Edward, you must put her feet up."

Edward found a stool.

"No, that is no good. What Sophia needs is a chaise-lounge so she can recline elegantly."

And with that Mrs. Harrington rang the bell to get her order executed post-haste.

When all the fussing and rearranging of furniture was over, Mrs. Harrington rang again for a fresh pot of tea.

"Don't let us delay you, dear Edward," she purred as she sat down with an air of satisfaction. "I am sure you have plenty to do."

"You aren't delaying me," Edward replied.

Mrs. Harrington sniffed. "Then I hope you are not being slovenly, sitting around all day."

With difficulty, Edward managed a mild response. "A man is permitted tea with his wife on occasion."

"Be that as it may, priorities have to be right," retorted the formidable woman with an air of finality.

She always says that if she has lost one argument and is thinking of another, thought Edward.

"But Sophia and I have some baby talk to do, and as a man you will neither be helpful nor necessary."

"Mother, you can't say that!" protested Sophia.

"My bank account may be helpful and necessary," joked Edward.

"My dear Edward," his mother-in-law said with a hand to her bosom, "I hope you are not begrudging my darling grandchild basic nursery necessities."

Edward drew himself to his full height. "Of course not. I by no means implied I was. In fact, I would delight in providing for my own."

And with that Edward kissed his wife and left the room.

And you need not forget that this baby, whom I am not allowed to join in any discussion about, is actually mine too! he thought quietly to himself as he left the house to inspect the farm.

As he walked, he kicked clods of mud angrily. *How could such an interfering woman produce such a wonderful daughter,* he wondered, then thinking with a shock, *What if the grandmother's traits come out in our offspring?* He pondered this vexing problem as he inspected and prodded the fattening pigs with Mr. Brookes. They were ready for the next market day. As he left the sty, Edward smiled to himself. *If mother-in-law were a pig, we wouldn't breed from her.* This irreverent thought tickled him and removed some of the irritation he had been feeling.

Edward wandered through a few meadows to an orchard. The last of the apples were being picked, and the workers were hurriedly loading full bushel boxes onto a wagon ready to be sent to Tunbridge Railway Station and onward to Covent Garden Market in London. The scent of earthy sweetness and the sight of full boxes of shiny apples usually produced in Edward a feeling of satisfaction, but today, despite handling and smelling the abundance of fruit, no such feeling arose. Edward helped the men heave the last bushel onto the wagon, joined in the jovial chatter, and then retraced his steps.

The dissatisfaction Edward felt could no longer be ignored or dismissed. For months, it had grown in his heart, and for months he had tried to suppress it, but the persistent nagging disquiet continued to intrude. As the feeling grew, its features developed and pervaded every area of his life, and only recently had he diagnosed the malady. It was not his shooting friends' rudeness, the servants' slovenliness, or his wife's family that were the root of the problem. It was not the responsibilities of the estate: the leaking roofs of farm cottages, the tenants behind with their rent, or the holes in hedges. It was not the agricultural cares: the foot rot among the sheep, the hail damage of the apples, or the hay stacked too damp. No, his problem was deeper than that, right down in the depths of his soul. He had lost his peace and purpose. He felt empty.

It was not a well-preached sermon that finally confirmed his diagnosis; rather, it was Sophia's announcement of her pregnancy. Suddenly he realised she would soon be facing possibly the most dangerous day in her life. After all, everyone knew of a woman who had died in child-birth. Sophia had all of this looming ahead, and he was responsible for getting her into the situation. Was she ready for eternity? He had never asked her this question; she seemed so good and sweet it almost felt rude to pose a question like this. But he was well enough grounded in doctrine to know that being good and sweet was not good enough. She needed to trust Christ as her personal Saviour. It was his duty to recommend Christ to her, but he was so distant from the Lord himself that he would feel like a hypocrite doing so. He thought of his unborn child and then of his own childhood. His mother had sacrificed a materially rich lifestyle to marry the man she loved, who also shared her love of Christ. They had very little worldly possessions but a treasure in heaven. They had made it their concern to bring up Edward to know the Lord. Had he sacrificed everything, but the other way around to his mother—Christ for lifestyle? Heavenly treasure for earthly gains?

These questions had dogged his mind for weeks and hung heavy on his soul. He pleaded with the Lord to forgive him for the weakness of his faith, but his prayers seemed to go unanswered. He had ignored God for a long time and now felt the situation was reversed. *And it serves me right,* thought Edward.

It had never been a conscious decision to side-line the Saviour. It happened as a gradual drifting away from Him. Now the distance seemed so great that the Lord seemed out of reach. Edward knew that God never completely deserts His people, but was he one of His? He doubted all his previous Christian experiences. Had he just been a little boy with a religious temperament and affectations? He envied people who experienced a remarkable, powerful, dramatic conversion. People who could name and date the day the Lord met with them and could clearly see how and when Christ had entered their lives, and by His Spirit had changed their character, conduct, and outlook. Edward had no special date to remember. There had never been a time he did not fear the Lord or pray. Could his religiosity after his parents' deaths have been some sort of emotional prop to escape from his sadness and help him cope with his abject loneliness? These plaguing questions removed any assurance, peace, and comfort.

Edward wandered around his land in turmoil, praying as he paced through the fields, and then re-checked his timepiece. *With mother-in-law about, I'm like a schoolboy who is not allowed home until bedtime. I shouldn't feel like this in my own house,* he thought rebelliously, and walked back with the determination of a rightful owner.

Before entering his study, he silently crept to the sitting room door and listened.

"*One* nursery, Sophia?"

"Yes, and a pretty one it is too."

"Pretty it may be, but one is insufficient. It is imperative that the child has different nurseries for night and day."

"Seems most unnecessary, Mother."

"Not in the least. Babies need different air to breath during the day and night, and to mix them is most dangerous. *Everyone* knows that."

Edward's eyes grew narrow.

"Many a baby sleeps in the same room as the rest of their family," Sophia said with assurance.

"But many a baby dies young."

"Then we will instruct the nursery nurse to open the windows and air the room."

"Never in the evenings! Night air is bad for babies."

"In the morning then."

"Draughts are also dangerous."

"The room can be aired when the baby is with me."

A pause indicated a truce, or so Edward thought.

" . . . and I can choose you a suitable wet-nurse of good nature and breeding, so your dear baby doesn't imbibe any bad traits from her."

"Mother," Sophia protested, "I am not having a wet-nurse, and that is that."

"You are being very unreasonable, my dear," answered her mother. "In your delicate condition, your thinking is not entirely rational."

"I am rational!"

"You need a wet-nurse to get your figure back quickly. That is what Edward would like."

Edward grimaced and forced himself to stay still. *As if she knows me at all,* he thought.

"Edward doesn't just love me for my figure!"

"Men are all the same, dear, and moreover, you need to produce a sibling as soon as possible. If you are breastfeeding, you are delaying the process unnaturally."

"There is nothing unnatural about breastfeeding, Mother. Think of all the animals!"

"Exactly, darling, think of all the animals! You don't want to be like some dairy cow, do you?"

Edward could bear it no longer. "Sophia," he said as he sprang into the room, "you breastfeed our child for as long as you like, and if your figure suffers, or if another child takes longer to come along, don't you worry. I will admire you the more for it!"

Sophia looked both relieved and embarrassed by his entrance and outburst, and Edward wondered if he had done the right thing. Mrs. Harrington had no mixed feelings though.

"Well, if you two will be so modern and unguidable, I wash my hands of you and will let you learn the hard way. My poor, poor grandchild!" she fumed as she stalked out of the room.

CHAPTER 6

REBECCA HEARD THE NEWS OF Sophia's pregnancy one morning as she queued at the bakery. She did all the right things: smiled happily, asked if Sophia was keeping well, and declared she was delighted with the news. But inside she felt as if she had been kicked in the stomach. Alarmed by her own reaction, she overcompensated by enthusiastically discussing knitting patterns for newborns with the other bread-buyers as the baker filled her basket.

On the short walk back to the vicarage, Rebecca mulled over the news. *Oh, of course Sophia has managed to expect a baby within eighteen months of marriage, and no doubt she will have a boy, as society most desires. She has always done the right thing at the right time. And has always looked beautiful doing it too.*

Rebecca dumped the basket of provisions on the kitchen table.

"You deal with them, and I'll make the bed," she instructed the surprised Violet. Normally she would have discussed the shopping trip and any bargains or encounters with her maid, but today she flounced out of the room.

Once upstairs, instead of making the bed, she flung herself on it and cried. How she hated herself sometimes! She was so unlike the serene vicar's wife she so wanted to be! Especially a few days every month, when she got cross with Violet, lost every trace of humour, and felt lukewarm toward her husband, even irritated by him.

Just like today! And why on such troublesome days as today did she always get that kind of news? Happy family news, the news she so much wanted for herself. She hated her own reaction. She should have been rejoicing with those that rejoice, but instead she was only acting. Of course, even Sophia couldn't control her future any more than Rebecca could, but it seemed that God heard her prayers more than Rebecca's, at any rate.

Why won't God answer my prayers? she thought. *Would I make such an awful mother? Would I make my child an idol? What does He think I would do wrong? What have I done to deserve this judgment? Or maybe He knows I will die soon, so is preventing a pregnancy. Or Jack . . . or . . . "* Rebecca tried to second-guess God's plan and tied herself in painful knots.

I've got a wonderful husband, lovely friends, a coop of chickens, and beautiful countryside right outside my back door. I should be content, I should be grateful, but I am just a miserable old hag. Jack will get fed up with me, my friends become too busy being parents, and Violet will give her notice because I am so grumpy. With that, Rebecca rolled over and cried again into her wet pillow.

If I had problems making a pie or cake, I would not hesitate to ask some experienced matron (probably Mrs. Brookes) for sympathy and advice. But in the area of producing a family—something far more significant than a pie or cake—I have no one to turn to. These things are unmentionable and therefore un-shareable. And with that thought came more unstoppable tears.

"Mrs. Hayworth, do ya need an 'and wiv ya bed?" Violet's question floated up the stairs

Rebecca sat up and wiped her cheek. "No, thank you, I'll be all right. I'll be down soon."

"Cos I think ya've got a committee meeting 'ere this afternoon."

Now Rebecca was on her feet. Indeed she had! She looked at herself in the mirror. What a state! How could she possibly look half decent within two hours? Quickly she splashed cold water on her face from her washstand and smoothed her hair before descending to the kitchen.

"Why, ma'am, you look rough" was Violet's honest but unhelpful reaction.

Rebecca's eyes filled with tears again. "But what can I do? All the ladies will be arriving soon."

"If ya don't mind, I'll 'elp you best I can," offered Violet.

"Please do," replied Rebecca meekly and allowed herself to be guided upstairs.

"First, you need more cold water on them eyes of yours, so 'old these cloths firm," instructed Violet. "Now find ya best dress, somefing bright and what suits ya."

"My new pink dress?"

"Exactly right!"

Rebecca almost began to enjoy the fun.

"Good, ma'am," said Violet with satisfaction. "Now ya just need to do ya hair in a nice playful bun, not all severe and scraped back like, but with a few of ya curls falling 'round ya face."

"For a committee meeting?"

"Yeah, show 'em all you are relaxed and 'appy."

Exactly what I am not, thought Rebecca as she sat down at her dressing table and allowed Violet to brush her hair. She looked at Violet in the mirror and saw her determined face, engrossed in her self-appointed task. *She's so kind to me,* realised Rebecca suddenly, tears threatening to well up again at this discovery.

When Violet had stuck in the last hairpin and twisted the last curl to her satisfaction, she stepped back. "What do ya think?"

Rebecca stared at the mirror in amazement.

"Violet, you are a wonder. I look okay!"

"No, ya don't, ya look beautiful, ma'am."

Rebecca could not resist giving her maid a hug. "Thank you, Violet. You have saved the day."

"And now I'd better get ya and ya 'usband ya lunch."

Jack entered the dining room shortly after Rebecca and gazed at her admiringly. "Darling, you look wonderful! Have you had a good morning?"

"Well," replied Rebecca, smiling, "as the old villagers would say, 'mustn't grumble, sir, mustn't grumble.'"

CHAPTER 7

AUTUMN GAVE WAY TO WINTER, and Capford village was enveloped in a thick, damp fog. But Jack didn't mind. He threw a log on the fire and relaxed into his armchair. In the kitchen, he could hear his wife humming a hymn tune as she prepared their evening drinks. He smiled with deep satisfaction. The day had gone reasonably well. It was only Thursday, and already his two Sunday sermons were fairly well under way. The members of the Prince Albert Memorial Committee had just left the vicarage, having finally agreed on the font of the wording. Maybe the disbanding of a committee was in sight. *What a rare occurrence*! Jack chuckled to himself.

Just as Rebecca was pouring the tea and hearing his account of the latest deliberations of the "Bertie Committee," the front doorbell rang. Jack groaned and looked at Rebecca as they sighed in unison. "Not again." They both recognised the long, insistent ring; it could be none other than Lord Wilson's footman. Jack eased himself reluctantly from his comfortable chair and, as a man resigned to the inevitable, went for his overcoat.

Rebecca followed him to the hallway.

"Well, I may as well say goodnight now."

"I'm afraid so, dear," replied Jack, giving her a parting kiss. "Please leave a lamp by the back door before you go to bed."

Jack sat himself in the luxurious carriage of Lord Wilson and contemplated what was before him—and it did not include sleep. A few weeks ago, Lord Wilson's elderly mother had declared she was on her deathbed. She was hastily removed from her dowager house and installed in the finest bedroom of Capford Manor. Her physician, Dr. Ward, was summoned and was barely permitted to leave her bedside. Last week the patient had tired of the familiar presence of her longsuffering, and by now somewhat cynical, physician and had demanded a man of the cloth. These were not short, mid-afternoon visits. It was normally at half past ten in the evening when Jack's presence was required, and he was only permitted to leave when the old woman was sound asleep. No one wished the invalid a deep slumber more than the groom, stable boy, and the Hayworths.

It was not easy to detect exactly when the lady was asleep. Evening after evening Jack sat at her bedside in the low, flickering light of the fire, willing her to sleep. Never once did she say a word to her guest; her only recognition of his presence was the beady gaze of her right eye. The left eye (if she had one), like her mouth, never opened. Eventually the right eye closed, and Jack would sit motionlessly, hoping to hear a gentle snore. Then he would silently stand to go, but quick as a flash the eye would open and shoot him a disapproving glare, which promptly made him sit down again. Jack found the unblinking, one-eyed glare somewhat disconcerting and often sat lost for words. The eye did not have the same effect on Lord Wilson, who frequently joined Jack in the bedroom. Totally ignoring his mother, Lord Wilson sat next to the fire, tankard in hand, propounding his own theories and decrying others. Jack wondered if the man saw any irony in the fact that he wanted a vicar to pray for his mother on her deathbed yet declared there was no God.

But tonight was different. Lord Wilson was not at his mother's side, and having been shown into the room by the nurse, Jack sat alone with the silent patient. She looked frail and tiny in the grand four-poster bed, but the grim set of her jaw and the glare of her eye dismissed any feeling of tenderness that normally arose when one is confronted with such aged humanity. Jack read a chapter from the Bible and then prayed for her and her family. Afterwards he tried as normal to make polite, general conversation about the day's events and the weather, but it was difficult to keep up the monologue with so little encouragement. He was tired, and the warmth from the fire and dimness of the room were both inviting him to sleep. But the eye was still upon him. *If I have to be here at this unearthly* hour, Jack suddenly decided, *I am going to make it worth my while.*

So, looking straight into her right eye, Jack started talking about eternity. As best as he could, he described the joys of heaven and the horrors of hell.

"And we are all going to die soon, maybe within days, and we can't take anything with us, not this grand house, or shiny jewels or fine carriages."

Undeterred by the lack of response, he told her how we would all be judged, "Not by how much we have given to charity, or how beautifully we have conducted ourselves. All that matters is what has motivated us and our relationship with Jesus Christ."

As much to himself as to the dowager, he enlarged on the suitability of the Saviour. "He, who is God's eternal Son, came from heaven to live a perfect life and die a death He did not deserve—in agony on a Roman cross—to save all who trust in Him. Would God have allowed His Son to suffer if we could get to heaven in any other way?"

After giving a description of the kindness, goodness, and mercy of Christ, then quoting some of His beautiful invitations and promises, Jack gazed into the eye and asked, "And are you trusting in Him?"

The eye closed, and Jack rested back in his chair, somewhat amazed at his own fluency and passion. As he prayed silently for the woman next to him, he felt content that he had done the right thing.

An hour later, the nurse crept in and beckoned him to leave. She grabbed his hand and shook it vigorously, then whispered with a tear-stained face, "And, sir, thank ye for ya sermon. Ya did me good, ya did me good."

CHAPTER 8

WHEN SOPHIA'S TIME ARRIVED, EDWARD felt hopelessly useless as he was ushered out of the room by the officious family doctor. He wished he could have a role, even if it was just warming up water and transporting it upstairs with the housemaids. Instead, he paced restlessly in his study, drinking numerous cups of coffee and silently pleading with the Almighty to spare his wife and child.

When he had parted from Sophia and was kissing her moist forehead, she had squeezed his arm and urgently commanded him, "Pray for me, Edward! Pray for me!" Her parting instructions had both touched and delighted him, and they perfectly matched his own impulse, so he prayed and paced, and paced and prayed as never before. He was reminded of the story of Joshua fighting the Amalekites and Moses praying for victory.

Was giving birth normally this prolonged? What was happening up there? Edward longed for information but knew he was not to disturb the goings-on. When, finally, in the small hours, he heard the welcome cry of an infant, relief and thankfulness flooded over him, but only briefly. *The stage immediately after a birth is the most dangerous for the mother,* he remembered. His praises were mixed with petitions until the proud physician came down to summon the new father to meet his offspring.

"May I be the first to congratulate you on the birth of your son and heir, sir," the doctor said as he shook Edward's hand.

"How are they? My son and wife?" Edward felt grown up and responsible as he asked the question.

"Tip top!" came the hearty reply as they climbed the stairs.

Edward was amazed that such a tiny scrap of humanity could cause such huge transformations within his household. His beautiful, perfect son not only had his doting parents at his beck and call (and yes, he freely admitted he was already a doting father), but also a highly experienced nursery nurse. And as no highly experienced nursery nurse can be expected to attend to a baby without someone to boss about, delegate to and, if necessary, blame for mishaps, a nursery *maid* was also employed.

But the transformation in staff numbers was nothing compared to transformation of his wife. The birth of little Bertie had been prolonged and very difficult. (When leaving the house with his wages and a bottle of port, the doctor admitted to Edward it was so.) Sophia looked so tired and pale, yet she was full of a new kind of vitality. The loving gaze she formally reserved for Edward was now lavishly bestowed on Bertie. Bertie was the centre of her universe, and everyone else had to orbit willingly around him and his needs. Edward looked with awe at the selfless attention his wife devotedly gave little Bertie. Breastfeeding was not easy, yet despite being tired and sore, Sophia tearfully persevered, day and night, until the nursery nurse was satisfied that Bertie was latching on and fully fed.

The bedroom and nursery became a hive of womanly activity and cooing. Using this analogy, Edward was unsure who was the queen bee—Sophia or Bertie. But one thing he did know: he was an intruder. This the nursery nurse made abundantly clear when she ordered the housemaids to make up a bed for Edward in a spare room. Sophia was not averse to his presence but was so pre-occupied by her new love that she hardly seemed to notice his kisses and congratulations. Edward sometimes sneaked into the nursery to hold Bertie, but more often than not he was caught red-handed and told off by the terrifying nurse.

"Don't touch him, he has only just settled!" was her stock phrase.

Edward had to content himself with quickly kissing the tiny pink fist of his son and stroking his soft sparse hair under the disapproving eye of the nursery dictator before being shown the door. Edward played with the idea of kidnapping his own son for an hour or two and sitting with him in the study, but with a smile he imagined the female furore it would produce and reluctantly dismissed the plan.

Edward was relieved to hear that Mr. Harrington would be accompanying his wife on her visit to meet the new grandson. No one quite knew how long their stay would be, but on hearing Mrs. Harrington declare it was "at least until after the christening," Edward wasted no time in contacting Jack for a convenient date for the ceremony.

In the meantime, he was enjoying his father-in-law's company more than he had ever expected. How such a sensible man had managed to remain sane throughout his long marriage to such an odious woman, Edward could only wonder. The man's main coping technique seemed to be a heavy involvement in various projects and a certain amount of selective deafness. Mr. Harrington's projects were interesting, and Edward found it refreshing to talk about non-baby matters without incurring disapproval. His father-in-law wanted to know all about the farm and estate, and the two men spent many happy hours plodding the land, commenting on potential improvements and exchanging ideas.

The evening conversations were interesting and yielded Edward much amusement. He secretly delighted in seeing how quickly any given subject could be related or reduced to the needs of the darling new grandson. Within minutes of Mr. Harrington mentioning the Napoleonic wars, Mrs. Harrington was fretting and praying that her little Bertie would never have to fight for king and country. The subject of the fattening pigs soon (and rather rudely, Edward thought) developed into a discussion about Bertie's amazing growth rate. And a conversation about coppicing part of a wood was taken over by the grandmother imagining what a fine young man Bertie doubtless would be by the time it needed coppicing again. Mr. Harrington seemed unable to hear these conversational side-tracks and plodded on with his chosen theme, unperturbed by interruptions. Sophia, probably through years of practice, managed to listen to both trains of thought simultaneously and give appropriate answers or noises as required.

The receiving of afternoon visitors to admire the baby and congratulate the mother was a duty mainly reserved for the womenfolk. But one wet afternoon, Edward and Mr. Harrington joined their ladies for afternoon tea and were rewarded by a visit from Rev. and Mrs. Hayworth. Once the right noises had been made over the new baby, Jack became engrossed in a conversation with Mr. Harrington about his involvement in the local cottage hospital. Edward was half listening but had heard most of the details before. From the other side of the room, he watched the ladies. Sophia, pale yet radiant with their dear child in her arms. Mrs. Harrington holding forth about something or other, and Rebecca looking just like always—reliable and wise. *What a dear friend she was,* thought Edward. *If only I could have a good ol' chat with her over tea and cake by the fireside. Jack has got himself a good thing.*

The sharp tones of his mother-in-law interrupted his musings.

"Still no baby on the way for you then, Mrs. Hayworth?"

Rebecca looked uncomfortable. "No, sadly not, Mrs. Harrington."

"Well, how odd! Must be something a bit wrong. Did you do cartwheels when you were young?"

"Why, yes, I did."

"How neglectful of your parents to allow such behaviour! I suspect your womb may well be dislodged. It could be all over the place!"

Edward saw Rebecca looking desperately toward Jack, and he followed her glance. Jack had his back to the ladies, oblivious of his wife's pain. Edward moved across the room rapidly.

"Why, Mrs. Hayworth, you must come and see our new conservatory. You left before we had it furnished."

Rebecca looked vulnerable and grateful as Edward guided her out the room and away from her adversary to the conservatory.

"Thank you, Mr. Thorpe," she said in a hushed tone.

Edward suspected she was close to tears. *I can't be dealing with that,* he thought and enthusiastically embarked on a botany lecture about the various plants he had brought to enhance the room. Rebecca made all the right remarks. *She always was easy to talk to,* remembered

Edward, and then he guiltily shook off a feeling of wistfulness that unexpectedly engulfed him.

"Mr. Thorpe, for some time I have wanted to say something about the unfortunate incident between Mr. Christopher and Violet, the maid, but lacked opportunity. I hope it didn't seem rude and unneighbourly that we took her on so soon after you had dismissed her."

Edward looked at Rebecca blankly.

"What incident? Whose maid?"

"Why, the romantic interlude between Mr. Christopher and your housemaid, Violet, which caused her to lose her job here."

With anyone else Edward might have bluffed, but he knew Rebecca knew him too well to try that now. He had to admit his complete ignorance to the whole affair and try to laugh it off.

Now I will look a complete fool in her eyes, he thought angrily. *What else am I kept in ignorance of by my wife in my own household?*

Rebecca was unusually quiet on the way home. *Cartwheels!* she thought. *Innocent and fun cartwheels. Could they really have rearranged my reproductive organs?* Again she wished she had known how to reply appropriately to the obnoxious Mrs. Harrington who dared talk about her womb in public.

On reflection, she now had the answer. Yes, if anyone else had the audacity to ask about her producing babies, she would reply piously, "We can only take what the Lord gives." That should shut them up. What a shame she always had a good answer an hour too late!

"A penny for your thoughts, darling?" Jack asked.

"Did you hear any of Mrs. Harrington's conversation with me?" replied Rebecca.

"I try not to hear Mrs. Harrington if possible, but was she talking about cartwheels, of all things?"

"Yes, she certainly was, she thinks—"

But Jack was not informed of Mrs. Harrington's opinion on cartwheels, for the couple was interrupted.

"Ahh, just the people I wanted to see!"

Jack and Rebecca looked around and beheld Mrs. Grey, the Sunday school superintendent's wife, puffing up behind them. She stopped to catch her breath.

"About the Sunday school prize giving."

"Yes, Mrs. Grey, that is next Saturday," said Jack.

"Indeed," puffed Mrs. Grey, "but Mrs. Brookes' hens were eaten by a fox last night."

Rebecca dared not look at her husband as she struggled to keep a straight face and asked, "And how does this effect the prize giving?"

"She normally makes the egg sandwiches."

"Why, of course, how could I forget? Well, mine are laying well, so I can make the egg sandwiches," Rebecca assured the woman.

"Thank you!" Mrs. Grey beamed before adding, "But not too wet, mind you, we don't want soggy sandwiches."

"I'll do my best." Rebecca hid a grin.

But Mrs. Grey hadn't finished. "Now, parson, you are a sensible man, aren't you? Please keep your remarks brief. The tea needs to be served promptly at five o'clock. If you over-run, the tea will stew and the food will dry out."

"Thank you, Mrs. Grey. I will bear that in mind," answered Jack gravely.

"Well then, I bid you good day and enjoy your walk," Mrs. Grey said with a warm smile before she scurried off in the other direction.

"No soggy sandwiches, my dear," teased Jack.

"And no lengthy discourse!" Rebecca wagged her finger playfully at him.

As they walked along arm in arm, Jack asked, "What kind of question is that? 'You are a sensible man, aren't you?' Would anyone answer, 'No, I am not'?"

Rebecca squeezed her husband's arm and laughed. How wonderful it was to live with such a sensible man—her definition of sensible, not Mrs. Grey's! How very different from life with someone like, for instance, Mrs. Harrington. Wasn't her husband worth more than ten sons? She must learn to be content.

CHAPTER 9

VIOLET ALWAYS ENJOYED THE MONTH of June. It was filled with hard work, but she still reckoned it was her favourite time of the year. The leaves, grass, and crops were still fresh, green, and lush. The strengthening of the sun's warmth indicated that summer was on the way. The bloom of the orchards had dropped, and in its place tiny fruits began to swell, promising a good harvest. The lambs that had been weak and feeble two months ago were now robust and stocky. June was a month of promise, anticipation, hope . . . and sheep shearing.

Shearing the sheep was a big event. All the farm workers were involved in gathering in the sheep, herding them down the lanes, then penning them up. Jokes and laughter mingled with the frantic baaing of the ewes and lambs as they were temporarily separated. The sun always shone on shearing days, for fleece cannot be shorn when wet, and the sunshine and noise made the atmosphere festive. There was also a great sense of camaraderie as the farm labourers worked together with a common sense of purpose.

The two main players in this scene, full of action, were Violet's father, Mr. Brookes, the shepherd, and Joe Mason. They were the head shearers, unbeatable in skill and speed, and Violet was their wool winder par excellence. Villagers could not resist wandering along to the shearing pens to watch Pa and Joe at work and admire their technique. With one easy move, they would select an ewe from the holding pen, turn her head to one side, and bring her to the ground. Resting the weight of the ewe on his thigh, Pa or Joe could hold her front legs and drag the ewe effortlessly out of the pen to the shearing platform. They could keep the ewe still with their knees and left hand as they clipped away at the wool with their right. They clipped close to the skin, just where the old wool was rising and loosening.

Their expertise could not be truly appreciated unless one also saw others trying the same feat. Violet had seen many a man or youth confidently asking for a go—only to fail spectacularly. A badly handled ewe would struggle, causing an uneven shear or cuts to the skin. Ewes seemed to recognise that they had no chance of escaping with Mr. Brookes or Joe and resign themselves to the process, but on being handled by an amateur, they put up a fight. With their hands fully occupied with a struggling sheep, the men looked as if they needed to grow a third to hold the shears. The watching crowd gleefully watched their predicament and offered contradictory advice. Not a few half-shorn sheep struggled free and escaped into the open field. Nothing was as determined not to get caught again as a semi-shorn ewe, and much time could be wasted sprinting after it. Joe normally joined in the laughter and said that at least it gave the spectators something to do, but inefficiency irritated Mr. Brookes, who at that busy time of year wanted to make the most of every dry day. "Leave it to Joe and me" was his stern command to anyone who dared step onto the shearing platform.

"Leave it to Vi" was also his plea when it came to wool winding. She too was unbeatable, and she had no qualms in admitting it. Other women occasionally stood in for her, but their loose fleece rolls often came undone when being thrown onto a cart or into the barn. Yes, she knew the job well. Once the shearers had finished with a fleece, she would remove all soiled wool, then deftly throw the fleece clean side down onto the floor. While standing on it, she would twist and pull up a corner of the wool to produce a strong rope. Then she neatly folded the fleece, rolled it, and tied it securely together with the woolen cord.

As well as winding wool, Violet was always at hand with the Stockholm tar. Occasionally even the best shearer nicked sheep, and the wound needed a dab of tar. Violet was quick to spot a cut and apply the tar in an efficient manner, not staining the fleece or delaying the shearer. Other girls came to watch the shearers and enjoy the spectacle, but Violet was there as an important part of the team. The other girls were happy standing around, looking pretty, and joking with the workers, whereas she was a worker herself.

Even Mrs. Hayworth had acknowledged her status as chief wool winder and allowed her a few days off for the work! Violet smiled to herself. No doubt her domineering mother had seen to that. Few people would go against the wishes of Mrs. Brookes, and Mrs. Hayworth was not one of the few. Violet normally resented her mother's interference, but with shearing, they were in full agreement about Violet's role and usefulness. *It's about the only thing she admits I can do well!*

Violet enjoyed working with her father. He was a man of few words, but what he did say was worth hearing, either for its wit or wisdom. Unlike Ma, who was always trying to organise her, Pa just let her be, unless, of course, she was too outrageous or foolish. But even then, unlike Ma, he always seemed to have a special rapport with her, which even his sternest disapproval could not completely obliterate.

Her father would never have said it, but Violet knew he enjoyed working with her. Her quickness suited him, and they worked well together. Away from the house and among the workers, she often spoke to him in a playful, slightly cheeky manner, which drew out a twinkly smile if not a reply in a similar vein. At lunch time, they sat together on a hessian sack, leaning against the sheep hurdles eating the ample lunch Ma had prepared. Violet commandeered the basket and handed out the food.

The basket was also a handy, innocuous barrier between her and Joe Mason. No one can be offended or hurt by the presence of a picnic basket, and she did not want to offend or hurt Joe, but neither did she want him sitting right up close, and he might well do so if he got half a chance.

A few years ago she wouldn't have minded. Why, they had always been the best of friends. He had started school with her, made the same dens in the bracken, and climbed the same trees. Ever since Violet could remember, Joe Mason had been around and had been sweet on her. His look of adoring devotion when she handed him a slice of meat pie at the sheep pens was exactly the same as when they were six and they had shared licks of a cough-candy.

Of course, he had changed. He was now a strong young man with a deep voice. Witnessing his metamorphosis from a boy into a man had been a strange, slightly hilarious experience for her. It was all a bit awkward, really. Friendship as children had been simple and straightforward, but now Joe was no longer satisfied with the status quo.

Violet knew that everyone, especially her mother, expected her to marry Joe. He was most suitable and would be a very loyal and reliable husband. He was nice, and she liked him, but he was not exciting. He was so . . . Capford! Capford born and bred, with no ambitions beyond the village boundary. He wasn't bad looking, and he was definitely manly, unlike some of the new male servants down at Biggenden, who looked so delicate and weedy. Marrying Joe wouldn't be bad—she could manage it—but her life would be so humdrum and predictable. Just like her sisters' lives. She would be the centre of attention for one day—her wedding day—after that her life would consist of babies, laundry, and kitchen chores. Joe would become a middle-aged man, interested in his vegetable garden and average rainfalls. Conversation would be limited to teething problems and toilet training, and his devoted glances her way would become a thing of the past. No, that would not do at all! Joe must find a wife elsewhere! But that was no good either, as she didn't like the idea of him falling in love with anyone else. No, Joe should remain a bachelor.

Another good thing about working with her father, Violet acknowledged privately, was the freedom it gave her to banter freely with Joe. Joe wouldn't dare flirt with her, or even worse, press his suit in front of her father. Safe in this knowledge, Violet could converse freely with him, just like old times before Joe had started getting silly ideas. Indeed, if the shearing was going well and the spectators were responsive, Violet and Joe could keep up a good banter and play to their audience. If luck was on Joe's side and he suddenly found himself alone with Violet, all her wit and sparkle would vanish. She became tongue tied and rapidly found a reason to disappear.

The Sunday school prize giving day dawned bright and warm. Rebecca was up early to cook the eggs, let them cool, and assemble the sandwiches. Between the stages of sandwich preparation, she helped the female Sunday school teachers decorate the church with flowers. Weather permitting, the tea would be served in the vicarage garden, so she had to also ensure everything looked as neat and tidy as possible. The hens complained indignantly about being imprisoned in the coop for the day.

The morning flew by, with many last-minute arrangements needing her attention. The kitchen was no longer her own, as each lady came with her contributions and crockery. Not her best crockery, mind you, for no child should be trusted with that. But not her worst either, for that was not fit for public inspection. Extra kettles filled the range, which Mrs. Grey instructed Violet to keep well stocked. Violet (Mrs. Grey also decreed) was to leave the service at the third hymn to ensure the water was boiling by the final amen.

Rebecca left the busy kitchen to change her attire and brush her wayward hair. She felt nervous and responsible for the proceedings. Would her class remember their verses? Would her egg sandwiches meet Mrs. Brookes' standard? Would the tea go well? She wanted to look her best. Her hair had to be done "Violet style." If only Violet wasn't so busy, she could have helped her. If Rebecca looked good, she would feel more confident and in control. The Harringtons would be among the guests, and she wanted to show Mrs. Harrington that although she was unable to reproduce, she was an able minister's wife.

The church was beautifully cool, and all the children looked unusually good and innocent in their Sunday best. Their normal mischievousness had evaporated as nerves set in. Rebecca sat in the second row with her little class of girls and smiled reassuringly at them as the gallery band struck up.

The building rang with the voices of the children singing "All things bright and beautiful," and Rebecca glowed with pride and pleasure. All indeed seemed bright and beautiful. The youngest class came to the front first to recite their verses. They were a darling bunch of five-year-olds, each looking clean and smart, even in hand-me-down clothes that covered if not fitted them.

The recitations had barely begun when beneath the children's feet, a puddle began to form. The puddle gradually expanded into a lake. The lake developed into various streams, slowly meandering over the memorial plate of a notable benefactor beneath. Rebecca looked in awe at the volume. Mirth welled up within her.

"Extraordinary!" gasped the teacher behind her in a whisper.

At this apt description, Rebecca began to shudder with suppressed laughter. The more she tried to control herself, the worse the situation became. *Rebecca, this is no way for a vicar's wife to behave,* she told herself sternly. The next class of children arranged themselves at the front. The line was somewhat disorganised as each child avoided standing in the puddle. Rebecca's group was next, so she severely reprimanded herself and nodded to her girls to come forward. *They are behaving better than me,* she thought as they filed to the front. One by one the girls recited their verses flawlessly. During the rehearsal, they had spoken loudly and slowly, but now they rushed their words in a small voice, so only those near the front could vouch for their accuracy, but Rebecca felt proud.

As they were walking back to their pew, Rebecca spotted the source of the puddle. He sat in the front pew, fighting back tears, with a tell-tale wet patch on his oversized trousers. A few pews back, his older sister sat helplessly looking on at her sad brother. Rebecca immediately knew what to do. She offered him her hand, took him back to her pew, sat him on her knee, and dried his eyes. Frankie was Agnes's little stepson. He was far too young to be in Sunday school but came with his big sister to give his parents an hour's peace. As he snuggled onto Rebecca's lap, she felt the dampness penetrate through her skirts and petticoat. She half regretted following her impulse, but on seeing his contented face, she knew she had done the right thing.

Before the recitations had finished, Frankie was fast asleep. He became heavier and heavier, and Rebecca became hotter and hotter. It was debatable who was most grateful to Jack for keeping his comments brief—she or Mrs. Grey. But as the *amen* was echoed by the congregation and Violet's kettles came to the boil, Rebecca gently woke Frankie and handed him over to his big sister.

Rebecca intended to disappear upstairs and get changed. But the opportunity kept evading her: the class needed congratulating, teapots needed filling, plates needed distributing, and people needed greeting. So many people! Rebecca was sure more people had come for the tea than for the service. The tea was primarily intended as a treat for the children, but anyone with the remotest link to them or the church had descended on the vicarage lawn and required feeding. Again and again, the teapots were refilled in the kitchen for a new round of "topping up." The children's nervousness had vanished, they had received edifying new books as prizes, and their tummies were full, so now they played happily among the guests and the gravestones.

Armed with a milk jug and tea pot, Rebecca approached the genteel group of ladies on the back lawn. Lady Wilson and her daughters had joined Mrs. Harrington and Sophia. *What a pretty picture they make in their finery,* thought Rebecca. *What a contrast to me, with my damp, smelly skirt and sweaty, windswept hair!* Mrs. Harrington must have had similar thoughts, for as Rebecca poured the tea, she commented in a kindly voice, "Oh dear, the day certainly has taken its toll on you, Mrs. Hayworth." Just when Rebecca thought she could not seem less like a capable vicar's wife, she glanced beyond Mrs. Harrington to see two boys opening her hen coop and the whole flock escaping.

CHAPTER 10

THE FOLLOWING EVENING FOUND JACK and Rebecca sitting by the fire in exhausted silence. Jack had conducted two services and preached twice that day. Three services in two days was heavy enough, let alone including all the small talk he had been obliged to engage in yesterday afternoon. On reflection, he decided, the hen's disruptive presence had been a good thing, as the ensuing commotion had hastened the departure of many of the visitors. Rebecca was still unable to see the amusing side of the situation, but Jack rewarded the hens with extra corn. Armed with one of John Calvin's commentaries, which he might or might not read, Jack sank gratefully into his arm chair.

Rebecca's book was open and her eyes rested on the words, but her mind was elsewhere. Today Agnes had confirmed her suspicions that she (Agnes, that is) was again expecting a baby. Agnes stated the fact with an air of reluctant resignation. Her youngest was only eleven months old. Rebecca mused on life. *How odd it is! If a neighbour has a glut of apples or leeks, for example, you might swap them for, say, potatoes. Or give them away. But you can't do that with babies. Imagine the conversation:*

"Agnes, you have too many children, don't you?"

"Yes, we don't know where to store them all."

"Then let's do a swap."

"What have you got?"

Rebecca looked around the room. *What is a baby worth?*

"Well, Agnes, our most precious and valuable possession is our grandfather clock. Jack brought it into the marriage. It is an antique. It needs winding only once a week, and it gains only a minute a day."

"What are you dreaming about, darling?" interrupted Jack. "With that half smile playing on your face."

Rebecca's startled gaze flew to his face. "Nothing important, dear," she lied. *Do we lie the most to people we love the most?* she wondered.

"Thinking about the hens?" Jack shut his book. "Actually, Rebecca, I keep meaning to tell you something."

"Oh?"

"Umm, last time I was called to sit with the old dowager, her physician, Dr. Ward, was there too."

"Oh."

"Well, the old lady was completely unresponsive, but we just had to sit there, so we chatted a bit. And in the course of our conversation, I just mentioned about . . . err . . . our problem."

Rebecca sat up. Talking about the *problem* over a dying lady! Mentioning it to a stranger, a doctor at that, was acknowledging there was a problem. Now it was real.

"Oh," she replied stupidly. *It was sweet of him to call it "our" problem not just "yours" though.*

"Dr. Ward recommended a specialist in London who may be able to help, a Mr. Gascoigne."

"I see."

"I have his address."

Rebecca looked into Jack's pleading eyes. This obviously meant a lot to him, and she was not being particularly helpful.

"Let's arrange an appointment," she said with more conviction than she felt, but she was rewarded with a look of relief on Jack's face. "And I can pay with my savings from Ma and Pa," she added. Her mind was working rapidly. "And we can combine it with a long-overdue visit to Uncle Hector."

"And I can take you to a London concert," added Jack, looking quite pleased.

Rebecca nodded. "And we can have fun."

If Jack had looked sharply, he might have noticed that Rebecca's smile was forced.

Proposing such a jaunt to London was one thing, but executing the plan was quite another. A country curate dare not leave his parish without the kind permission of the local landlord; and a landlord is unlikely to give permission when his mother is on her deathbed. Jack knew better than to ask. But he would have been too tired to formulate a plan anyway, for night after night he was called to the bedside of the dying lady. She no longer knew he was there, but Lord Wilson did. Why evening visitations in particular were so vital was open for debate, but Jack suspected that his presence freed up Lord Wilson for dinner parties and other social commitments. Or, if Lord Wilson was in a debating mood, provided a conscripted opponent to discuss higher criticism or evolution. Neither of these reasons were laudable excuses for requesting—nay, demanding—a pastoral visit, and Jack was utterly sick of the situation.

Rebecca harboured un-Christian resentment toward Lady Wilson. She was no biologist, but the absence of her husband on a nightly basis was not conducive to conception. And the old lady's lingering existence postponed any medical action plan that might have been beneficial. In short, Lady Wilson stood in the way of Rebecca attaining motherhood.

Finally, when no one was looking, the dowager slipped out of life, and the whole of Capford was thrown into a state of respectful, if not sincere, mourning. Despite the hours of pastoral care Jack had bestowed upon the old lady, he was not asked to conduct the funeral service. Rebecca took this as a personal insult, but Jack was downright relieved. What would he have said anyway? The sermon preparation would have dominated his week. As it was, the Bishop of Rochester (for who less could worthily conduct the dowager's funeral?) delivered a sugary sermon to the praise of the deceased rather than to the praise of God. He and the Wilson family were delighted by his discourse.

CHAPTER 11

VIOLET HURRIED THROUGH HER MORNING chores. Every minute she spent inside on such a hot July day seemed an utter waste. Today was her half day, and she was determined to be out of the vicarage at one o'clock sharp. To ensure such a prompt finish, she brushed the floor dust under the rugs and was a bit hit and miss with the dusting. *Dust never killed anyone,* she reasoned as she flew on to the next job. She washed the kitchen floor without sweeping it first, and the result was disappointing.

She sighed at her lot—few other housemaids had the misfortune of having a mistress who had once been a housemaid and then a housekeeper! The vegetables were hacked rather than chopped. *They'll taste the same however odd they look.*

When the hall clock struck one, Violet threw off her apron and hung it on the broom cupboard door. Then, quietly as she could, she slipped out the back door into the sunlight. There was only one possible obstacle standing between her and an afternoon in the barley field: her mother. This afternoon, she didn't want her interfering mother cross-questioning her plans.

On arriving home in Shepherd's Cottage, Violet was relieved to find it empty. She ran upstairs to change out of her uniform and into working clothes. She felt a slight pang of guilt about her plan, but only the merest twinge. Today her father and Joe Mason would be shearing the last of the sheep, and they would be expecting her. But they would have to cope with the disappointment, for Violet had arranged for Molly to take her place with the shearers so that she could go to the barley field. Violet preferred sheep to barley, but according to Clara, a new seasonal farmhand had arrived who was well worth a look. Violet still expected Mr. Christopher to reappear and claim her, but meanwhile, there was nothing wrong with looking.

The new man surpassed Clara's most glowing recommendation. Violet spotted him across the field. He was tall, dark, handsome, and very muscular. He had abandoned his shirt, so as he wielded his scythe, Violet admired his manly torso. She just had to make sure she worked near him. Clara was there already, but being a shyer sort, she was admiring from afar. Violet had never been plagued by shyness so, passing her friend, she boldly walked closer to the reapers and started gathering bundles of barley near the newcomer.

The hot afternoon sun burned on her back as she set to work making sheaves and stooks. No one could work like Violet when she wanted to. With rolled-up sleeves and her blouse unbuttoned as far as she dared, Violet toiled away and was finally rewarded with a greeting from the stranger and a swig from his cider flagon. When the foreman halted all work for a quick break, Violet sat down wearily in the shade of a cart and rested her aching back against the wheel. Her tiredness evaporated when the stranger himself joined her.

"Madam, is this seat taken?"

"No, sir, do make yourself comfortable," she replied, echoing his elevated vocabulary and gathering in her skirt to make more room.

"I 'aven't 'ad the pleasure of meeting you afore," he said, flopping himself onto the stubbled ground.

Violet passed him a jam tart.

"I've been working."

"Thought so, I would 'ave remembered ya pretty face."

Violet blushed and looked demure before speaking again. "You ain't from around 'ere, are ya?"

"Na," he replied, mouth full of pastry.

"Where do ya come from?" she continued.

He drank deeply from the cider flagon, wiping his lips with the back of his hand before enigmatically answering.

"I come from 'ere, there, and everywhere."

"Mysterious!"

"That's me—mysterious."

"Mr. Mysterious."

He grinned, and his brown eyes twinkled. "But you can call me Reuben."

"And I'm Violet."

"Pretty name for a pretty lass."

By now everyone was heaving themselves up and getting back to work, so Violet and Reuben followed suit. Violet smiled to herself as she bent down to gather up an armful of barley stalks. *Clara won't 'alf be jealous!*

CHAPTER 12

REBECCA SHOULD HAVE GIVEN VIOLET a sharp reprimand for her slapdash work the previous day, but she was far too busy. Correcting Violet was always problematic, for she frequently got huffy about it and had a habit of answering back. This was not how maids were expected to react, but then Violet was not the typical maid. She was more than that. Despite her faults and immaturity, she was a good friend and ally. Her lively and bold character made her interesting company. Giving her a few days off appeared to be rewarding bad behavior, but it could not be helped. Tomorrow Rebecca and Jack were off to London, the vicarage would be shut up, and Violet could help with the barley harvest. Rebecca was impressed at Violet's eagerness to help in the field—she really was a tough and willing worker!

Rebecca anticipated the trip with mixed emotions. It would be lovely to meet Uncle Hector again, and she was curious to see his residence, where they had been warmly invited to stay; but seeing the specialist was a different matter. Jack had arranged everything, which was just as well, for venturing into London seemed as adventurous and daunting as a trip to Timbuktu.

The journey from Tunbridge Station to Redhill Junction took them through beautiful countryside. Familiar scenes of harvesting could be observed through the carriage window as they rattled by, but once out of the rural parts of Surrey and on toward Victoria

Station, the fields disappeared, and the buildings became taller and closer together.

Rebecca stood bewildered and agog on the platform. She had never seen so many people or heard such a cacophony of noises in all her life! But she was jostled into action by the moving masses; standing still was not the thing to do. She had to keep up with Jack and not lose him in the crowd. This was not easy, for all London men seemed to be wearing black hats like his, not the assortment of flat caps found in rural villages. As she stepped out onto a busy London street, she felt her heart swell. *This is London, the home of Queen Victoria, Prime Minister Viscount Palmerston and our government, and the beating heart of the great British Empire!* Meanwhile, she clutched her bags and kept her trunk close to her skirt. *This is also home to many pick-pockets and scoundrels.*

Jack hailed a waiting hansom cab and gave the driver Uncle Hector's address: 27 Milton Square, South Kensington. When Jack, Rebecca, and all the luggage had been unceremoniously squeezed into the small cab and the driver had moaned about too much baggage, he set off with speed. Rebecca hardly dared look as he weaved the horse through the busy traffic, narrowly missing pedestrians and overtaking stagecoaches. The journey was only two miles, but the excessive fare for the nerve-wracking experience convinced Rebecca that walking would have been the better option, luggage or no luggage.

Uncle Hector's house was one in a long line of tall terraced houses. They had been built in the last decade and bore all the hallmarks of comfortable, modern living. Each shiny front door had five steps leading up to it, large sash windows on either side, and a small railed balcony above. The effect was beautiful, elegant, and welcoming. As Jack and Rebecca climbed the steps and pulled on the heavy bell chain, they looked at each other. Could a relative of theirs really be living in such a salubrious abode?

They had little time to wonder for Uncle Hector welcomed the couple with delight. Rebecca was encompassed in a warm embrace, and Jack's hand was gripped by both of Uncle Hector's and shaken heartily. As he ushered them into the sitting room for a cup of tea, their luggage disappeared upstairs to the large guest chamber by means of an unobtrusive footman.

If the exterior of the house was impressive, so much more was the interior. Even Barton Manor and Biggenden could not boast of the luxury of gas lamps and piped hot water. *How much easier for the servants,* thought Rebecca. Her feet softly sank in the deep carpet as Uncle Hector propelled her to a comfortable leather armchair. Jack was making his way to another seat via one of many glass-fronted book cases, surreptitiously perusing the contents.

"This truly is a great pleasure," said Uncle Hector, sitting down heavily in an armchair surrounded with piles of books and papers.

"Indeed, it is," replied Rebecca.

"How rare it is for me to welcome a blood relative to my abode!"

"We are most grateful, Uncle."

"I have government advisers and academic students visit me on an almost daily basis, but now I have an actual niece staying."

Rebecca smiled as she was elevated above the rank of advisers and academics, but whether it was due to her kinship or the intended duration of their visit with him remained ambiguous.

"I presume Ma and Pa never stayed here."

"No, alas, I never had that pleasure," replied Uncle Hector solemnly, apparently forgetting how critical he so often had been of his brother and his choice of wife.

The tray of tea arrived.

"Ahh, Becca, you can be in charge of the pot."

"Happily," responded Rebecca, and she lavished her uncle with all the attention one can offer in preparing a cup of tea to the desired taste of the recipient.

"Sir, what is your area of expertise?" asked Jack, who until then had been excluded from the conversation.

"For many years, I was a government adviser for income tax."

Rebecca looked hopefully at Jack. What could one reply to such a conversation-killing job? This is where husbands can be very useful—even husbands like Jack, who hate anything financial.

"How interesting," he commented cautiously. "Gladstone has reduced income tax, hasn't he?"

"Indeed, only this year he reduced it from nine pence to seven pence, despite cuts in duty. Why, he is a remarkable chap. When he became chancellor, the government coffers were nearly empty, but Gladstone has managed to replenish them somewhat without squeezing the pockets of the working man too much. He rightly believes that Parliament is too extravagant and wasteful with taxpayers' money, and this has made him more popular outside the Commons than within it."

"Remarkable indeed."

"Yes, he is a dear friend. Why, he has often sat right where you are now and discussed the country's finances with me."

"I thought you had retired, Uncle."

Uncle Hector's gaze returned to Rebecca. "Ahh, advisers don't really retire, dear Becca," he replied in a rather paternalistic, patronizing tone. "I no longer attend Whitehall, but ministers of the Treasury often visit me to discuss policy."

"You must be a busy man," said Jack.

"But that isn't the half of it." Uncle Hector shifted in his seat. "Since withdrawing from Whitehall, I have become a private mathematics tutor for university students."

"Do you enjoy that?"

"To be perfectly honest with you, I am appalled at the ignorance of many of the pupils; they come from privileged homes, have had the best education money can buy, but still have not grasped basic mathematical principles. Either they have wasted their parents' money in fooling about in class or are naturally, frankly, rather dim."

The conversation, which almost amounted to a monologue, continued. Rebecca's mind drifted as she gazed around the room. And what a masculine room it was! She tried to analyse this impression, wondering what made it so very male. The numerous bookcases that lined the walls were mahogany. The dark, shiny wood seemed masculine. Was the word for mahogany *le* or *la* in French? Even the glass doors on the cases, with their gothic arches, looked unfeminine.

The fashion of the day was greenery; ferns and evergreen pot plants, like Biggenden Manor now boasted of, but in this room, there was not a plant or flower in sight. Instead of lace mats and ornaments on any table top and windowsill, there were piles of books, papers, and pens everywhere. Strictly speaking, it was not untidy. Rebecca was sure Uncle Hector knew exactly where everything was located, but the room definitely felt cluttered in spite of its lofty ceiling and spacious proportions.

The phrases "Prime Minister Palmerston," "stabilizing the colonies," "consolidating the Empire," "abolishing paper duty," and "money for the common man" drifted past her in soporific waves. She looked at her husband. She could not think of a subject he was less interested in. Politics was bearable, but economics and taxation? But Jack looked interested and engaged.

What a dear man he was! Imagine being married to a verbose man like Uncle Hector! Did women in that predicament realise before plighting their troth that their men were garrulous, or did the awful realisation dawn too late? Did some women actually enjoy being the captive audience to a chatterbox? Did they routinely feign headaches and retire early, or did they learn how to switch off while retaining an interested facial expression? Dear Jack, she must give him an extra big hug tonight for being just right in conversational matters.

The next morning after a leisurely start, Uncle Hector proposed a guided tour of the important sites in the metropolis, somehow making it sound like a landowner suggesting a trip around his estate. From her previous experience of her uncle's inactivity, Rebecca was surprised he offered to be their tour guide rather than just pointing out places of interest on a map. But Uncle Hector's commodious hospitality included the hiring of a private carriage for the day, arranging a copious picnic, and devoting the whole day to his guests. What Uncle Hector did not know about the Palace of Westminster, Westminster Abbey, Buckingham Palace, and The Mall was not worth knowing.

"And here is Buckingham Palace, my dears, home to our dear Queen Victoria," stated Uncle Hector after cautiously descending from the swaying coach and heading toward the iron railings. "Notice the new façade, complete with a central balcony, which, by the way, was Prince Albert's suggestion. All this was built with money from the sale of the Brighton Pavilion, after Queen Victoria complained to Robert Peel, the then prime minister, that Buckingham Palace lacked space for entertaining."

"I think nine children could comfortably live there," joked Jack.

"She doesn't do much entertaining now, does she?" asked Rebecca.

"Oh no, my dear." Uncle Hector's chins wobbled as he shook his head. "Since Prince Albert's death, she has been in seclusion, and hardly anyone has seen her. She hasn't opened Parliament since. Rumour has it that her husband's private rooms are just as he left them and she insists that hot water for shaving be taken up daily."

"How odd!" exclaimed Rebecca.

"Yes," added Jack, "and people are beginning to think her mourning has become rather self-indulgent, considering her coronation vows."

"Quite!" agreed Uncle Hector, lowering his voice to add in a conspiratorial tone, "and this is giving republicans ammunition. Their voice is getting much bolder."

"Surely, *you're* not a republican, Uncle?" teased Rebecca.

"Certainly not!" sputtered Uncle Hector. "But with power and privilege comes duty and responsibility, and I think the queen is ill-advised to prolong her seclusion indefinitely."

The trio gazed a little longer at the impressive palace. Rebecca wondered if the grieving monarch was gazing out at them. Did her massive abode feel like a lonely gilded cage? Were the iron railings keeping her inside as much as they kept the people out? As the cramped coach swung into The Mall, Rebecca felt a sense of freedom and contentment, worth more than the crown jewels.

Nelson's column at Trafalgar Square was an awe-inspiring sight. Though Uncle Hector declined to alight, Jack and Rebecca were keen to explore the elegant fountains and magnificent statues in front of the National Gallery. It was a delight to enjoy the monument in silence and marvel at the skill in designing and fashioning such sculptures, but on returning to the carriage, the lecture resumed.

"You can't begin to conceive how much trouble that colossal column has already caused. There was a competition for the design, which had to be re-run due to organisational problems. The proposed material for the shaft was changed from sandstone to expensive granite. Then four years into the project, the Nelson Memorial Committee ran out of funds, and the Government Office for Woods and Forests—of all departments—took over."

"Oh dear," said Jack and Rebecca in unison.

"Then one of the bronze reliefs on the pedestal was found to be adulterated with iron, and the partners in the company that produced it were imprisoned for fraud."

And you have managed to tarnish our enjoyment of it too, thought Rebecca.

The carriage took them down Whitehall, and Uncle Hector continued his running commentary. If Rebecca was looking out of the right window, he seemed to comment about something on the left side, and vice versa.

"And here is Downing Street, of the famous Number 10 Downing Street." Rebecca followed his plump finger to the right but missed the road all together.

"Pitt was the last prime minister to reside there. It is said to be in a terrible state, built on soft soil with shallow foundations. Many walls are cracked and floors are buckled. Over the decades, numerous attempts have been made to restore it, but now it is either vacant or used only for occasional meetings. It may well get demolished."

"Rule Britannia," muttered Jack under his breath, making Rebecca shake with suppressed laughter.

"Now coming up ahead is the Palace of Westminster—housing our parliament. It was once a beautiful building, but in 1834 there was a terrible fire that took five days to extinguish. In its place, as you can see, they are constructing this hideous building in what they call Gothic Revival Style." Uncle Hector almost spat out the last three words.

"Sir Charles Berry, the architect who designed this monstrosity, died three years ago, so never will see his creation completed," Uncle Hector added with some satisfaction. "The limestone he chose to build with is already showing signs of decay, and the project isn't even completed, so it probably will not last for long anyway."

Rebecca strained her neck to see past her uncle, through the steamed-up window, to the Houses of Parliament. What she saw seemed very impressive and in no danger of collapse, but she dared not voice her opinion. Instead she squeezed Jack's knee and was rewarded with a fleeting wink.

All this sight-seeing produced a hunger that turned Uncle Hector's train of thought from the crumbling architecture of London to the picnic basket. Tapping hard on the ceiling of the coach with his walking stick, Uncle Hector gained his chauffeur's attention and redirected him to St. James's Park.

Rebecca was relieved to step out of the stuffy, swaying carriage and was astonished at the beauty that met her eyes. The reflection of the late summer sun danced on the shimmering lake. The trees and bushes around the water were attractively set out, contrasting and complementing each other in colour and shape to produce a most pleasing sight. "Like the Garden of Eden," whispered Rebecca to herself.

"Rather a lot of Adams and Eves," teased Jack.

Rebecca was annoyed and embarrassed that anyone had heard her comment. "I meant the beauty."

"Yes, it is nicely laid out."

"Such a great designer."

"Yes, Nash is a clever man."

Turning on her heels, Rebecca marched back to help Uncle Hector with the picnic basket. Sometimes it just wasn't worth trying to share her thoughts. At least the picnic occupied both men's mouths and probably their minds, and Rebecca was able to observe the business of the park without Uncle Hector's critical comments or her husband's flippant ones.

St. James's Park was clearly the place to meet, to see, and to be seen. Ladies promenaded elegantly along the paths, their full, bell-shaped skirts skimming the grass as they glided along. Each dress was uniquely beautiful in its colour, design, lace, folds, and tucks, but all were uniform in lavishness and extravagance. The slightly exaggerated way the young ladies flicked their heads, played with their parasols, and smiled so readily suggested they were very satisfied with their own comeliness and expected others to comply. The men must have been hot in their long, dark dress-coats and tall top-hats, but most looked as if they considered it a price worth paying for the refined silhouette it afforded them.

They all looked so smugly satisfied with themselves. Surely none of the fine ladies could be barren like her; none of them would have an appointment with a specialist tomorrow. That appointment was casting a shadow over everything, even a picnic in the Garden of Eden. They all looked too perfectly feminine to be suffering with any sort of inadequacy. Barren, what an awful word! Very biblical, of course, but very fruitless, hopeless, disappointing. Yes, very disappointing!

"Would you like me to grow Piccadilly weeper sideburns, darling?" Jack asked, drawing her attention to a particularly bushy set nearby.

"Don't you dare!" Rebecca giggled at the idea. "They would definitely come between us." *However wretched I feel, I must try very hard to be nice and enjoy today, and not spoil it for my poor, probably disappointed, husband.*

"Would my good lady care to promenade around the park?" asked Jack, gallantly offering her a hand up.

Rebecca was just about to reluctantly decline in order to keep Uncle Hector company, but one glance in his direction was enough to assure her she would not be missed, for he was flopped against a tree, fast asleep.

"We will not be long," she whispered apologetically to her uncle and accepted Jack's arm.

There were delights to discover in the park. Right there, in the middle of busy, bustling London, in among the bushes sat the idyllic

Duck Island Cottage, looking as if it had been transplanted from some remote rural village.

"Oh, I'd love to live there!" cried Rebecca.

"Apparently, it is for the Keeper of the Birds in the park."

"Then you had better become an ornithologist instead of a parson."

"Yes, waterfowl may be easier to handle than Lord Wilson."

"And swans than sermons."

"And ducks than deacons."

CHAPTER 13

VIOLET COULD HARDLY BELIEVE HOW things had worked out. Actually, she thought with pride, it was due to some cunning planning on her part. It was one thing to have time off from work during harvest; it was quite another to have that time remain unfilled by one's organising mother. But, without exactly telling fibs, Violet had left Ma with the distinct impression that there were still daily chores to be done at the rectory. To give her her due, there had been chores to do, but Violet had completed them all, and now she was free. As much as she liked Pa, she was pleased he was too busy sorting fattened lambs to be involved in the wheat harvest. Having Joe in the field was awkward enough, but she could dismiss his disapproving glances in her direction as she flirted; her father's would have been harder to ignore. And the flirting was going so decidedly well that she certainly did not want any unnecessary interference.

Reuben was by far the most intriguing man Violet had ever met. He was so strong and manly, able to keep up with the head reaper with ease. The harvesting team was pleased with his assistance, acknowledging him to be well worth his daily rate, and yet he kept aloof from them all. Violet was the only local who had been able to draw more than a few words out of him, and she was proud of the distinction. If Violet was in the field, Reuben would sit with her at meal times; if not, he would sit alone. But whether alone or with

Violet, the area he chose was always away from the group and out of sight. Violet heartily approved of this arrangement, since away from prying eyes, they could lark about. They could playfully feed each other mouthfuls of bread and cheese, tease one another, and kiss. Their deep, mutual understanding bypassed the need for conversation, Violet reasoned.

The little Reuben had revealed to her of his past was very romantic. He was a real, proper gypsy, born and bred in a tiny horse-drawn wagon, roaming the country with his family as they sought seasonal work. Every year they took the same route across the country from Cornwall to Kent, picking snowdrops, daffodils, cherries, apples, hops, or whatever was in season. Violet imagined the star-lit evenings around a camp fire, rabbit stew simmering in a big cauldron. Reuben's father would be telling tales of yester-year, his mother putting a baby to bed, and the other children sitting on the wagon steps, spell bound by their father's stories, staring into the glowing fire while the aroma of the stew whetted their appetites. What an idyllic childhood!

Violet longed to be part of the close-knit gypsy community, which was despised by others yet fiercely protected their own. Their ancient traditions and customs were fascinating, and she would embrace them wholeheartedly. Her wagon would be kept as spotless and polished as any gypsy wife's, and she would lovingly lavish Reuben with the respect and attention gypsy husbands demanded. She would gladly abandon her plain, boring frocks for bright colourful dresses, and her ears would just suit big golden rings.

Violet understood Reuben's reserve. Wherever gypsies traveled, they were treated with disdain and suspicion. He had grown up knowing he and his loved ones were loathed and misrepresented. His aloofness was a natural response to the hostile world around him. His acceptance of her was an acknowledgement of their natural affinity.

She felt somewhat guilty by entertaining such thoughts when she should have remained loyal to Mr. Christopher, but his delay was inexcusably lengthy, and she was beginning to entertain some doubts about his fidelity. Anyway, would a grand country house really have suited her? Oh yes, she could very easily get used to the idea of never scrubbing a boiled over milk-pan again; but always having to be genteel and lady-like would be stifling. Never again to experience the delight of walking barefoot through a dewy meadow, nor the satisfaction of swinging an axe and splitting a log, let alone to enjoy the camaraderie of a reaping team. These were high prices indeed to pay for a life of fine frocks, elegant meals, and enforced ease. No, the gritty life on the road, where one relies on one's sheer hard work and wit to keep alive, was more the stuff she was made for. Living close to nature, dictated to by the seasons and shunned by society, she could cope with that; within months she would prove herself to Reuben's family, and they would forget she was ever a non-gypsy—a "gorder" girl.

Reuben was lodging at The King's Head on the village green. After a meal at home with the family, as the dirty dishes and tired children vied for their mother's attention, many a villager slipped out of his noisy house and made his way to the snug interior of the bar. Here his voice would be heard and his opinions respected; here he could relax after a hard day's graft, away from squawking offspring and a grumpy spouse. This escape was the breadwinner's right, despite the united chorus of disapproval from over-zealous parsons, the interfering Temperance Society, and nagging wives. Indeed, as the men sat together, pint mug in hand, chewing on tobacco and gazing into the flickering fire, they became invincible. Safe in the knowledge that no woman was allowed to cross the threshold, a husband could tell tall tales without the inconvenience of a wife's correcting voice. He could elaborate on subjects he knew little about without encountering the dampening effect of a skeptical look. Here he was a man among men, the very pinnacle of creation.

Violet had often walked past The King's Head on a dark, damp evening and looked longingly and unseen through the steamed-up windows. The flickering candles and fire light gave a warm, inviting glow. The waft of beer and tobacco escaped the open window, along with laughter and loud male voices. How she longed to sneak in and witness the masculinity of it all! Men had all the fun. And now the attraction was even greater, for somewhere among all the males was Reuben. She imagined him sitting in a corner, silently observing the action, listening to the conversations but never adding his voice.

Due to the warm summer weather, the pub was not quite the closed cocoon it became in winter. On hot harvesting evenings, when even more men felt the need to quench their thirst, the drinkers spilled out onto the benches outside. This situation was a rare opportunity for the local lasses. If they just happened to have gathered on the village green, they might be invited to share a pint with some generous lad. Any respectable woman would never place herself in such a situation, Violet had repeatedly been told by her parents. But as her father never frequented public house and her mother disapproved of most things, Violet dismissed their advice as old-fashioned and ill-informed. They carried on as if they were Georgian, not

Victorian, wary of any changes in society or new inventions. Anyway, this evening Violet was not going to hang around outside the pub, hoping to entice some lads, and one in particular. Oh no, that would be far too unsubtle.

As soon as the washing up was done, Violet disappeared from the house and started rounding up her friends. Molly and Clara were up for a laugh and walked with her to the vicarage. Having found the key in the woodpile, Violet approached the back door.

"Vi, ya can't do this!" protested Molly.

"Don't worry, scaredy-cat, there's no one around."

Molly shook her head. "I don't mean that."

"Well, what do you mean?"

"Ya can't just walk into someone's house when they're away."

"But I happen to work here," reasoned Violet, turning the key in the lock. "And I am only borrowing something."

She swung open the door and walked in.

"Are ya coming to help or not?" she called back. Molly and Clara giggled nervously as they followed her down the dark hall and into the study.

"I feel bad, being in a vicar's study like this," said Clara.

Molly glanced around. "'E ain't 'alf got a lot a books."

"We ain't looking for books, girls," Violet reminded them. "It's the skittles we're after."

"Vicars don't normally keep skittles in their studies," Clara said, frowning.

"Well, my one does and we need to find them."

Molly placed her hands on her hips. "Ya should know where they are cos you dust in here."

"But I don't dust skittles."

"No?" queried Clara in a posh voice, "Then I fear you are rather negligent in carrying out your domestic duties, my girl."

"Sorry, ma'am," replied Violet. "Next time I'll dust 'em and polish 'em till I see my own beautiful reflection in 'em. Until then, just keep on looking."

"'Ere they are," cried Molly triumphantly, "in the sideboard."

"How dare you look in there!" Violet grabbed the heavy bag from Molly.

"At least they're found," said Clara with some relief.

Once outside in the sunlight, the girls inspected their find.

"They're beautiful and smooth."

"'E's a clever man, all right."

"Nicely painted."

"How did he make the balls so perfectly round?"

"Vi, we can't borrow them," said Clara. "They're too good."

"Oh, come off it, Clara." Violet waved away her friend's concern. "He made them for the good of the community and for the enjoyment of others, and that is exactly how we are going to use them."

"But what if we smash 'em?"

"You just said how clever he is. He made them strong enough to get hit. That's the whole point of the game, isn't it?"

"But the paint might chip."

"Have you ever seen skittles without chipped paint?"

"No, but I've never seen skittles anywhere else before anyway."

"Well then," said Violet decisively, as if she had won the argument. "Anyway, I reckon I know where to find more paint if we need it." And with that she locked the door, returned the key, and walked toward the green, the other girls trailing behind.

Having reached the village green, they realised there was a problem.

"The grass is too long."

"And the ground is too bumpy."

"Then we'll have to go on the road."

"Where?"

"Well," said Violet as she thought aloud, "we need to be near enough to the pub for the lads to see us, but not too close, or we would look 'unrespectable.'"

So, at a suitably discreet distance, the girls set up the ten pins.

"How do they go?" asked Molly.

"In a triangle."

"Five or four at the back?"

"Dunno, but come on, we don't want to look like idiots who have never played it before."

"Well, we haven't."

"But that isn't the point."

The lane was disappointingly rough, and every little bump or stone could send the ball flying off at an unexpected angle, but the girls laughed at the misses and cheered at the hits. As their skill increased, so did their enthusiasm and competitiveness. Violet's cunning plan worked splendidly, for within five minutes the lads outside the pub were cheering raucously. Within ten minutes they had wandered over, pint in hand, to watch and then to join in the action.

Violet was surprised that Joe was among the lads, as he was not a regular pub-goer. She was even more surprised at the familiar way he flirted with Molly. Not that there was anything particularly wrong with Molly, but there wasn't anything particularly amazing about her either. Violet was stunned at Joe's lack of taste. Not that it had anything to do with her, of course, but Molly's replies were so boringly predictable. She, Violet, could have given Joe much more of a laugh. She knew the kind of replies he liked, wit that Molly was totally incapable of. Anyway, each to their own, she thought with a shrug. It didn't matter at all, because right now Reuben was strolling over in her direction.

CHAPTER 14

LIKE A CRIMINAL TO THE gallows, thought Rebecca as she hurried along the busy pavement with Jack toward Harley Street. Her mouth was dry and her palms were sweaty, but she marched on with determination. She had to do this for Jack, and anyway it was good to be actually doing something that might make motherhood a reality. She would do whatever the specialist said. The day would not be easy, but already she felt the Lord had helped them. They had been very concerned about what to say to Uncle Hector and how to sneak out without any questions being asked, but all anxiety was swept away when a housemaid apologised for her master's absence from the breakfast table and explained he was indisposed due to the strenuous activity of the previous day. Of course, Rebecca would never actually pray for someone to feel indisposed, but his indisposition did seem like an answer to prayer.

The streets were bustling with people going about their business, but it was the birds that caught Rebecca's attention. *Oh for the wings of a dove, or even a pigeon,* she thought as she saw one of the latter flying away from danger. *I would fly far away, and be at rest.* Away from infertility, physicians, and surgeons. Would a dove or a pigeon feel bereft if they never laid an egg or hatched a brood? Would other doves and pigeons despise them for not producing offspring? On reflection, no. She remembered that the Sermon on the Mount teaches that the birds are content with whatever their Heavenly Father provides. Now she envied them, not only for their wings but for their contentment too. But Jack had stopped and was addressing her, and she must attend.

"We're nearly there and are a bit early."

They had turned into a street of houses even more imposing than Uncle Hector's, but Rebecca was in no mood to admire architecture. "Let's just wait here a bit then."

"Or shall we find the place first, then loiter out of sight?"

Rebecca shrugged. "Whatever you like."

Jack put his hands on Rebecca's shoulders and turned her to face him. "No, I want to do what you prefer, darling."

Rebecca's gaze fell from his. "I don't know, and I don't care."

"Oh, Rebecca, I wish I could help you." Jack grasped both her hands.

She looked up at him then. "You are helping."

"I really feel for you, my love."

"Thank you," croaked Rebecca, "but please, no sympathy now, or I will cry."

Jack kissed her gloved hands silently.

"Jack, I love you, but just for now I can only manage business-like and matter-of-fact."

"Okay," agreed Jack. "Here we come, Harley Street, Mr. and Mrs. Business-like and Matter-of-fact, and we demand the very best you can offer."

Rebecca had hoped that the specialist would be a kindly, greying man with sympathetic eyes and an understanding manner, but the man before her was stern, with eyes that pierced her soul. His huge waxed moustache seemed to convey a certain smugness unbecoming to his profession. As he ushered them into his consulting room, he looked them up and down, and Rebecca suspected he immediately decided they were below his normal class of clientele, wondering if they could afford his fees. *My dear Pa's hard earned money is as good as any of your genteel patients' brass.*

With an air of extreme condescension, he offered them a seat before sitting down behind a large polished desk. Immediately, he began to finger a gold fountain pen while he addressed Jack.

"So, your wife is barren?"

"Well, she seems to be struggling to conceive."

"For how long?"

"Two years, sir."

Mr. Gascoigne looked accusingly at Rebecca over the top of his half glasses. Feeling like a naughty school girl before a schoolmaster, she nearly apologised. The questioning recommenced, not involving her, but all directed at Jack. Rebecca blushed and curled her toes as information was sought and given that should never be discussed outside the marital bedroom. But if these made her feel uncomfortable, worse was to come.

"So how is your wife's mental state?"

Surprise caused Jack's jaw to drop. "Mental state? Why, she is of a sound mind!"

"Easily agitated?"

"No."

"Easily flustered with trifling cares?"

"No."

"Easily dissolves into tears?"

"No."

"But, Jack," interrupted Rebecca, wanting to be open and honest. "I sometimes get agitated or tearful just prior to . . . err . . . once a month."

The steely schoolmaster eyes fixed on her, silently daring her to speak again.

"Is that so?" he asked Jack.

"Not that I would notice."

"But your wife confesses to these agitations, and they may be very significant. The female body is of weak frame and subject to all manner of influences. Undue worry, stress, or emotion can greatly affect the female reproductive organs and result in wandering of the womb. The worst scenario in the female is hysteria, when uncontrolled, unbalanced emotion completely displaces her womb, rendering her barren and mentally infirm."

"Mrs. Hayworth does not suffer that, sir," said Jack firmly. "She is a most rational and balanced woman."

Mr. Gascoigne ignored this interruption.

"But even a small degree of disequilibrium can render a woman infertile. She needs to learn to check her emotions and seek to maintain calmness at all times."

"Yes, sir."

"And now I wish to carry out a physical examination of your wife." He seemed to be asking Jack for permission, not Rebecca. He rose and led her out of his opulent consulting room to a leather-covered couch in a small, tiled examination chamber en-suite. It reminded Rebecca of the cold room at Barton Manor where fish, pheasants, and geese were disemboweled. Lying on the hard couch in a most compromised position, Rebecca tried to disassociate herself from the present, but one glance at the large, shiny speculum made her eyes widen, and she gulped in horror.

"That would fit a horse!" she said.

Mr. Gascoigne refrained from replying but merely raised one of his black bushy eyebrows and continued with the examination.

Rebecca grasped the sides of the coach and looked up intently. There was a crack in the ceiling that looked like the outline of Wales. She nearly verbalised her thoughts, then immediately thought better of it. Such a random comment would certainly activate the eyebrow and might lead to a firm diagnosis of madness. The pushing and poking made her feel nauseated and faint, not helped by the way his ridiculous waxed moustache bobbed up and down as he carried out his inspection.

When she felt she could bear it no longer, Rebecca prayed for help and comfort. What a wonderful thing the Christian faith is, she thought, when even in this awful position, I can freely pray to my Heavenly Father, not having to fear that it is irreverent but confident of His sympathising ear. Could any other religion offer the same consolation? All others would think it most unseemly and prescribe rituals and ceremonies before approaching a distant deity. If the Lord blessed this undignified investigation and would give the obnoxious man wisdom about a treatment plan, maybe this time next year she could be cradling her very own baby.

At last the examination was over, and Mr. Gascoigne silently exited the room, leaving Rebecca to sort herself out. As she pulled down and straightened her skirts, she wished her emotions could be put right as easily. From the next room, she heard the drone of Mr. Gascoigne's authoritative voice. Was she expected to join the men or wait to be invited back in? A rush of rebellion seized her. It was her body after all that was at stake, so she opened the door. Mr. Gascoigne had lit a fat cigar and was giving his verdict amid a cloud of smoke.

"Yes, as I say, the findings are fairly inconclusive—as they so often are in this difficult specialty. There are so many factors involved, all very complex. The mind of a woman and her body are so uniquely and intricately connected that any exertion of the mind, whether through intellectual effort or strong emotion, may create obstruction of menstrual effluent. This may in turn result in congestion of the brain and lead to irreparable psychological damage, insanity, or death."

"I see," whispered the couple in unison.

The smoke billowing from the accoucheur's nose did not help to relieve Rebecca's feeling of nausea.

"To keep the physiological, mental, and emotional economies of womanhood in equilibrium, Mrs. Hayworth will need to cultivate a calm and even emotional state. No unnecessary taxing of the brain through study. Nothing to encourage a wandering womb. No hard physical labour or exercise that disturbs the abdomen, but daily gentle walking— vigorous enough to warm the body but not to produce perspiration. In the morning when the air is fresh and invigorating, but not in the evening, for evening dew is a source of ill. Gentle walking is a tonic to general health and does not put undue strain on the structures supporting the reproductive organs. Of course, no tight lacing of the corset. A good corset will provide warmth, support, and protection to the delicate female organs and ligaments. It will help maintain a good digestion and healthy bladder as well as averting back injury. But a tightly laced corset could do untold internal damage and dislodge your vital organs. Finally, I suggest a daily sitz bath, by which I mean sitting in a few inches of cold water."

Mr. Gascoigne put down his smoldering cigar and fingered his fountain pen.

"Now Rev. Hayworth, may I give you some advice. I detect that you, like many other men of less privileged class, are at risk of viewing your wife as an equal. This is a grave and dangerous error. Indeed, you, of all men, should remember how even Scripture refers to women as the weaker vessel. Do not require her to share the burden of care that ought to fall on your shoulders."

Was it Rebecca's imagination, or did her husband stiffen his shoulders at this statement? Was it in disagreement, or was he flexing himself to shoulder the parish burdens alone?

"Keep her from the strains and alarms that come your way and demand the attention of men like you and me, who are called upon to assist the suffering and unfortunate. Do not encourage mental exertion—for example, the reading of your theological tomes. Women are weak and need to be treated as such. Light reading, moralising tales, and ladies' periodicals are suitable, but no study books or emotionally disturbing novels."

The flow of advice then ceased, but the Hayworths sat silently, unable to formulate a sensible reply.

"So that will be all. Come back in several months if there is no change, and we can consider surgery. That will be ten guineas. Thank you and good day." The fountain pen pointed toward the door, and they obligingly exited.

They walked in silence all the way to The Regent's Park. Carriages rattled past them, and street sellers advertised their wares loudly, but

Rebecca was oblivious to everything except her battle to fight back tears. What an incapable specimen of womanhood she was! She appeared to have no control of her emotions or her wandering womb. She must change beyond all recognition before she could ever hope to be worthy of motherhood. As they sat down on the first available bench, she was blind to the trees, flowers, and beauty that would have normally enchanted her. All she could see were legions of nannies and young mothers proudly pushing perambulators.

She could bear it no longer; the tears she had held back since the humiliation of the examination chamber flooded out, and her whole body shook with their force. Jack pulled her to himself and held her close to his chest. He bent down to kiss her hair, but it landed on her bonnet.

"My darling, don't take it so badly. The man is a buffoon." The sobs continued. "What he said about women was outrageous! Especially applied to you. You are the most rational, energetic, and sane woman I know. If we can't have children, it is nothing to do with your . . . whatever did he call it? . . . equilibrium or whatever. It is just what the Lord sees best for us."

"The specialist despised me!" Rebecca shakily replied from the depths of his waistcoat.

"He despises all women," her husband said in a low voice.

"Why did he choose that profession then?"

"To charge ten guineas, purchase gold fountain pens, and smoke cigars."

The sobbing recommenced. "I've cost us so much money."

"I'd have paid more, just to escape." Dear Jack and his humor.

"Do you think he has a wife?"

"Probably—in a specimen jar somewhere," he whispered in Rebecca's ear.

"Pickled?"

"Exactly!"

Unaware of any passersby, they clung to each other, mingling tears and laughter.

CHAPTER 15

THE TEN-PIN BOWLING IDEA HAD really taken off in Capford. One of The King's Head regulars, Tim, was the undergardener for Lord Wilson and had access to a lawn roller. After meticulously cutting a strip of grass on the village green, he rolled it to the standard of the Wilsons' croquet lawn. Now no one could blame uneven ground for a poor shot, and the arguments were reduced. Every school boy was eager to get his hands on the vicarage skittle set, but Violet guarded them with an eagle eye. "As a paid member of the vicarage household, I am entrusted with safeguarding their property," she explained haughtily to a bunch of boys who dared to ask.

"But 'e made 'em for the Sunday school tea, and so they're for us Sunday school children."

"Is that so?"

"Yes, it is."

"Then, before leaving, he would have instructed me to give them to you, and I can assure you, he did not."

"Maybe 'e forgot to say."

"Maybe he did, but to play with them without his permission would be terribly wrong of you, wouldn't it, and I don't want to see you getting into trouble. Now run along and carry on playing skittles with upturned logs."

"But they don't fall down as easy."

"Then you'll have to throw a bit harder, won't ya?"

Thus Violet remained centre stage in the ten-pin bowling craze, and every evening The King's Head regulars looked out for her and the big canvas skittle bag. But Violet was running out of time on two fronts: the Hayworths were to return from London in two days, and Reuben was leaving Capford at the end of the week to go hop-picking in Flimwell, a village ten miles away. She was certain she had won his heart, but she needed also to win his hand in marriage, or at least a promise of his hand. The whole village knew of their attachment, and she would be a laughingstock if he slipped away without an acknowledgement of their position. Not that she doubted his intentions, but he did need to verbalise them. That is common a weakness in men, she had noticed. They couldn't express their intentions and often needed women to help them.

Tonight the lads were in a celebratory mood. The back-breaking job of harvesting the turnips was completed, so now at Biggenden only the apples were left to be picked.

The moment Reuben approached her, Violet could see he had drunk too much. She had never heard him talk and laugh so much. He was too demonstrative in public, and she felt uncomfortable. Whatever her plans had been for helping him articulate his intentions, they would have to be shelved until he was sober. A drunken proposal was no proposal at all. How was she supposed to treat him? She had had no experience of dealing with an intoxicated man. Should she ignore his loud, befuddled declarations of love or try to humour him? She felt embarrassed in front of her fellow villagers.

She glanced at Joe and saw his look of disgust. She wanted to go home but was responsible for the wretched skittles.

She tried to mingle with the crowd and lose Reuben, but he followed her relentlessly. Now she was scared. If and when he went to refill his tankard, she would slip off into the shadows, and the skittles would have to look after themselves.

It was twilight before she could carry out her plan. She crept past the public house and disappeared down the path by the woodshed. She walked fast, her heart beating louder than the exercise required. Then she heard her name being called. It was Reuben, and his voice sounded harsh. When she heard footsteps behind her, she gathered up her skirts and started to run. She could not tell if Reuben was catching up with her, for the leaves under her feet and her own heartbeat drowned any other noise. She realised she was running away from help as well as toward harm. Down this lonely path, no one would find her. She was about to lose her life or her virtue or both. She ran and prayed as she had never run and prayed before.

Now she could hear his footsteps, fast and close. She screamed and was about to scream again when his hand suddenly muzzled her mouth. Now he had her.

"You've been dallying with me for long enough," he hissed, "and now you can give me my dues!"

His other arm crossed her chest, and his hand grasped her shoulder, forcing her backward. She kicked as hard as she could, but with one movement of his leg he had her down on the ground. He crashed to the ground on top of her. Her whole body was jarred with pain, but she fought on. Her kicks, bites, and scratches only provoked from him expletives and punches. His weight pinned her to the ground, and a firm slap around the head made her so faint she wondered if she would ever rise again. She could taste blood in her mouth. She was too weak, faint, and bruised to put up any more resistance. She was no match for him. The inevitable must happen, and she must submit and die.

Just at that moment they were surrounded by lamp lights, and someone kicked Reuben so hard he weakened his grip of her. The kicking continued until he was right off.

"Get out of 'ere, you brute!"

"Leave our Vi alone!"

Now Violet recognised her saviours—they were Tim and Joe. They were pulling Reuben to his feet and with a few more swipes, sent him on his way.

"And don't ya dare show ya evil face in these parts again!"

Violet felt dazed, relieved, and embarrassed. When she tried to sit up, her head reeled.

Out from the shadows a shaken Molly came to assist. "We'll get ya safely home, Vi."

The three hauled her to her feet. She staggered along between them. Her dress was torn and covered in mud, and her hair roll was half undone. She felt so disheveled and foolish, and they were all so kind and decent. She really needed their assistance, but all she wanted was for them to be gone.

I must look awful, 'cos even Ma is sympathetic, thought Violet as she collapsed into a chair by the stove. Her rescuers explained the situation, received hearty thanks, and then bade them all goodnight. Even when they had gone, her mother fussed around her lovingly. Pa looked ready to grab a shot gun and go after Reuben, but instead he laced Violet's warm milk with brandy and drew her chair closer to the stove. Such tender love after such hateful violence broke Violet's brave composure, and she wept like a baby. She desperately wanted her parents to understand, but her sobs and swollen top lip made stringing a sentence together nearly impossible.

"Ith all right," she lisped. "He didn't acthually do anything."

Her parents looked at her battered face, swollen lip, and bruised body, but they knew exactly what she meant.

"That's all right then," they said with relief.

"Yeth, ith all right."

CHAPTER 16

AS SHE WALKED UP THE vicarage garden path, Rebecca paused to take in some deep breaths of fresh country air. How wonderful it was to be back in quiet, unhurried Capford. Early that morning as they had left Uncle Hector's house, they saw that an autumn mist had descended on London. In the country, a light morning mist could beautify the scenery with mystery, often heralding the dawn of a warm day, but in London the damp droplets caught the acrid smoke of a thousand chimneys and refused to let the sun penetrate its density. On seeing the smog, Uncle Hector refused to take a step outside.

"You'll choke to death," he warned the couple as they prepared to walk to Victoria Station.

They ignored his predictions of an early demise, not wanting the expense of a cab, and coughed their way through the miasma and murkiness of the shrouded streets.

Yes, it was wonderful to be back in rural Kent, where the sun still conquered the mist and where farm animals still outnumbered human beings. In this calm and pleasant environment, where nature and man lived in greater harmony and where life was not unnecessarily rushed or mechanised, she would school herself in the art of serenity, indulge in sitz baths, and pray for results. Thus resolved, she made her way indoors to greet Violet.

Violet! What a state! Rebecca could scarcely believe her eyes. With two black eyes and a thick lip, the poor girl looked utterly miserable and incapable of work. Over a cup of tea at the kitchen table, Jack and Rebecca heard Violet's abbreviated version of the incident.

"Violet, you should not be here. You need to be in bed."

"Needs must," replied Violet.

"Well, I am grateful for your loyalty and courage in struggling here to light the stove and get things ready for us, but please, go home and rest."

"It would be nice."

"Then go."

"But what about your supper?"

"I can manage that and everything until you are fully recovered. For I guess you have a lot more bruising than we can see."

Violet nodded with downcast eyes. "You wouldn't want to know, ma'am."

"But what I do want to know is that you will not return until you are fully recovered. Shocks like you have experienced can take their toll, especially on young women." *Now I am sounding like Mr. Gascoigne.*

Violet must have been in pain, for she put up no resistance but, with tearful apologies, left Rebecca to don her apron, stoke the stove, and prepare the supper. The trunks needed unpacking, and the parlour fire needed lighting. The log baskets were empty.

News traveled fast. The back doorbell hardly stilled between messengers. Old Mrs. Foreman had fallen and broken her arm. Mrs. Pearson had delivered two weeks early. The school teacher had run out of text cards. The deacon had forgotten to announce a collection last week, so it would be a week late.

With specks of London soot still adorning her face, Rebecca hurried between pantry and parlour, back door and bedroom. She peeled vegetables, exchanged pleasantries, issued sympathy, promised help, and wrote messages for Jack. Back to normal life, just as she liked it—right in the centre of village activities, but was it compatible with cultivating calmness?

Life at the vicarage fell back into its normal rhythm and routine. Jack rarely left the four walls of the study unless he was visiting the sick, at a committee meeting, or taking a service. Rebecca arranged the harvest display, visited the sick, prepared meals for the helpless, cooed over newborns, and endured committee meetings. During their short evenings together, Jack never mentioned Mr. Gascoigne's advice. Rebecca wondered if it ever even crossed his mind. He never mentioned buying a sitz bath, and Rebecca dared not ask for such an expensive item—not after the specialist's fee. One did not need a fancy bit of equipment to sit in a few inches of cold water. In the privacy of her own room, when she was completely sure Jack was out visiting, she tried various receptacles. The copper bath took far too much water. A bucket was too deep and narrow. The biggest mixing bowl, used for making Christmas puddings, was too wobbly. The only thing that came anywhere near being suitable was her jam-making saucepan. She could just about sit in it without the fear of falling over or getting stuck. It took only two jugs of water to reach the required areas, and it could be hidden in her wardrobe. Perching herself on it was laughably ridiculous and precarious, but it did the job. It was more of a contortionist's feat than a relaxing soak, but then again, would sitting in two inches of cold water ever be relaxing? Especially when fearing that any moment you may be discovered in such a ludicrous position? Neither Jack nor Violet must ever know.

Walking was a much easier instruction to follow. She walked miles every day, crossing the parish on various missions, and she enjoyed it. Whatever the weather, it was wonderful to step out the back door, feel the wind tug her skirts, and take a lung full of fresh air. Along the lanes there was always plenty to observe and delight in. Even the bare branches on a grey winter's day had a knotty beauty of their own. The crispness of a frosty morning and the bleak dusk of the early evening—both were lovely when you had a warm house awaiting your return. But instead of being merely absorbed in her surroundings, Rebecca now had to be careful; she did not want to jiggle her internal organs around too much, so skipping was strictly forbidden. And she must not perspire. That was easier said than done when she was carrying a large basket of provisions for an infirmed parishioner or returning from the grocers. Slow, sedate walking did not come naturally, and she felt a bit silly walking like a fine lady in a London park when she was actually negotiating streams on a country track. Walking with Jack had always been pleasurable, but now it was fraught with problems. She either lagged behind or jiggled and perspired.

Rebecca had never indulged in the fashion of tight corseting. Only the idle rich could afford to lace themselves in so severely they could barely breathe or stand up without feeling light-headed. The Wilson ladies were like that—unable to sing in church due to their tiny, whale-boned cages. Their figures were stunning, but the price to pay was their lack of independence. No women thus trussed up could possibly touch her own toes or pick anything up off the floor. They could never sit in a chair, merely perch on the edge. Yet

Rebecca had to admit to herself she had been tugging on her corset strings rather more of late. Marital happiness had added an inch or so to her waist, and a well-tied corset disguised the fact nicely. Any expansion of the waist in a wedded woman could get the village gossips hinting at the patter of tiny feet, and she could do without such unfounded rumours.

All the medical ideas about careful walking and supportive corseting made Rebecca imagine her womb to be like some sort of badly set blancmange or soufflé. The sort of culinary disaster that keeps cooks awake at night and makes others question their ability. Her early cartwheeling activities, the trauma of losing both parents at a critical age, and her monthly moods were like a cook failing to whip the eggs enough, having the oven the wrong temperature, or undercooking the dish. But did God really make such a precariously sensitive arrangement when He created woman? The regularity with which many women seemed to reproduce contradicted this theory. *The Bible itself states we are "fearfully and wonderfully made," suggesting something rather better designed than a sunken soufflé.*

God may have purposely created her barren—that was possible. He being the Divine Potter and she being the clay meant He could do with her as He saw fit. It was true but difficult. How did Christian folks who were blind, deaf, or lame come to accept their Heavenly Father's design of their bodies? Could they really be like Paul and "glory in my infirmity"? Their faith must be outstanding. So much better than her own, faltering and weak, which seemed to waver at every hardship, even though her affliction was light compared to what many other people had to suffer. *I really must school myself in counting my blessings,* thought Rebecca.

Yes, maybe if she counted her blessings, showed great faith, and gloried in her infirmity, God would reward her by giving her a child. But surely that was against all she knew about grace—God's undeserved love and mercy. God never asks sinners to earn His favour; it is a free gift, and as a believer the terms are no different. God loves because He wants to love. Our goodness is not what we are or what we do, but the imputed, perfect righteousness of Christ. Time and time again Rebecca had to take hold of all the biblical truth she knew so well, like a drowning man grasping onto an overhanging branch as he is swept down a fast-flowing river. When she lost her grip, she either struggled in a whirlpool of anger against God and self-pity, or was dragged into a strong current of pharisaical good works as if they were meritorious and could sway God's opinion and plan.

As fact and fable, theology and theory struggled for supremacy in her ruminations, she wondered if Mr. Gascoigne had been correct, after all. Was her problem due to inappropriate levels of brain activity? Maybe she was thinking too much. She wondered what Mr. Gascoigne would think of soul activity. Where in his medical model of things did that come in? Did he consider it a waste of energy and a threat to equilibrium? *"Don't worry your weak womanly head about your destination for eternity, it may displace your reproductive organs, Mrs. Hayworth."* It was ludicrous, and just imagining the conversation (and fountain pen movements) made her smile, but it also propelled her thoughts in a different direction. Eternity is unimaginably long, and heaven unimaginably wonderful, so why should she get all upset by a little problem that, at the most, would last for only a couple of decades? What are decades compared with eternity? If in heaven there is no marrying or giving in marriage, there would certainly be no fertility or barrenness.

The mundane business of vicarage life became a welcome distraction. Hens needed to be fed, clothes needed to be ironed, meals needed to be prepared, and villagers needed to be visited, come what may. She would rejoice over newborns in the congregation, despite the vicarage nursery standing empty. She would delight in her Sunday school infants, despite not being the one who tucked them into bed each night. She must and she would. *So help me God!*

CHAPTER 17

EDWARD TOOK A POLITE SIP of his tea before replying to his wife. A man should never sound delighted at the news of one's mother-in-law's indisposition, and he checked his response with the appropriate proportion of filial concern.

"Laryngitis can be nasty."

"She can hardly manage a word."

What a marvelous situation, thought Edward, then meeting his wife's eyes, he realised she too was smiling.

"It must be most unusual at home." She seemed unable to suppress a chuckle at the thought.

"No wonder she is concerned. Do you suppose she is very ill?"

"Of course not, Edward. If she is capable of organising the exodus of the whole household to the South of France for the winter, she can hardly be as ill as her letter implies."

"What does your father think?"

"He and his wishes are not mentioned in her letter, but I suspect he is secretly delighted. Dear old Pa has longed to winter in southern France for years, but a sense of duty has always held him back. Now that the cottage hospital is up and running and his dependents are off his hands, he can at last contemplate the idea." She stopped to nibble her buttered toast before continuing. "Pa denies himself pleasure, but if he can tell himself that going to France is a husbandly duty prescribed by a physician, he will overcome all his puritan scruples and thoroughly enjoy the experience."

"No excuse is better than a medical one."

"Exactly."

"Do you think her physician really suggested the South of France?"

"Of course not!" Sophia dropped her toast on her plate. "I can just imagine it. Mother would have suggested the idea to the doctor as he was packing up his bag and considering his fee. Absent-mindedly he would have nodded his consent, and she would have presented it to Father as a medical edict."

"I got the impression she could not live without seeing her dear little Bertie every few weeks."

"Mother greatly exaggerates her feelings toward anyone other than herself."

Edward was taken aback. "Darling! Isn't that a bit harsh?"

"Edward, I have had to live with her most of my life and have had to learn this from bitter experience."

"Was it that bad?"

"Maybe I am guilty of exaggeration too, but she blew so hot and cold, one minute praising us and the next minute undermining any confidence we had, that we learned to be wary of her favour."

Edward gazed at his wife with new respect and insight.

"And the way she treats you, Edward, is appalling—as if you are not good enough for me, just like she has undermined me for so many years."

Edward leapt from his seat and kissed his beautiful wife.

"My own sweetheart! You are lovely. And the one subject on which I heartily agree with your mother is my unworthiness of you."

"Are you not greatly distressed by the idea of not seeing your mother-in-law for three months?" asked Sophia, deflecting the subject from herself.

"As a true Englishman, I will take this blow with fortitude and a stiff upper lip."

"You are lovely!" Laughter played on Sophia's lips. "But may I say that you look a bit ridiculous eating that toast with your lip elongated like that."

"Fortitude, my good lady, fortitude."

"I bet you couldn't kiss looking like that."

"Then, I will prove you wrong."

Edward was still smiling as he entered his study to peruse the plans to drain boggy-meadow. At the moment things weren't bad. Not bad at all! Only last week Sophia had surprised him with her determination and courage by dismissing the awful nursery nurse. The old battle-axe could have made the best of men quake, but Sophia had confronted her, ordered her bags to be packed, and saw her off the premises forthwith.

She had every right to terminate her contract immediately, for the nursery maid, when searching in a cupboard normally kept locked during her dictator's absence, had found a half-used bottle of laudanum. Having experienced months of abuse at the nurse's hands, the maid lost no time in showing the bottle to Sophia and explaining her theory that little Bertie was sedated every night. The maid had long suspected this to be the case, since the nurse had boasted of good nights every time *she* put Bertie to bed, implying it was all thanks to her many years of experience and superior skill. The bottle was the proof the maid had sought for so long.

Of course, the nursery nurse denied all allegations most vehemently. She maintained that the laudanum was for her own use for backache. But Sophia was adamant: even if the nurse was being truthful (and she was convinced otherwise), Bertie was not to be nursed by a woman doped up with drugs. She had grown to dislike the overbearing woman, and this was the ideal opportunity to dismiss her. So, dismiss her she did!

The domestic team had certainly shaped up nicely. The loss of Rebecca Stubbs as housekeeper had been a huge blow, and Edward imagined he would never again have such a dedicated team of staff. But now, after a rocky couple of years, peace had been established below stairs—mainly, he suspected, due to the growing confidence of his lovely wife. The grumpy, sore housekeeper who Mrs. Harrington had triumphantly appointed to replace Rebecca had gradually lost her sourness and seemed, like a cox apple, to mellow over time in the country air. Both the haute men-servants that Mrs. Harrington had thrust upon them had found the sights and smells of rural life beneath them and had obtained positions in London, leaving Edward free to dress himself again, just as his mother had taught him to do.

Actually, Edward had always dressed himself. The thought of another man assisting him seemed ludicrous, but now he could do so without feeling as if he was slighting his servant or denying him the opportunity to advance his career. Employing only women in the house, Edward was no longer required to pay the male servant tax. Paying less tax is always gratifying.

The appointment of a new male member to the outdoor team demonstrated Sophia's kindness. Benny was the simple son of one of the farmhands. Benny could neither read nor write, and his speech was hardly understandable, but his winning smile made him a favourite of everyone, including Sophia. She persuaded the gardener that Benny could be helpful around the grounds and in the green-houses. Benny loved his new job and especially the shiny boots he was given. Everyone who met him, whether in church or in the lane, had to admire his boots, the laces, and the sturdy soles. Every day, against all the normal rules, he knocked on the front door and presented Sophia with a bunch of seasonal flowers or foliage. His wide grin and enthusiasm were infectious, and Sophia found it no hardship to admire his footwear as well as his flowers every day. She always had a candy or biscuit to reward him. The simple arrangement received pride of place in the drawing room, as if they were from a London florist.

It still troubled Edward that he did not conduct morning and evening prayers with all his household. Many other Christian households gathered together twice a day for Scripture reading and prayer. For a long time he excused himself by admitting he was in no spiritual state to teach anyone, but now, thankfully, things were much better. Reverend Jack Hayworth's series of sermons on Hebrews had been excellent and had rekindled Edward's love for the Lord. He had feared that his spirit was so starved, shriveled, and close to death that it was beyond stirring, but as Jack spoke of Christ's excellency and superiority to all the Old Testament types and shadows, Edward was drawn to his Saviour afresh.

His Saviour, what a staggering thought, that the eternal Son of God should deign to become man and die for his sins. Not like some Old Testament calf for sacrifice, struggling and being dragged to the altar, but willingly out of unfathomable love. Not like an unapproachable Old Testament high priest who, though a fellow sinner, was distant and haughty, going about his routine, but as the Great High Priest—sinless yet sympathetic and approachable. Approachable and sympathetic, even to those who have wandered off and are returning for the umpteenth time.

Grace is amazing in first converting a person, but Edward thought it was even more amazing in restoring and bearing with people like him who had been greatly blessed but had proven to be such mediocre Christians. Why hadn't he been cut down like the barren fig tree? Why did God still bother with him? It was all thanks to God's undeserved, patient, persistent, and unexplainable love. Truly He is "rich in mercy."

Yes, the Lord was indeed very kind to him. He received good teaching at the parish church, his household was peaceable, his mother-in-law was out of the country, and his farm was profitable. The only thorns in his bed of roses were his pheasant-shooting companions who would soon be issuing invitations to shoot on their land and dine at their tables—and expect reciprocation. But, he reflected, he could stomach their arrogant ignorance and fine dining if it gave Sophia pleasure. She deserved a few evenings mixing with the great and good of Kent and Sussex. Just watching her be the attentive hostess to enchanted guests almost compensated for the inconvenience. She still impressed him with the grace and ease with which she circled the room, charming the corpulent men and pleasing the languid ladies.

His shooting companions were annoying, but his sharpest thorn lay closest to his rose and pained him daily. His Sophia was wonderful, but had she yet understood her need of the Saviour? She went to church, she kept Sunday, she sang a bedtime hymn to Bertie, but had she committed her soul to Christ? Edward loved her soul as much as he loved his own. He would have forfeited his place in heaven if she could have gained it. But that was all theoretical—she had to trust the One who had given up His place in heaven and forfeited his life for sinners. Edward prayed for her many times a day, yet speaking to her seemed impossible. So often he had good intentions, but when an opportunity arose, he somehow failed to make use of it, and the conversation soon moved on, leaving the important subject untouched.

Reading the Bible and praying after each meal when they had no visitors was now their regular habit, and he was pleased about that. He could say more in prayer than he would dare in an ordinary discussion, but Sophia's only response to his devotions was a reverently whispered echo of *amen* at the end.

The doorbell rang and a maid attended to it, and it happened many times again. Safely closeted in his study, Edward listened to the cheerful distant hubbub of female voices and remembered that today the village charity knitting group was meeting in his parlour. How Rebecca had managed to persuade Sophia to open her doors to the gathering, he could not imagine! Mrs. Hayworth was turning into a real little vicar's wife, delegating here and twisting arms there in such a charming manner that one ended up agreeing to things without knowing it. Imagine if the country was run by women like

Rebecca and Mrs. Brookes—so much more would be accomplished in a far quieter and more reasonable way. A parliament full of determined women would be quite formidable—but this was fanciful thinking! The only women in Parliament were the tea-ladies and cleaners. Fancy the knit and natter group, as he called them, sitting in his parlour! They were probably putting the world, or at least the parish, to rights over a cup of tea, in a manner not unlike the House of Commons—plus knitting needles. *I bet there is full attendance today, as they all want to inspect our interior and assess our china tea-set.*

CHAPTER 18

VIOLET'S FEET CRUNCHED ON THE white frozen grass as she walked from the vicarage to the church. Her buckets of hot water steamed in the chilly air. This would have been good weather for Christmas, although snow would have been even better.

Instead it had been grey and dreary—similar to her mood. She just couldn't help always anticipating Christmas with the butterfly stomach of the little girl she used to be. Carol-singing around the village in the dark had seemed such an exciting event. Ma would dress her up warmly and send her off with the rest of the family, while she stayed behind to prepare food for the singers. Pa would lead the singing, so he delegated the care of Violet to one of her older siblings. They in turn forgot her as they found their friends in the crowd of singers, leaving Violet to giggle and whisper with her school chums. She wasn't really big enough to go door-to-door with a collecting bucket while the singers sang, but she would make it her business to pester a bucket-holder into relinquishing his role so she could take over. Of course, she wanted the householders to give generously to the collection for the church, but she also knew that a well-timed smile could earn her several sweets or mince pies. None of her friends were brave enough to knock on a door, but they admired her bravery and happily shared in her gains.

After the singing, at what seemed midnight to the young Violet, everyone would gather at the Brookes' cottage for soup and mince pies (Reverend Brinkhill would never have countenanced such an invasion of his vicarage). Ma would rush around the hot kitchen directing her daughters in serving the guests. Violet knew if she set foot in the kitchen she would be roped into service, probably passing around plates of mince pies to the elderly, who hadn't even done any singing. Instead, Violet would sneak upstairs with a loaded plate, a few candles, and her group of giggling girls. Had Ma realised Violet was in her bedroom with flickering candles and fidgety girls, she would have been horrified, but she was too busy bustling about to notice her absence.

Christmas day—for her younger self—would be equally as exciting. Thanks to Reverend Brinkhill, the morning service lacked any seasonal warmth or joy, but this passed Violet by. She had a pocketful of cough-candies from the toe of her Christmas stocking and was content. Once again, the Brookes' cottage would be filled with guests, food, and excitement. All her many brothers and sisters returned home, the older ones bringing spouses and babies. There was no one of Violet's age to play with, but she enjoyed her tiny nieces and nephews and the teasing she received from her brothers-in-law. The married sisters congregated in the kitchen and chatted their way through the chores while Violet was left to mind the babies. Once the work had been done and the babies were asleep, the games began. The very games and exuberance that Reverend Brinkhill had solemnly warned against in the morning were played out to the full. This was the one day in the year that work, debt, and bills could be forgotten and the riches of family life and friendship enjoyed. Prince

Albert had introduced the country to the Christmas tree, and Violet longed to have one in their parlour, but Mr. Brookes believed them to be papal or pagan and firmly forbade it. *How can a tree be Roman Catholic?* wondered Violet. Holly and mistletoe were acceptable in her Pa's Protestant eyes, so the cottage was liberally decorated with greenery. The branches wilted and yielded to gravity as the rooms heated up, and Violet was instructed to take them outside before the babies would wake up and sample the berries.

Those years had gone, and the babies were now school children. The brothers-in-law still liked to tease her, but she no longer accepted piggyback rides. The games she had loved and that the rest of the family still seemed to love, now seemed ridiculous. And there were now far too many nephews and nieces. The married sisters were much too busy fussing about their broods to help in the kitchen, so Violet had become the family's scullery maid. *I could be at the vicarage,* she moaned to herself, *then at least I would be getting paid to scrub the pans.* Even the caroling had let Violet down: Mrs. Hayworth had taken over the responsibility for refreshments when her husband became the vicar, so instead of singing, Violet was stirring the soup. Many of her former school friends were absent due to work commitments, but those who were present seemed far too busy flirting and devouring the food she had prepared to take time to visit her in the kitchen.

Today marked the end of all seasonal celebrations. She and Mrs. Hayworth were cleaning the church and returning it to its non-high-day normality. The activity suited Violet well, and as she scrubbed the floor, she imagined life as a nun. Until recently she had seen life in monasteries (along with purgatory and Christmas trees) as a terrible Roman Catholic heresy, but to her amazement she had discovered there were Anglican nunneries. The Hayworths had returned from London with various old editions of the St. Martin-in-the-Field's Parish Post. Being one of the few things she was permitted to read on a Sunday, Violet has perused them and found an interesting article on the Sisters of Mercy in Windsor who devoted their lives to God and the church. These noble women worked tirelessly among the poor and outcasts of society. They befriended unmarried mothers and fallen women. They provided shelter and an opportunity to learn a trade, as well as giving spiritual advice and education. *You never hear of unmarried fathers and fallen men,* thought Violet. *The women always take the blame, while the men just disappear.*

Violet imagined herself in the convent. Nobly resisting all temptations of the flesh, she would devote her life to communion with God and the service of others. She would look pure and angelic in a nun's habit, far beyond the reach of males. She would rise early, sing beautiful plainchant in the chapel as the morning sun, like a ray of blessing from heaven, shone through the stained glass windows onto her serene face. With a heart devoid of selfishness, she would work hard in the monastery for the good of her sisters—and in the community for the good of mankind (but especially womankind).

Violet was aware that if things had gone differently in September and she had not been rescued by her friends, she too could well have been a fallen woman. Society would have treated her with repulsion and contempt. She was thankful to God for sending help. She was also thankful that God is more merciful than society. She knew that He had given fair rules about this sort of attack. If she had cried out for help, even if her cry had gone unheard by human ear, according to God's rules to Moses, she would be innocent. The realization that

God is kinder to us than we are to each other was new to Violet. The more she thought about it, the more convinced she was. We give up on people easily, find it hard to forgive, expect loyalty, and easily take offence. God describes Himself as longsuffering, rich in mercy, ready to forgive, and patient. This was exactly the sort of God she needed.

Violet was busy polishing a brass memorial plaque when a messenger boy entered with a letter for Mrs. Hayworth.

Rebecca dried her hands on her apron and opened it. Her face looked grave as she read the contents. "It is from Uncle Hector's housekeeper," she told Violet. "Uncle Hector has suffered a stroke. I must go to him right away."

Violet stood up. "I'll help you pack your trunk, ma'am."

"Oh, but Jack is far too occupied to come with me. I daren't even ask him. What shall I do?"

Mrs. Hayworth looked unusually agitated.

"Let me come with you," suggested Violet.

"But you are needed to run the house here."

"I am sure Ma could see to that for a few days."

Mrs. Hayworth looked at Violet thoughtfully. "I'll discuss it with my husband. Meanwhile, please gather the things here and hurry to the vicarage to help me get organised."

Violet scurried around collecting the mops, buckets, and dusters. She desperately wanted to go to London. What an adventure it would be! She often wondered what the capital was like. Something about it had affected Mrs. Hayworth. Since her visit there in September, she had changed. Violet could not put her finger on the problem, but somehow her mistress was unnaturally aloof, even slightly haughty. She no longer laughed freely at comical situations and didn't become animated as easily as she used to. Violet missed her spontaneity and wondered why she was suppressing it. Maybe London ladies were all calm and dreary.

Much to Violet's delight, Jack decided that his wife was more in need of her services than he was and gave permission for her to accompany Rebecca. Instead of helping pack at the vicarage, she was instructed to go home and pack her own clothes. She ran and skipped through the village and arrived at the cottage out of breath but exuberant.

"Whatever is going on?" asked her puzzled mother.

"Uncle Hector is ill," exclaimed Violet with what little breath she could catch. "Mrs. Hayworth is going to see him. I am going too."

And with that she raced upstairs to pack. Finding a trunk was difficult as no one in the family had ever been away. But Mrs. Brookes found an old case in the attic and dusted it off while Violet sorted through her clothes.

"How long are you going for?" her mother called from the attic.

"No idea."

"Then take your Sunday best and next-best frocks."

"Is it warm or cold in London?"

"I've no idea, but take plenty of vests."

"I don't have a decent hat for the journey."

"Well, you need to look respectable. I'll pop down the road and borrow one from your sister."

"And the cape to match, please."

CHAPTER 19

HAVING WAVED THEM OFF AT Tunbridge Station, Jack and Mr. Brookes were soon out of sight. Rebecca sank into her seat and prayed for a safe journey. It had been kind of Mr. Brookes to take them to Tunbridge with his horse and trap, and it had been kind of Jack to accompany her to the train. In her hand she grasped the instructions he had written.

Alight at Redhill.

Train to Victoria Station. Ask porter which platform.

Front of Station, Cab to 27 Milton Square, South Kensington.

She knew all the details but would have felt lost had she mislaid the note. What a relief it was to have Violet with her! Violet had never set foot outside Kent, but she had a good deal of common sense, was intrepid, and above all was good company.

The windows were steamed up, making it hard to see out, but Violet sat opposite her, nose to pane, staring through a section of glass she had wiped clean. Three gentlemen entered their carriage at the next station. After heaving their bags into the overhead racks, they settled down, unfolded their newspapers, and began reading. Two of the men seemed to be business acquaintances and continued a sporadic conversation through or over their papers.

"Mrs. Hayworth, I have been thinking," Violet said abruptly, turning her attention from the outside to her mistress. "I believe that as I am accompanying you on a visit, I should be promoted from housemaid to lady's maid."

Rebecca glanced at their fellow travelers. The carriage fell silent and, as one, the men buried their heads in their newspapers, but Rebecca knew she had their undivided attention.

"And would this promotion you propose include a pay raise?"

"I think that would be appropriate."

Rebecca felt acutely aware of the three pairs of ears behind the headlines. Not a page turned. She leaned forward and lowered her voice in the hopes that the rattling of the carriage and the noise of the engine would drown her answer.

"You do indeed have many skills appropriate to the role. Technically you are employed by my husband and not by me, but as your wages come out of the household budget for which I am responsible, I will agree to your proposal."

"So, I am now a lady's maid."

"You are indeed, and I am now a lady who has a maid."

Rebecca imagined reproachfully raised eyebrows from behind the newspapers. Did their wives conduct their domestic arrangements in such an unorthodox manner? Not a newspaper twitched. *How very English!* Violet silently rewiped the window and once more turned her attention to the passing scenery, while Rebecca marveled at her maid's artfulness. *Violet is many things, but you can never accuse her of being dull.*

The change of train at Redhill Junction went remarkably smoothly, thanks to a kindly porter. *Quite a portly porter,* Rebecca noticed. He would probably have been helpful anyway, but Violet galvanised him into action by asking him to deal with "her lady's trunks." She and Violet could have easily managed them alone, but the chubby man hurried off to find a sack truck, loaded their luggage onto it, and whisked them away to the correct platform, leaving the women to scamper along behind and deliberate, in whispers, the etiquette of tipping. Rebecca was not the sort of lady to watch a man perspire on her behalf and not offer a little for the services rendered, so the good man received his due. With a wide smile and a doff of his cap, he ushered them into the ladies' waiting room; when the London train eventually arrived, he reappeared to ensure they and their luggage were safely stowed before bidding them good-bye. *He wouldn't have treated the queen herself any better,* thought Rebecca as she thanked God for kind people.

Her thoughts went ahead of the train to Uncle Hector. How would he be? He must have been gravely ill at the time the letter was written, for it was penned by his housekeeper, not himself. It was hard to imagine him anything but hale and hearty, although for a long time he had occasionally mentioned a chest complaint. She hoped that he still could communicate and that she could understand him. She had heard of people having strokes and finding it difficult to articulate, even swallow. The family would struggle to make sense of the slurred speech, and the poor patient would become frustrated and withdrawn. How awful it would be for Uncle Hector to suffer like that. Fluency had been such an important part of who he was, as a relative, government adviser, and teacher. How would she feel toward him? She prayed that, even if he was confused and dribbling, she would feel a surge of love toward her one and only uncle, and not instinctive repulsion. She felt guilt even thinking that, let alone having to pray about it. Surely good Christian women should feel only tenderness and compassion for the sick.

At Victoria Station, although there was no porter available to take their luggage, all went smoothly and, once they had jostled their way to the exit, there was no shortage of cabs waiting for their custom. Rebecca hoped she could choose which carriage she took, for she wanted one driven by an older man in the hopes that he might be steadier and less erratic. But after nearly causing a fight by approaching a mature man farther down the road, she realised that she was obliged to take the first in the queue and hope for the best. Violet stared around her.

"It mus' be market day, surely."

"I think it is always this crowded."

"I don't know what they're all doing, but they ain't 'alf busy."

"It makes Capford seem slow."

"It makes Tunbridge seem empty!"

"Do you think you'll like London life?"

"If we survive this cab journey, I might get used to it."

The welcome Rebecca received at 27 Albert Way was second to none. When all the staff lined up to greet her, she feared the worst. Maybe she had arrived too late. Her mind was put to rest by the housekeeper's greeting.

"My dear," she said, sounding like her master, "we are so pleased to see you. Mr. Stubbs has been asking for you ever since he took ill."

"So he can talk?"

"Oh yes, my dear. Mind you, it's a bit slurred."

"May I go and see him?"

"Of course, but will you not take some refreshment first?"

"A cup of tea when I am with him would be most welcome. I am sure my maid, Violet, would also appreciate something."

After they had been relieved of their outer garments, Rebecca and Violet parted company. Rebecca ascended to Uncle Hector's chamber, and Violet descended to the kitchen for tea.

Uncle Hector greeted Rebecca with a wide, lopsided smile. His right hand was weak, so he grasped her hand with his left as she leaned over the bed to kiss him.

"Ith tho good to thee you."

"I'm pleased to be here, Uncle," replied Rebecca, drawing up a chair to perch on. "How are you?"

"Noth thoo bad."

Still holding her hand in a vice-like grip, Uncle Hector described how he had experienced a sudden pounding headache, then collapsed when attempting to rise from the dining room table. His physician had examined him later that day and explained that he had been afflicted with a stroke. Not a bad one, but not one of the mildest kind either. He had prescribed rest for body and mind, and blood-letting.

By now the teapot had arrived and, with her free hand, Rebecca poured the tea. Uncle Hector looked exhausted from so much talking, and once he finally released her hand to take the cup, it shook violently. Rebecca hastily relieved him of the cup and put it to his lips. Tea dribbled down his chin from the drooping corner of his mouth. With tears of frustration Uncle Hector called himself a baby.

"There, there, Uncle, you're nothing of the sort." Wiping his chin with her handkerchief, Rebecca blamed the cup and her own inexperience. She rang the bell and asked for a more suitable receptacle to be found. The maid returned with a ceramic cup with a spout. It was very suitable, but Rebecca was hesitant to show her uncle for fear of offending him. "Uncle," she said at last, "they have found this for you. It isn't the most elegant china you possess, but it may just help you for a few days."

Uncle Hector gave a resigned shrug and let Rebecca use it. The tea behaved itself this time, and Uncle Hector quickly drained the cup. Realising that he probably had not drunk much since his collapse, Rebecca refilled his beaker again and again until the tea pot and milk jug were dry. Once he had finished the last drop, Uncle Hector leaned back into his pillow and, mouth sagging, fell asleep.

Rebecca drank her now cold tea and studied him. Sunk into his pillow with his drooping face, Uncle Hector looked pale, old, and vulnerable. The surge of love Rebecca had wanted to feel did not materialise, but looking at him now, she felt a huge wave of mixed emotions—compassion, responsibility, duty, and tenderness—threatening to overwhelm her. She followed Uncle Hector's example and closed her eyes, but not to sleep. She was asking for God to help her.

CHAPTER 20

THE DAY BEGAN PERFECTLY. THERE had been a sharp frost overnight, giving a satisfying crunch underfoot and a beauty to the landscape. The cloudless blue sky created a magnificent backdrop to the frozen foliage. Edward, dressed in his tweed shooting outfit, mingled with his guests on the driveway. Each man, dressed in almost identical garb and with a double-barrelled twelve-bore gun on their arm, greeted Edward, helped himself to the sherry and fruitcake that maids were handing around, then mingled with fellow-shooters. The sound of boots on gravel and male voices filled the air with excitement and anticipation. Today it was the turn of the Biggenden pheasants to be shot at and decimated.

In the stable yard the gamekeeper was trying to organise his motley team of beaters. He had no great faith in their ability to operate in a professional manner, for they always failed to recognise the seriousness of their task. Relieved of farm work for the day, the Biggenden workforce was enlisted to flush out the pheasants and drive them toward the guns. Instead of listening to the gamekeeper's meticulous directions and orders, the team, as excited as the shooters, were jovially bantering together as if on some sort of day trip. This was the most important day in the gamekeeper's calendar, and no one was paying it the respect it deserved—except maybe Mr. Edward

Thorpe, who frequently approached him to discuss wind direction and tactics. Frustrated and with a hoarse voice, the keeper marched off toward the woods with his dogs and was relieved to find that the men followed on after all.

Edward led his group of equally jovial men toward an open area beyond the woods, which had been designated as the shooting line. He too had misgivings about some of his party. Lord Wilson arriving late and stomped into the gathering like an angry bull. He huffed and puffed at the peg position he drew out of the hat and snapped at his servant, who attended him as a loader, for no apparent reason. Lord Wilson had clearly got out of the wrong side of the bed, but Edward also wondered if he was slightly tipsy already. As they neared their positions, the conversation ceased and an expectant silence descended on the shooters—or Guns, as the keeper insisted in calling them.

"A gun with a small *g* is the firing arm they use, but the Gun with a capital *G* is the person who fires the gun with a small *g*," he explained to his bemused, then mocking team.

"'Ow can we tell whether ya talking with a capital or a small *g*?"

"It's all about context."

"I 'ope the ol' pheasants understand all ya jargon."

"Silence, please." The gamekeeper held up his hands as if pressing back the noise. "We need to spread out and take positions quietly now, before raising the pheasants."

"Keep quiet . . . so we don't scare 'em before we scare 'em," joked Joe.

"Wow, boy! You've really got the 'ang of this!" teased the gardener.

"I know," whispered Joe. "I'm a natural."

"But keep ya eye on Benny too," cautioned the gardener. "I don't want him near any gun, capital letter or otherwise."

From his allotted position, Edward looked down the line at his participating guests. Each stood in alert silence surveying the woods with the intensity of a soldier on watch. The snapping of twigs and the rattling squawk of a few surprised pheasants were the only indication of the forthcoming excitement. The gamekeeper was flushing out the birds, but not alarming them enough to take to their wings before reaching the clearing. Edward's pulse quickened as he watched the first pheasants appear. For a few seconds the view was magnificent as the beautiful birds fluttered their colourful wings and launched themselves into flight. Their guttural alarm calls were soon drowned by the noise of gun fire, and stricken birds fell from the sky. Edward was too busy shooting to notice his companions, but when he paused to reload, he glanced Lord Wilson's way. He was alarmed to see Wilson's erratic and dangerous shots. Sometimes he aimed too high, resulting in an injured but not dead bird, condemning it to a lingering and painful death. Sometimes he aimed too low, blasting the pheasants to pieces. This was not sportsmanship, this was massacre!

From his place in the woods, Benny saw an injured bird flapping helplessly among the bracken. Breaking rank, he ran toward it. At that moment, Lord Wilson fired low.

Benny's scream and stumble indicated a direct hit. The noise of gunshot was immediately replaced by shouting. The beaters ran out of the woods to their bleeding friend. Edward was nearer, so arrived first and pulled out his handkerchief to stem the blood flow from Benny's leg. It was soon saturated. Benny's father ripped off his shirt and used it as a bandage, and Joe used his garter as a tourniquet. Mr. Brookes ordered a man to send for Dr. Ward. With the utmost care and gentleness, a few men eased Benny off the ground and carried him toward Biggenden.

When Edward saw that the situation was being well managed he turned toward Lord Wilson, who spluttered, "Whatever happened, Thorpe?"

"You shot him!"

Lord Wilson puffed out his chest. "Rubbish, utter rubbish."

"You did. I saw it with my own eyes." Other shooters gathered around and testified to having witnessed the shot too.

"Well, what is all the fuss? The boy isn't dead. He shouldn't have been near the guns. How ridiculous to bring the village idiot on a shoot!" Lord Wilson looked pointedly at Edward. "It is asking for trouble."

It took every ounce of self-control Edward possessed not to punch Lord Wilson in his fat, arrogant, and ruddy face.

"Sir, please leave my land now!" he ordered through gritted teeth, and then, turning to the other shooters, "Sorry, gentlemen, the shoot is over, please be so kind as to return home." With that, he turned on his heel and headed home to check on Benny, leaving the guests to pack up, divide the spoil, and chew over the day's events at their leisure.

By following a trail of mud and leaves through the house, Edward found Benny and half his workforce in a spare bedroom. Sophia, smeared with blood and mud, was clearly in control. Dr. Ward soon arrived and examined the wound. Benny's mother had been sent for, and the maids had been ordered to serve the lunch that had been prepared for the shooting party to the workmen instead. At the centre of all the activity lay Benny, pale and drifting into unconsciousness.

Sophia stroked the patient's hair, and the room was silent with all eyes on the physician as he painstakingly extracted leadshot from the wounds. The housemaid's call that lunch was ready went unnoticed by the audience.

At last the doctor straightened up and flexed his back. "I believe all the gunshot is out. Now to clean the wounds and dress the leg."

Hot water was sent for and bandages were extracted from the doctor's bag. There was no lack of volunteers to hold up the wounded leg for bandaging, or to arrange Benny under the covers.

"The femur is peppered but not shattered, and I don't think the nerve or any other bone or organ has been affected. But those leg wounds are nasty and could easily get infected." Dr. Ward addressed Benny's father. "If he had been a couple of yards nearer the gun, the story would have been very different. As it is, he has lost a considerable amount of blood. What he needs now is rest, analgesia, and—when he wakes—plenty of fluids."

Satisfied that Benny's life was not in immediate danger and that he was comfortable, the men left the room and headed to the laden lunch table.

"Dr. Ward, you have done a splendid job. Will you not join us for a bite to eat?" asked Sophia.

Edward had very little appetite, but his men did not seem to be similarly afflicted. He leaned back in his chair and watched them, the doctor, and his wife chatting and munching away. The dining room was at its best, with the daintiest china and hot-house flower arrangements, in stark contrast to the men wearing their rough, patched-up work clothes. What an incongruous scene it was! *But what a decent and agreeable bunch they are. Vastly superior to the intended guests!* Their love and concern for poor Benny had been deep and genuine. *That is what unites us all,* thought Edward. Dear Benny, whose ambitions in life were limited to giving flowers to Sophia, keeping his boots polished, and smiling broadly. How dare Lord Wilson call him the village idiot! There was only one man that day who looked like an idiot, and that was Lord Wilson himself.

CHAPTER 21

EVEN LONDON WAS BORING IN February, Violet decided. January and February were her least favourite months, and out of them both she probably liked February the least. The best thing about it was its shortness. Whoever had invented the calendar must have disliked it too and knocked a few days off the end. But a February in Kent was nothing compared to one stuck in a house in South Kensington. Apparently, it was a fashionable place to reside, and she was among the good and the great, but if there were such beings, *they are either in hibernation or look remarkably like the rest of us.*

The crisp frosty weather had turned to drizzle or smog. Once Violet had looked around the streets around Milton Square and found that they all looked the same, she had little to motivate her to venture outdoors. Mrs. Hayworth was fully occupied with caring for Uncle Hector, who in Violet's eyes was lapping up the attention. They had been there for four whole weeks, and the man was more or less recovered, yet he seemed to cling to his niece as if he would wither and die without her.

Violet felt sorry for Reverend Jack Hayworth losing his wife to an uncle-in-law. She felt sorry for herself for having to be stuck in a town house for so long. She felt sorry for Mrs. Hayworth, who was such a conscientious sort and the epitome of a dutiful niece. She had fed the man, read to him, sung to him, and played the piano for him. The first two nights she slept in a chair by his bed. Violet had felt bad about that. There she was, sleeping in a comfortable bed in her lady's maid's room and being waited on by the housemaid, while her mistress roughed it out on a chair. If, as was suggested by the gossipy cook, the Hayworths were the uncle's sole beneficiaries, well, they deserved every penny. But what would a cook know about her master's monetary arrangements anyway?

Being a lady's maid was the easiest job in the world. Well, it was if you were the lady's maid of Rebecca Hayworth née Stubbs and were visiting. The expectation of the household was simple. Violet was to assist her mistress as required and keep her room clean and tidy. That was it. But it came with a heavy price: boredom. She was no reader, but even Mrs. Hayworth, who enjoyed reading, found Uncle Hector's collection of books disappointing. If they had wanted to delve into economics, history, politics, or the history of politics, there would have been plenty to read. But they did not, so there was not. Mrs. Hayworth found a whole pile of *Bentley's Miscellany* monthly periodicals in the study and had become gripped by a story called *Oliver Twist,* written by a certain Charles Dickens. The frustrating thing was that some issues were missing, so there were big gaps in the plot. Violet tried to read it but found it too wordy and depressing.

Every afternoon when Uncle Hector was asleep, Rebecca and Violet escaped from the house and went for a walk, come rain or shine. Kensington Gardens was their favourite destination. It seemed amazing to be able to walk around a part of the grounds of Kensington Palace, where Queen Victoria was born and lived until she became queen. She had graciously opened some of the park to the public, but only on the condition that they were respectfully dressed. Violet longed to see some un-respectfully dressed individual being forcibly removed, but this never happened. Her favourite part of the ornate park was the Italian Gardens, a gift to Queen Victoria from her doting husband, who had loved gardening. Violet doubted whether he had even lifted a spade once during the construction of the garden, but it was certainly a lovely gift. The garden was not of the grass and trees type but had terraces, fountains, urns, statues, and flowerbeds. Violet felt almost regal as she promenaded along the stone terrace with her lady, following in the footsteps of their monarch.

A steam engine provided power for the fountains, and Mrs. Hayworth found out that the poor stoker worked throughout the night on Saturday to keep the engine running and the pump going so that on Sunday there was enough water to run the fountains without the engine working. If Sunday went from midnight to midnight, the reasoning seemed illogical. Surely the exhausted stoker flopped into bed after his night's work, not into a pew. *Did Queen Victoria ever visit the garden now?* Rebecca and Violet wondered, and would it be painful or comforting to her after Albert's death? They decided she probably did not, as she seemed to have shut herself away from everything and everyone.

Shutting oneself away—that reminded Violet of something she wanted to discuss.

"I spoke to an Anglican nun yesterday," she said as they reached the fountain.

"Oh?" Rebecca turned and looked at her.

"I asked her if I could enter the convent."

"Violet! You in a convent? Tell me you are joking." Rebecca frowned and pursed her lips, as if unsure whether to laugh out aloud or show firm Protestant disapproval.

This was not an encouraging start. "No, ma'am, I am not joking. I have been thinking about it since September. Nuns do a lot of good, you know."

"Is that why you want to join them?"

"One of the reasons. Anyway, it won't be that easy. The nun wasn't too encouraging. She said I would need my father's written permission and a dowry."

Rebecca was grinning. "Both very unlikely."

"Can you imagine Pa agreeing to me joining a convent? He would throw a fit. And then asking him to give money." Violet sighed. "No, it won't happen."

"Are you disappointed?"

"Yes, I am a bit. I think religious life would be good for me. I would have time to meditate, I would be away from men, and I could do good works."

"You can do all of that now."

"But it isn't so dramatic and romantic."

"I can't see anything romantic about being a nun."

"I don't mean falling-in-love-romantic. I mean the atmosphere, the singing, the stained glass windows, and all that. The nuns do really good work. They rescue fallen women and get them back on the straight and narrow. They run a laundry—the girls get some kind of moral cleansing as they learn the trade of laundering."

"Do you think it will bring you nearer to God?"

"I should hope so. But the nun didn't look exactly serene."

"So that is what you are after—serenity?"

"Yes, I suppose so. I need to know I am forgiven."

"Then you are looking in the wrong direction. We can't find peace by doing good things, being devout, or trying to be perfect. We will fail. The Bible says our righteousness is like filthy rags in God's sight."

They both stared at the fountain, and Rebecca continued:

"The Lord Jesus has made perfect righteousness by living a perfect life and dying a sacrificial death. He is willing to transfer that righteousness to whoever asks for it."

"Why would He want to?"

"Because of love."

"How could He possibly love me?"

"That is what we all ask ourselves, and no one knows the answer, but His offer is genuine. His love is greater than anything."

"But what if I ask Him and He refuses?"

"He has never done that, and He promises 'Whosoever cometh I will in no wise cast out.'"

"But what if I am not one of His elect?"

"Who has made you feel that you need forgiveness? That isn't something you initiated. God has been making you uncomfortable for a reason. That is a sign of His love."

"So, what do I have to do?"

"Nothing." Rebecca spread her arms wide. "Jesus did it all one thousand, eight hundred and sixty or so years ago. Hand over your sin and guilt to Him and ask Him to give you His righteousness."

"Is that what you have done?"

"Yes, and have to keep doing."

"Are you at peace?"

Rebecca thought hard.

"Yes, I think so. Not in some amazing floaty sort of way, but somewhere deep inside me I know that I trust the Lord Jesus for my eternal salvation. He is so trustworthy I can leave it all to Him, and I will get to heaven because of His life and death."

"Not some floaty way? Do you mean you are not constantly full of joy?"

"No, I'm afraid not, but that is my fault and not the Lord's. I should think more of my union with Christ and of heavenly things, but I get bogged down with earthly things. My father always said, 'We should trust God's unchangeable promises, not our changeable feelings,' and that is what I must do. The wonderful thing is that God is so understanding. The Bible says 'He knoweth our frame and remembereth that we are but dust,' so He knows that we are weak, yet He continues to love us."

"That is good," Violet said. "Trust God's unchangeable promises, not our changeable feelings."

"Trust Him, Violet, and you will never be disappointed."

It was good to talk, and somehow talking while out walking or staring at flowing water was easier than trying to do so indoors.

As they re-entered 27 Milton Square, a gloom descended upon Violet. She had never stayed in such a beautiful and luxurious dwelling, but as the door shut behind her, she felt imprisoned. Two envelopes were awaiting their attention on the hall table—the regular, almost daily letter from Jack and one addressed to Violet. *Good old Ma,* she thought. Now that she was the offspring farthest away from home, she seemed to have gained favour and significance in her mother's eyes. The frequent letters were cheerful and chatty, full of the events of Capford. Violet had always considered the goings-on in the village rather mundane and unremarkable, but compared with the four walls of 27 Milton Square, they seemed utterly captivating.

Rebecca smiled to herself and pocketed her letter.

"Another love letter, ma'am?" asked Violet cheekily.

Rebecca's smile broadened. "Well, it is a letter, and from the man I love, so maybe yes."

"You're lucky."

"Yes, I am. I have got a lovely husband."

"Not *'out of sight, out of mind'* then?"

"Oh no, more like *'absence makes the heart grow fonder.'*"

At the stairs they parted, Rebecca to see if Uncle Hector had woken up, and Violet to her room to read the letter.

"Benny had a week at Biggenden Manor and is now at home. He is getting on well and is his normal smiley self—except, of course, he is still in bed. Mrs. Thorpe visits him a couple of times a week and always takes flowers, picture books, and biscuits. She is turning out to be a good sort. Since Rebecca is away, Mrs. Thorpe has taken over some of her visiting, and the folks like her. The apple pruning is nearly done. Pa and Joe are getting ready for lambing. Joe is repainting the lambing hut. He and Molly are engaged. She is a good, steady girl and will make him a good wife. Agnes soon wants her hat and cape back. She did not realise you would be away for so long. Mrs. Hayworth senior is coming to Capford to help her son while Rebecca is away. I've offered him a few meals, but to be honest, he is a bit too independent to help very easily. He was a bachelor for a long time before getting married, and you can tell. Lord Wilson has not been to church since the accident. He don't seem to want to show his face. Good he has some sort of conscience. I hope the Thorpes send him the doctor's bill. As far as I have

heard, Wilson has not even asked over Benny, let alone sent him anything. I think it is disgusting."

Violet smiled at her mother's opinions—she had always had a view on everything. Maybe Violet took after her a bit. She thought about that sudden insight. If she did, at least her opinions were a bit better than her mother's, who tended to be a bit old-fashioned in her views. Molly a good wife! In an old-fashioned way, maybe. But she would be such a boring fireside companion. She would never offer any original thought about a subject, but just be an attentive and agreeing audience to Joe. Is that what he really wanted? If so, he had changed. He used to like a good old discussion, a good bit of banter, and a good laugh. He was now a church member, so maybe he had become all serious. But there was nothing wrong with a good sense of humour. Pa and the Hayworths were good Christian folks, and they all knew how to have a good laugh. The Hayworths bantered with each other—you could almost call it flirting. She, Violet, would never marry a man she couldn't tease a little. Without fully understanding the reason why, Violet laid on her bed and cried. She felt so lonely and bored and empty.

As had become their routine in London, Violet took their evening drinks to Mrs. Hayworth's bedroom and sat with her chatting. The other staff probably thought she was helping with getting her lady to bed, but her ma'am was quite capable of doing that herself and preferred a chat instead. *She is probably as bored as I am,* decided Violet.

"Violet, are you all right? You don't look your normal bright self."

"Oh, sorry, ma'am."

"No, I'm sorry. What is the matter?"

Tears began to flow again.

"I don't know. I just feel down and very lonely."

"Did you get bad news today in your letter?"

"No, just the normal village news."

"Including?"

"Benny is getting better. Mrs. Thorpe is visiting him a lot and doing other good works around the village. Your mother-in-law is coming, and Joe and Molly are engaged."

Rebecca was slow to answer.

"Does it bother you that Joe is getting engaged? Wasn't he your best friend once?"

"Yes, he was. I shouldn't be bothered, 'cos I had decided I didn't want to marry him. But all the same, I didn't want him to marry anyone else."

"So, that has made you feel down?"

"Maybe." Violet sighed before continuing. "But I am also so lonely and bored here. Sorry, ma'am, I shouldn't moan to you, but I have nothing to do all day. I even miss scrubbing pans and mangling cloths."

"Oh, I am sorry, Violet," Rebecca exclaimed. "I have been selfish keeping you here for so long. I sensed you were unhappy, but I underestimated the extent. I've kept you here because I do so enjoy our walks. I have been selfish. "

"Not at all, ma'am. You are never selfish."

"I have been, and I will rectify the situation. You must return to Capford."

"And leave you here alone?"

"Yes. Hopefully I will follow you down shortly. You could prepare the house for my mother-in-law. Jack is a good man, but I am sure the house hasn't seen a duster in the last four weeks."

"I will gladly make it spotless, ma'am."

"Good, and get a good joint of meat for her arrival."

"I'll make sure she has a right royal welcome." Violet paused before adding, "But I can't really be a lady's maid being so far from you."

Rebecca pondered the dilemma.

"Then why not return to the title of housemaid but continue with the pay increase."

"That sounds good."

"Yes, very suitable."

"But will you be all right here alone, ma'am? You are hardly having a fun time yourself, and you don't half look tired and pale."

"I'll be fine, thank you, Violet." Rebecca pinched her cheeks to bring colour to her face. "Hopefully I can follow you down to Kent soon. Uncle Hector is almost back to his old self, I think."

CHAPTER 22

TRAVELING INDEPENDENTLY WAS FUN, VIOLET decided. Mrs. Hayworth had waved her off at Victoria Station, and someone from the village would be at Tunbridge Station at her arrival, but in between she was alone, anonymous, and free. No one in the carriage knew the first thing about her and probably had no desire to, either. The feeling was one of liberation. Some people in her situation—going from A to B—had just disappeared. They had failed to arrive at B. If she wanted to, she could get off the train at any station, board one going anywhere, and start a new life for herself. She had a bag of clothes and a few shillings. The fantasy excited her, but only for a few heady minutes, until her sensible side shouted down the idea. She would cause such alarm to all the people she loved and trusted—her parents, the Hayworths, and lots of the village folks. Would Joe be upset, or would her disappearance reinforce his opinion that she was too flighty for marriage? Was that his opinion? It probably was after the bad year she had experienced with the opposite sex. He probably thought she wasn't trustworthy. And she was beginning to think that too. Could she actually trust herself?

As she despondently tried to analyse her own character, she was reminded of Mrs. Hayworth's advice about finding peace. Violet had never really considered whether the Lord Jesus was trustworthy. As far as she could remember, the Bible didn't use the word, but if she was asked to sum up Jesus's character in two words, she might say He is kind and trustworthy. No, loving and trustworthy is better, for one can be kind, in a professional way, but not loving. Violet thought of all the texts with gospel promises she had learned in Sunday school. They are trustworthy. She looked outside at the beautiful Surrey countryside—its Maker is trustworthy. *The One who organises the seasons, feeds the wild-life, and created the rolling hills is worthy of my full trust,* she thought. But as the train moved on, so did Violet's thoughts. Back to the vicarage for dusting! Boring old dusting! But at least after four weeks it would seem worthwhile. *Normally you can hardly see where you have polished and where you haven't, but with a good layer of dust, it will be easy. Maybe monthly dusting should be the rule.* She imagined the conversation:

"Why Mrs. X, what a lovely layer of dust you have on your sideboard."

"Yes, Mrs. Z, I've been watching its growth with pride and interest."

"I can never seem to get my layer that deep."

"Patience, Mrs. Z, it takes patience, open fires—and self-control."

"Now that is where I go wrong, I can't stop myself reaching for the duster."

"Poor you, Mrs. Z, displaying such weakness of character."

Violet smiled to herself, then looked around anxiously to see if anyone had noticed. A little boy was staring at her, so she quickly crossed her eyes and stuck out her tongue before staring out the window with feigned interest.

Of all the people in Capford and of all the workers at Biggenden Farm, why did it have to be Joe who went to Tunbridge Market that day? Violet tried to hide her disappointment as he tossed her bags onto the wagon and gingerly took her place on the bench next to him.

"How was the big smoke then, traveler?" Joe asked as he picked up the reins and set the horse in motion.

"Nice, thank you."

"Did you see the queen?"

"No, but we saw her Italian garden, which is very beautiful."

"Good."

Violet stared straight ahead at the horse's rump.

"Congratulations on your engagement."

"My engagement?" Joe looked at her in surprise.

"Mother informed me you are engaged to Molly."

"Then, for once, your mother is wrong."

"Oh, sorry, I don't know how that happened."

"Neither do I 'cos, actually, Molly and I are no longer courting."

"Oh, Joe!" exclaimed Violet, turning toward him. "I'm sorry to hear that."

"Well, don't be too sorry. She is a nice girl and all that lot, but we didn't really suit, and it took us a long time to realise. In the end, it was her decision to stop the relationship—she didn't like my plans."

"What plans?"

"I want to immigrate to Canada."

A feather would have knocked Violet clean off the bench.

"For the gold rush?"

Joe laughed.

"No, I don't want to dig or sieve for gold. I want to be my own boss, have my own farm in a country that values the labourer and has fertile soil."

"What an adventure! I envy you, being a man and able to make a bold, independent step like that."

"Yes, I am excited about it."

"Don't you think you could be your own boss here?"

"Just look around you, Vi. Half the country is owned by idiots like Lord Wilson. In Scotland, they have cleared ship-loads of crofters off their land, almost starving them, not allowing their animals to roam freely on the vast estates, just so the rich landlords can rear a few more sheep. Up in the Midlands, hundreds of millers are starving or hunting for work they have no skill in due to mechanisation. Even here, fewer farmhands are needed with the threshing machines and stuff that's coming in. Village life is under threat as more and more folks are forced to the big cities for work. The new factories in the cities are destroying all cottage industry—no one can compete with them. It is only going to get worse."

"Wow, Joe, I didn't know you were a radical."

"You don't know me much these days, Vi. I'm not the little lad in knee breeches anymore."

"I know that." Violet paused and once again studied the horse. "And I am not the silly girl you think I am either."

"I've never thought you silly!" replied Joe, eyes firmly on the road ahead.

"But I have been foolish, what with the Mr. Christopher situation, then with that awful Reuben."

"You can't help being attractive to men."

Violet didn't know how to respond to that comment.

"But I should have been a better judge of character."

"We live and learn, Vi."

"I hope I've learned."

They jogged along in silence until reaching Capford.

"When are you planning to set sail, Joe?"

"Oh, not for a while. I mean to save all I can first. Buying my passage across won't be cheap, and then I need cash to get started over there. Anyway, I can't leave your old pa to do the lambing alone, can I?"

"Oh, good."

"Why good?"

"Because Capford will be odd without you."

Joe stopped the cart outside the Brookes's cottage. He heaved down Violet's bag and plonked it at her feet. "Then let's make the most of my time here. How about joining me for a Sunday afternoon walk?"

"When?"

"This Sunday."

"Fine."

"Good."

"Yes."

"Good-bye then."

"Good-bye . . . and thank you for collecting me."

"'Til Sunday."

"Yep, 'til then."

CHAPTER 23

JACK WAS ALARMED AT THE despondent tone of Rebecca's last few letters. Gone were the cheerful humour and witty observations. Instead they read like a weather report. If Rebecca could no longer think of what to say and had to fall back on the very English subject of the dreary weather, something was amiss. After cancelling committee meetings and delegating visits, Jack caught the next train to Redhill Junction. Several of his nieces had contracted chicken pox at school, and his mother had delayed her planned visit to help his sister cope with a bedroom of irritable and itchy girls, so that all worked out very nicely.

If anything, Rebecca looked paler than Uncle Hector, who was now up and about and functioning as normal. Jack couldn't help thinking that the old man was milking his illness rather too much and basking in the care and attention he was receiving as a result. One thing Jack knew for sure was that when he returned to Capford, he would be taking his wife with him. But now that he was up in London, it seemed reasonable and economic to kill two birds with one stone and to consult Mr. Gascoigne again. Rebecca was far from keen on the idea, and it did seem rather undiplomatic even to mention it to her.

"But he did say to come back in six months, darling," he argued.

"But one month out of those six we have been apart anyway."

"We don't want to have to come back in a month's time, do we?"

"Not unless Uncle Hector needs me."

"Then we will be apart anyway, so the situation will be the same."

"I doubt if you will be able to arrange a consultation with him at such short notice," replied Rebecca triumphantly.

"If there is an appointment available, will you come?"

Rebecca nodded reluctantly.

An appointment was available, and the Hayworths found themselves sitting face to face with Mr. Gascoigne again.

"By your presence here today, I assume there has been no progress in the matter you consulted me about before."

"That's correct, sir," answered Jack, to whom the question was directed.

Mr. Gascoigne fingered his gold pen and looked at Rebecca over his glasses as if she was an uncooperative schoolgirl.

"I'm sorry, sir," she muttered, studying her hands on her lap.

"And did you follow my advice regarding calmness, moderate exercise, and sitz baths?"

Jack looked at Rebecca in alarm. He had forgotten all the instructions, but she was giving a confident answer.

"Yes, doctor, I have done as you advised."

Jack looked at his wife in admiration. How had she managed? He felt a pang of guilt. He had done nothing to help, not even supplying a suitable bath. She wasn't lying, was she? No, Rebecca was always truthful.

Mr. Gascoigne's steely gaze turned again to Jack.

"Well, I could do another internal examination, if you insist, but I doubt very much that anything has changed."

Rebecca looked pleadingly at her husband.

"No, I don't think that is necessary, thank you, sir," Jack replied decidedly.

"The next line of treatment I can offer is the application of internal leeches."

Rebecca gasped, shuddered, and crossed her legs. "Is that a recognised medical procedure, Mr. Gascoigne?"

Rising a few inches in height, Mr. Gascoigne drew in a deep breath. "Of course, it is a 'recognised medical procedure,' Mrs. Hayworth. I am no quack." Then, as if to offer some comfort, he added, "Naturally, the leeches detach themselves and fall out once they are engorged."

Jack had never seen Rebecca look more horrified and was about to refuse the treatment when the surgeon went on to say, "But, on consideration, you look rather pale anyway, so perhaps the treatment is not advisable in your case at this time."

"Thank you, sir," chorused the Hayworths with united heart and voice.

"We are drawing near to the limits of modern medical treatment for infertility," the doctor concluded. "As mere mortals, we cannot provide what the Almighty deigns to withhold."

Jack agreed, but doubted if Mr. Gascoigne believed in the Almighty for other reasons than convenience's sake.

Then rising from his chair, Mr. Gascoigne unexpectedly said, "But I would like to discuss a little more about this delicate matter with Reverend Hayworth, so I request that you leave the room please, Mrs. Hayworth."

Looking bewildered, Rebecca was ushered out of the room.

"Do find a seat in the hall. We will not be long," instructed the surgeon before he shut the door with unnecessary firmness.

Now I am in for it, Jack thought, shrinking into his chair.

Mr. Gascoigne returned to his imperial position behind the polished desk and fingered his gold fountain pen. He seemed to be choosing his words carefully.

"You are a young man, Reverend Hayworth, with a bright future ahead."

Jack could neither agree or disagree with this strange comment so remained silent.

"To produce no offspring can be a great disappointment, not only to a man but also, in a sense, to his ancestors. Indeed, producing an heir is often perceived as a duty rather than mere choice." The pen rolling continued. "Our laws recognise this expectation and thankfully make suitable allowances." He paused and continued in a lower tone. "Reverend Hayworth, I have good, respectable colleagues who would be willing to help you."

"How?" asked Jack, truly puzzled.

"I have observed your wife making some unusual remarks. My colleagues could assess your wife and pronounce her deranged as a result of chronic hysteria. This would allow you a legal divorce, and you could re-marry."

Jack stiffened. "And what would happen to Mrs. Hayworth?" he asked through gritted teeth.

"We would find her a suitable asylum to live out her days in quietness. Why, some of the newly built asylums are splendid buildings with beautiful parks and gardens."

Jack's hands curled into fists.

"Mr. Gascoigne, you have totally misunderstood both my character and my relationship with my wife."

By now Jack was standing and had thumped the polished table with his fist. The fountain pen bounced slightly. He could no longer keep his speech slow or quiet.

"How dare you suggest such a hideous solution! I love Rebecca, with or without children. How could I conspire to have her locked up in a madhouse?"

Mr. Gascoigne slid down his chair, and Jack noticed how breakable his horn-rimmed glasses looked. He resisted the temptation.

"Many men avail themselves of this option, Hayworth."

"Well, they need locking up themselves—along with all your colleagues!" retorted Jack, putting on his hat and striding toward the door. He stopped half way and, reaching in his pocket, pulled out some money. He stomped back and flung it on the desk.

"And take your filthy lucre. Buy a new fountain pen."

"Men of the cloth are often awkward and opinionated," muttered the surgeon. Jack hesitated, then chose to ignore the comment.

On exiting the room, he grabbed Rebecca in the hall and stormed out of the building, slamming the door behind him. Rebecca's feet hardly touched the ground as they hurried away from Harley Street and toward the park. It was not until they were seated on a bench and Rebecca had caught her breath that they exchanged a word.

"Whatever occurred?" asked the perplexed Rebecca.

"That man!" growled Jack. "That odious, pig-headed man!"

"What happened?"

"He should be lynched."

"Whatever happened?"

Jack rubbed his forehead. "Oh, it doesn't matter!"

"Jack, you can't shout at a surgeon, almost slam his door off its hinges, frog-march me down a London road, then not explain. Did he want to operate?"

"Operate?" Jack got up and paced around the bench. "I hardly want to tell you what he proposed."

Rebecca remained silent as he composed his thoughts.

"He said he could have you falsely diagnosed as mad and have you locked away."

Once the sentence had left his lips, Jack bitterly regretted it. Rebecca looked so shocked and vulnerable.

Jack sat next to her and took both her icy hands in his. "It is an unthinkable idea. It is what some unscrupulous men do in order to marry again and produce an heir."

"That is terrible."

"Criminal."

"Does he think I am mad?"

"I bet he thinks we both are."

They sat in shocked silence.

"Does this really happen in this country?" asked Rebecca in a small voice.

"Apparently so."

"Poor women."

"Who did he think I am? Do I look like a man who gets his wife locked up? Clergymen can't get divorced and re-marry anyway—not that I'd want to," he hastily added.

Rebecca still looked unhappy and was unusually quiet. Finally, she broke another long silence.

"Jack, do you regret marrying me now that we realise I am barren?"

Looking at her drawn and tear-stained face, Jack was almost overwhelmed by the surge of love that erupted from his heart.

"Never, never, never!" was all he could reply as he hugged and kissed her passionately.

"We now know what happened to his wife. She isn't pickled in a specimen jar—she is locked away."

That night, in the comfortable London bed, Jack snuggled up to Rebecca and cradled her in his arms until she was asleep. She had never seemed so lovely and precious. Gazing at her innocent sleeping face and tousled hair, every fibre of his being wanted to protect her from everything malicious. *What a beautiful wife I have,* he thought, gently lifting one of the brown ringlets that lay on the pillow and winding it around his finger. One thing he was sure about: he was taking her home with him tomorrow.

Jack had not been asleep long when he was awakened by Rebecca grabbing his arm and screaming. His dull, drowsy mind took a while to realise she was having a nightmare and needed waking.

"You're all right, Rebecca."

"No, I'm not!" came back the irritated reply. "They want to take me away."

Jack fumbled for a match and lit a candle.

"Wake up, darling, it's only a dream."

Rebecca awoke, but her eyes were wide with terror, she was drenched with sweat, and as he held her close, Jack felt her heart racing. Gradually she relaxed next to him.

"Oh, Jack, that was awful."

"I know, my darling."

"They were going to lock me away."

"Don't even think of it," replied Jack. "Tomorrow I am taking you home."

"That will be lovely."

"Yes."

Jack reached over and blew out the candle. "Now let's get to sleep, and if anyone else dares to creep up on you, I will punch them in the nose."

"Then they would take you as well."

"Let them try."

"At least we would be together."

"That is the important thing." He agreed, squeezing her hand.

"Good night."

"Sleep well, darling."

CHAPTER 24

JACK POLITELY BUT FIRMLY INFORMED Uncle Hector that Rebecca was run-down and needed to return home. Uncle Hector looked crestfallen and Rebecca wavered, but her dear husband remained firm. The kind housekeeper sided with Jack and assured Uncle Hector that they could manage his care, and admitting defeat, the recovered invalid capitulated. Rebecca's heart felt lighter with every mile the train removed them farther from London, Milton Square, and Harley Street. It was only early March, but the countryside through which they traveled was already showing signs of spring and the promises of renewed life. New hope and optimism seeped into Rebecca as she gazed out the window. She smiled as she watched a field of newborn lambs skipping and playing chase together.

"That's good," Jack said. "You've got a smile back on your face. All we need now is some colour on your cheeks."

He seemed determined to wrap Rebecca in a protective blanket. Violet could run the home; his mother was soon to arrive and could also assist, and Rebecca was to relax. But she did not want to relax. She had done enough sitting about aimlessly at Uncle Hector's. She couldn't wait to be out and about, visiting friends and parishioners and catching up on the news.

A thrill ran through Rebecca as she crossed the threshold of Capford vicarage. *Whoever would have imagined I could fall in love with this draughty, dull house*! She smiled to herself as she resisted the temptation to kiss the doorstep. And what a beautifully clean doorstep it was too! Violet had done an amazing job of the housework and had a delicious meal waiting for them. Her genuine pleasure at seeing Rebecca touched Rebecca's heart.

The next day, against her husband's advice, Rebecca made her rounds to the baker's queue, the Brookes's cottage for a cup of tea, and the bedside of an elderly villager. And against Jack's doleful prediction, she returned to the vicarage with a spring in her step and plenty of interesting gossip.

The arrival of Mrs. Hayworth senior was another source of enjoyment for Rebecca. The nimble little lady breezed into the vicarage with arms outstretched to embrace both Jack and her daughter-in-law. She always reminded Rebecca of a chirpy little sparrow as she flitted around the house, chatting happily. Everything she said was accompanied by emphatic head movements, which, combined with her warm character, added enthusiasm and sincerity. Within minutes she was teasing Jack and cooing motherly over Rebecca.

"You've had a hard time, my dear," she said.

"Oh, Mother, it was not so bad."

"Jack told me how selflessly you cared for your uncle."

"Maybe he exaggerated."

"Oh, no, no." Her head shook firmly. "For all his faults, Jack does not exaggerate. His letters to me are so terribly brief, exaggeration is impossible."

"Mother, I write to you regularly!" protested Jack.

"I wasn't talking about regularity, was I?"

Rebecca thought about the lovely letters Jack had penned to her when she was away. If he disliked letter writing, she would never have suspected it.

"At least I make use of full stops and other punctuation," retorted Jack. "Reading your letters makes me breathless."

His mother smiled mischievously. "The Greeks didn't use punctuation."

"But most subsequent civilisations have deemed it necessary."

Rebecca grinned as she poured the tea. *Families are such a great invention.*

The next two weeks were pure delight. It was wonderful to be back in the Kent countryside, and it was wonderful to be back with Jack. Getting back into normal vicarage routine was easy and enjoyable, especially with Jack's mother by her side. After a few hesitant attempts, it was easy to call Mrs. Hayworth *Mother.* The word would have stuck in her throat for any other woman, but ever since Jack's ma had heard of Rebecca how she had lost both her parents to typhus fever within six weeks of each other, she had unreservedly taken Rebecca into her heart and truly mothered her.

Being an only child, Rebecca would have been totally desolate, were it not for her dear and kind friends. Looking back, she saw how amazingly the Lord had provided her with loyal, trustworthy friends throughout her life: Mrs. Brown had taken her in after her parents' deaths. Emma had befriended her while she was a housemaid at Barton Manor and had put a smile back on her face. Edward Thorpe had provided a strong though complex companionship for a few years and had been the means of bringing her to Capford. How she had loved Edward! As his housekeeper she had devoted herself to him. More than ever before she had struggled to submit to the Lord's plan for her life when he gave his heart to Sophia, but with the benefit of hindsight, she saw it was all for the best. Jack had soon moved to the area with his mother, and his love for Rebecca soon eclipsed all others. How blessed she was to be part of the Hayworth family!

Mother had resided in Capford for only six months, and even then, she had been outside the village, in a cottage at the end of a muddy lane. She had been unable to socialise during that time as she was recovering from cataract operations. Yet despite all of this, she seemed to know and remember all about the parishioners and, when out visiting, charmed everyone with her genuine interest and apt enquiries. Rebecca enjoyed sitting back and watching her at work. Head tilted to one side, she listened attentively to whoever she was visiting, drawing out of them more than they ever intended. She had plenty of amusing stories to tell about her children, grandchildren, and neighbours without ever being disparaging. Her comments jumped from the temporal to the eternal, the physical to the spiritual with ease, yet without flippancy. *What an asset she must have been to her vicar husband,* thought Rebecca, slightly jealously. Was it purely an amazing character trait, or had she gradually learned through making mistakes? Was it a social talent or evidence of sanctifying grace? Rebecca thought of Elisha watching Elijah and his prayer, "Give me a double portion," and prayed it for herself.

It was with mixed feelings that Rebecca anticipated her forthcoming, and in fact any, visit to Biggenden Manor. Mrs. Sophia Thorpe had kindly invited her and her mother-in-law to afternoon tea. At least Mrs. Harrington would not be there, although it would have been amusing to see how she and Mother interacted. Armed with her mother-in-law, Rebecca felt almost sufficiently reinforced to take on the outspoken woman.

Some sentences are hard to utter without smirking, and "Mrs. Harrington has gone to the South of France to recover her voice" was one of them. But Mrs. Harrington was not the only difficulty. Ever since they had met, Rebecca and Sophia had kept each other at arms' length. They were as polite and respectful of each other as could be expected of any English lady, but there was no cordial warmth. Visits consisted of superficial pleasantries and polite manners but little more and were in the end rather unsatisfactory.

Rebecca was unsure whether she wanted to expend energy on deepening their relationship or remain content with the status quo. She had read many good things about Sophia when in London—her visits and care for Benny and others in need, but even those had left her with mixed feelings. Instead of rejoicing in her kindness, Rebecca found herself questioning Sophia's motives and, if she were honest, resentful of the villagers' growing regard for Sophia. Rebecca knew that her reaction said more about herself than it did about Sophia. How could another woman, a pleasant woman at that, bring out the worst in her?

The visit began, like any other, with pleasantries and politeness, bone china tea cups and cake. Bertie was presented to them. He was such a handsome little boy and had such a winning smile that their admiration of him was totally genuine. His mother beamed as they picked him up and fussed over him. Sophia's face glowed with the love and devotion exclusive to motherhood.

Eventually, the tea pot was drained, and only crumbs remained of the cake. With her head tilted and her voice full of interest and concern, Mrs. Hayworth senior asked, "Were you brought up in a Christian family, Mrs. Thorpe?"

Sophia hesitated before replying, "I thought I was, but really it was only Christian in the sense that we went to church on Sunday and would have described ourselves as good Anglicans." She paused and her listener nodded. "It wasn't until I met Edward that I realised Christianity is much more than having a moral framework or a Sunday routine. Edward showed me that it should influence one's whole life and outlook, during the week as well as on Sundays." An encouraging nod allowed Sophia to continue. "It is a personal relationship with God."

"That's right."

Sophia took a building brick from Bertie and fiddled with it. "That is what I really appreciate about Capford. Your son's preaching is so clear and searching. He leaves us in no doubt about why we need salvation. Until I came here, I thought religion was just about doing good and being decent and upright. Through Revered Hayworth's ministry, I have also seen my husband grow stronger spiritually."

"Are you growing, my dear?" asked Mrs. Hayworth gently.

Sophia turned the brick around. "If I am, I am just a weak little blade of grass. Most plants grow, but I seem to grow then shrink, grow then shrink."

Mrs. Hayworth nodded sympathetically. "I think we all do that. But the Lord said faith is big even if it is as tiny as a mustard seed. It is not about the size of our faith, but where our faith is resting. We are weak, but the Lord Jesus is almighty."

"But my motives, even in spiritual things, can be so mixed."

"We carry a mixed heart with us right to the grave, my dear. The Lord Jesus doesn't invite us to trust Him once we are sure of pure motivations. He invites us just as we are. Confess your struggles to Him. He knows them anyway."

"Why would He want me?"

Rebecca could no longer keep quiet. With tears in her eyes, she exclaimed, "That is exactly what I keep asking myself—'Why me?'—and the only satisfactory answer is because God is love—love itself. It is not about who we are but about who He is."

"And pride doesn't like that," added her mother-in-law. "We like to try and come up with a reason in ourselves why God should love us and want us, but there isn't one. We can even proudly reject His love because we can't understand it."

Sophia, as if she could not trust her voice, just nodded.

"We should accept God's love like little Bertie accepts yours—unquestioningly, trustingly."

Sophia nodded again. "Thank you . . . thank you," she croaked.

At that moment, the nursery maid came in to take Bertie away for his afternoon nap. Mrs. Hayworth got to her feet. "We had better be off, my dear."

Sophia rose too. "Well, thank you for coming. Please come again, and you too, Mrs. Hayworth—er—junior." She laughed.

"Please call me Rebecca." The smile on her face was sincere.

"And call me Sophia, like the rest of my friends do."

The two Mrs. Hayworths wandered home along the country lanes. The brisk north wind made their shawls flap and tugged at their bonnets.

"What a lovely young lady!" Mrs. Hayworth said at last.

"Yes, she is."

"And what a beautiful baby."

"Indeed."

"Sometimes it must be hard for you."

Rebecca was shocked. "Why, I never complain, do I?"

"No, you don't. But wanting a baby is very natural for a woman, and it can be hard to wait. I waited four years for Jim, and they were probably the longest four years in my life."

Rebecca gazed into the far distance. "I long for a baby so much, maybe too much. For Jack's sake, as much as for my own."

"It is hard not knowing why we have to wait, isn't it?"

"Yes, it is." Rebecca stopped walking. "But it is even harder wondering if it is just waiting or whether the answer is a firm 'No, never.'"

Her mother-in-law nodded sympathetically.

Folding her arms across her chest, Rebecca added, "And I don't want to be an object of pity."

"There is nothing wrong with pity, my dear. Don't call it pity; call it sympathy. Even sympathy is easier to give than to receive. Our silly old pride doesn't like it. But accept it when it comes because it shows people care for you."

"But I can't go around crying at every christening."

"No, my dear. You need a lot of grace to remain cheerful and optimistic, and to be able to rejoice genuinely about the blessings of others—and from what I have seen of you, you are doing very well."

"Do you really think so?"

"Yes, I really do."

"But inside I am not. I am questioning the Lord's wisdom and wondering why He is doing this. Wondering what lesson He is trying to teach me. I get so confused, and it is easy to think, 'If only I am nice and gracious about it this month, maybe next month He will bless me with pregnancy.' I seem to want to bargain with Him."

"We don't deserve God's blessings any more than we earn our salvation. They are gifts."

"I know, but the Bible does say, 'As ye sow, so shall ye reap.'"

"I don't think that is the right application of the text. That verse is talking about wrong actions having consequences. Your situation is different. You are struggling with unanswered prayer, prayer for something perfectly legitimate."

Rebecca took a path that would make the walk home longer but allow them to avoid the centre of the village. The conversation hadn't been easy, but she did not want it to stop quite yet.

"How can I be totally submissive to the Lord's will for me?"

"Are any of us totally submissive? When we delight in the Lord and fully trust Him, His character, and purpose for us, we can be submissive, but like any other spiritual fruit, it can come and go. Remember, my dear, I was widowed relatively young. I struggled with God's purpose in that loss. I questioned myself about everything. Had I not been a good enough wife? Had I relied on my husband too much for my own spiritual life? What had I done wrong, and why was I being punished? Why did God remove a useful and gifted minister so early? God doesn't answer all our questions, but He gives grace and peace to rise above this the quagmire of questions and simply trust Him." Rebecca walked on silently, and her mother-in-law continued. "Samuel Medley's hymn 'God Shall Alone the Refuge Be,' was a great comfort to me in my early widow-hood, especially the line, 'Too wise to be mistaken, He / Too good to be unkind.' Once the devil has convinced you that God can be unkind, he can rob you of any joy and comfort. That is when you are at risk of self-pity and becoming bitter, sour, thinking 'poor little me.'"

Rebecca sighed. "I know. Sometimes I have to make myself count my blessings: I have a wonderful husband, a good maid, some lovely friends, and I live in a beautiful part of the world."

"Yes, that's good. Sometimes if you look around and see everyone else's burdens, you come to realise you wouldn't want to swap theirs with yours even if you could."

"Some burdens are hidden from sight."

"Yes," agreed Mrs. Hayworth. "Imagine living with a violent or disagreeable husband. Or a private struggle with an unfortunate character trait. Or an unspoken-of miscarriage."

They walked on in silence. Rebecca shuddered as she imagined a loveless marriage: the stony silence and icy atmosphere. How quickly one's concept of home would change! Home should be the place of refuge and solace, not a battle scene. Surely nothing could be more draining and wearying than an unhappy and hostile domestic situation.

With her mind's eye Rebecca ran through the pews at church and their Sunday occupants. To the left of the aisle, there was a case of unrequited love, various cases of constant pain, a rocky marriage, an overly-fertile and worn-out woman, and an unhappy spinster. To the right she saw an insomniac, another spinster, three constant pains, two difficult dispositions, and a recently bereaved. And those were only the burdens she knew about! Surely, all people gathered are included, when they unite in the prayer that says:

Have compassion on those who suffer from any grief or trouble;
That they may be delivered from their distress.

CHAPTER 25

VIOLET WONDERED WHY SHE HAD accepted the offer of a Sunday afternoon walk with Joe. It would seem so odd. Everyone knew what Sunday afternoon walks meant—it was almost courting! A walk and chat with Joe would be pleasant enough in an uneasy sort of way, but she could hardly bear to think of the smugly satisfied look her mother would wear if she heard about it. And she was bound to hear about it, for this was Capford, not anonymous London. She could decide simply not to show up and pretend to have a fever or a headache, but that would not do: a promise is a promise. Joe's opinion of her would plummet even further if she stood him up. She was not quite sure what she thought of him, but one thing she knew: she wanted him to have a good opinion of her.

The whole idea of a Sunday walk was awkward. As it was only early spring, the second service on a Sunday was still at half past two. Not until after Easter did the time change to six in the evening. The idea was that, during the winter months, there was enough light left after the service to do the chores and feed the animals before dusk. So, when could one fit in a walk? It would have to be straight after the midday meal—just when her mother expected her to don her apron and wash the dishes.

Violet walked home in the dusky pale light of the evening sunshine. The birds were singing their last songs of the day, and in the distance a sheep was bleating. Well, she decided, it was best to stop worrying about it. If Joe wanted to see her, he would have to arrange the details himself. Perhaps he was just being polite about meeting up and had already forgotten his suggestion.

Suddenly, heavy footsteps fell behind Violet. Panic immediately rose within her, and her heart began to pound as the incident with Reuben flashed before her mind's eye. She wanted to run.

"Hey, Vi, wait up!"

Her consternation evaporated on hearing Joe's voice. She turned and waited for him.

"Sorry, Vi," he puffed as he came alongside her. "I can't make it for the Sunday walk."

Violet's heart sank.

"Lambing has already started," Joe explained, "and this year I am in charge of half the flock."

"That's new," Violet responded in surprise.

"Yes. Mr. Thorpe decided not to stagger tupping but to put all the rams to the ewes at the same time. This means lambing will be intensive, but hopefully more lambs will be fat for the early markets, when the price is higher."

Violet smiled to herself at this information. Her father was terribly old-fashioned and never discussed the details of either tupping or lambing. Such information was thought not to be suitable for young, female ears, and she had never been encouraged to visit the lambing field.

"So, you'll be busy for the next month or so."

"Yes, I have even got my own shepherd's hut to sleep in. Your pa is having a hundred ewes in the Orchard Meadow, and I am having the rest in the next field—Four Acres."

Violet could see Joe was excited about the prospect of shepherding his own flock, but she could not wholeheartedly share in his pleasure. He would be too occupied to do any socialising.

"Will you come and visit me, Vi?"

Violet stared at him with delight and surprise. "Could I really?"

"If you would like to."

"Can I help with lambing?"

"Of course, if that is what you want."

"I most certainly do."

"Good. I'll expect you at Four Acres then. Wear old clothes and bring your own cup if you want tea from my little stove."

"When shall I visit?"

"Any time after tomorrow. Tomorrow I am setting up the hurdles and getting the hut towed out to a good spot."

It is amazing how quickly a new routine can be created if there is the will and enthusiasm. Every evening, however cold and wet, found Violet hurrying through her chores at home, dressing up warmly, and filling the lantern to head to Four Acres. Everything there was welcoming: the shepherd, the cosy hut, the snug sheep shelter, and the motherly baas of the ewes to which the newborn lambs replied with high-pitched bleats. Joe taught her how to latch a hungry lamb onto its mother, how to spot an ewe about to give birth, and then, most exciting of all, how to deliver a lamb. An ewe's womb was surprisingly warm compared with the cold evening air, and many lambs seemed reluctant to cooperate with being delivered. Their slippery legs would slide out of Violet's grasp as they pulled them back into the ewe's warm environment.

"They are playful even before they are born." Violet couldn't help but laugh.

"Ahh, the cheeky chaps like a fight. Show 'em who's boss, Vi."

So, pulling with all her might, Violet eased the slimy front legs and head out, after which the body followed easily, and soon another perfect lamb was lying steaming on the hay, soon struggling to get up. Quick as a flash Violet cleared mucus from the mouth and pulled the lamb around to its mother for licking. Violet never tired of observing the first loving communication between mother and baby: the ewe's reassuring baas between licks of her offspring's face and the first shrill bleats of the lamb in reply as it lunged toward its now-standing mother, looking for milk.

"Get your arm washed first, or you'll freeze," said Joe.

"I just want to see the lamb find its feet." An icy breeze whipped stray wisps of hair into Violet's eyes and chilled her slime-covered arm. But she stood entranced.

In silence they watched the wobbly lamb try out his lanky legs for the first time and launch himself toward his mother's udder.

"He's aiming in the right direction."

"He's latched on."

Jack swung his lantern away from the ewe and lamb and toward the hut. "They'll be fine. Now we can have a well-deserved cuppa."

"Unless another ewe has started."

The hut was warm and snug compared to the chilly sheep pen. Joe threw another log in the tiny stove and, after washing her hands, Violet made the tea. A bushel box under the bed was Joe's larder, and Violet dragged it out to find the tin of tea leaves and jar of biscuits. The hut was a strange mixture of shepherding equipment—Stockholm tar, shears, and a shepherd's crook—muddled in with saucepans, logs, lamps, and a bed. Joe often tipped the logs out of the box, letting them roll anywhere, to make room for a weak, chilly lamb in front of the stove. The diverse aromas of rabbit stew, tar, damp clothes, and wet lambs added to Violet's fascination. It was all so male, business-like, and intriguing.

At first it had felt somehow amiss to sit on Joe's bed, but there was nowhere else to perch in the cluttered hut, so Violet soon overcame her scruples.

"How can you sleep on this lumpy hay mattress?" She asked, trying to get comfortable.

"I sleep like a log."

"I bet you have never shaken it about since it was made."

"Alas, my housemaid is somewhat negligent," said Joe in an upper-class voice.

"Then dismiss her forthwith," replied Violet in like vein.

Looking around the functional hut, Violet could not help wondering if Joe would have a similar wagon for traveling across Canada. She had seen drawings of settlers making their way along the American Oregon Trails in covered wagons. Probably in Canada they used something like that, unless the weather was much colder up there. The thought of Joe leaving caused her enjoyment of the moment to evaporate, and Violet tried to dismiss the prospect from her mind.

"Do you get many visitors here?" she asked.

"Mr. Thorpe wanders along every so often to see how things are going—he likes to lend a hand if it is busy. He's quite decent like that. After school one of my young siblings comes along with a casserole from mother and to raid my biscuit tin. Other than that, it is pretty much me, myself, and I."

"Do you get lonely?"

"Lonely? Never! I'm too busy or too tired to get lonely. Anyway, what more would I want? I like the work, the landscape, and the night sky. Most other people would spoil it."

Violet wondered at the last comment. It sounded like a compliment.

But tea breaks never lasted long. After downing the scalding tea, Joe set off to work again. As he opened the door, a blast of cold night air chilled the hut. Violet left her half empty mug on the stove and followed. Joe stood on the steps and gazed at the stars.

"It's clear tonight. There's old Orion."

"I only know his belt."

"There's two stars up and two down as a basic shape, a bit like a sand timer, then some people say those over there are his bow."

"I can see the Plough."

"Who have you been star gazing with?"

"My dear father, of course."

The night sky was awesomely vast and beautiful, and Violet felt tiny. Joe must have had similar thoughts, for he began quoting Psalm 8.

"When I consider Thy heavens, the work of Thy hands . . . "

"The moon and stars, which Thou hast ordained," continued Violet.

"What is man, that Thou art mindful of him?"

"Or the son of man, that thou visitest him?"

Neither of them moved, but after some time, Violet sensed Joe's attention shifting from the heavens to the earth.

"You can tell a lot from just listening," he explained, breaking the silence. "Even when I'm in bed, I have a pretty good idea what is going on. The normal sounds are the contented noises between the ewes and their lambs, the ewes chewing their cud, and a bit of moving around. Anything else usually means action. Loud baa-ing and bleating means a lamb has got lost. Grunts and groans mean a sheep is struggling to deliver. All of them baa-ing means a fox or dog is at them or they have broken out of the pen. I wouldn't even stop to lace up my boots if I heard that noise."

"Do you have a gun?"

"Yes, somewhere behind my larder box," said Joe.

If the live births were beautiful to behold, the stillbirths could be heartbreaking. After sometimes hours of labour, the exhausted ewe would nudge and lick her dead lamb, puzzled by the lack of movement and response. Violet could have wept as she heard the mother's noises of love go unanswered. As often as possible, Joe would find a spare twin lamb, skin the dead lamb, and cloth the lively one in the skin, then present it to the confused ewe. Meanwhile, Violet ran to the adjoining field and borrowed the sheep dog from her father. The dog sat placidly near the new family. The ewe would stamp her front hoof at the perceived threat and was so busy protecting the lamb that her inspection of it was cursory. Meanwhile, the lively lamb got down to business, found the udder, and had a good drink. By the time the interloper was full and ready to curl up next to its new mum for a snooze, she had accepted it as her own.

"She thinks a miracle has happened," said Joe with a smile for Violet.

"It has—thanks to you." Violet gazed at the happy pair. "It's the miracle of adoption, not resurrection."

CHAPTER 26

THE VICARAGE WAS QUIET, IDEAL for sermon preparation. Rebecca was at the charity knit group at Biggenden Manor, and Jack's mother had gone back to his sister's house at the end of last week. Yet Jack was unable to apply himself to any work. He had received post that morning, the contents of which had rendered studying impossible. Once again, he unfolded the letter and read the now familiar lines.

> My dearest Jack and Becca,
>
> Words cannot express my gratitude to darling Becca for her loving care and devotion rendered to me during my recent illness. I am feeling bereft and lonesome without her, and the house is empty without her cheerful presence. Since our happy reunion two years ago, I have hinted to my darling niece, (who is as a daughter to me), that all I have will be hers once I depart this life. I wish you to be fully aware and assured of this arrangement. For your immediate enjoyment, I enclose a bank cheque for £100. I have instructed my solicitor to make this an annual gift.
>
> Yours indeed,
>
> Hector Stubbs

Jack fingered the cheque. *How easy it would be to tear it up!* He was slightly alarmed at such a thought, but there was something about the whole arrangement that grated. The cheque was payable to him, not Rebecca. This was, of course, exactly as was proper and correct, for solicitors are always proper and correct, but somehow it seemed wrong. Now that Rebecca had committed herself to him in marriage, all she ever had or would earn, inherit, or be gifted was legally his. He hardly knew Uncle Hector, was not sure if he even liked the man, and being the recipient of such generosity made him feel guilty. One hundred pounds! It was more than he earned in a year. He balked at the idea of another man providing better for his wife than he did. Could he still call himself the breadwinner? Such a liberal amount would definitely make their lives more comfortable, and he was delighted for Rebecca—she would enjoy ordering a new frock and Sunday bonnet. *If only she were here now!* Jack willed the charity knitters to drop their stitches, lose their voices, and disband early. But with his intimate knowledge of committees and charitable gatherings, he realised an early finish was a vain hope.

Jack leaned his elbows on the desk and put his head in his hands. Running his fingers through his hair, his mind continued to whirl. Such generosity comes at a price. They were duty-bound as relatives to help Uncle Hector in his hour of need. Such assistance was right, proper, and biblical. But the monetary gift bound them to Uncle Hector with golden handcuffs. From now on they would doubt their every motive—was it pure Christian charity or for ulterior motives? How murky things would become! Money is not the root of all evil, but the love of it is. Jack and Rebecca did not love money, but who was totally immune from liking it, just a little?

Time and again he heard the back door creak on its hinges and sprang up to greet Rebecca, only to sink back into his chair when recognising the footsteps as Violet's. His Greek dictionary lay unopened on his desk as he doodled on the paper intended for sermon notes and mulled over the implications of the letter.

When his wife did finally arrive, he barely had time to screw up the doodling and toss it in the bin before she swept into the study.

"I've never enjoyed a charity knit so much in my life," she announced.

"Good."

"Instead of being trapped in a corner near Mrs. Grey, I sat next to Sophia Thorpe, who by the way is an excellent hostess and conversationalist. I really do rather like her."

"Good."

"And how was your morning?" she asked, removing her bonnet.

"Very interesting."

"Oh, have you had visitors?"

"No, a letter."

"From whom?"

"From Uncle Hector."

"You said it was interesting."

"It was. Sit down and read it yourself."

Jack watched Rebecca's face as she read the letter. Her eyes widened and her eyebrows rose, and then she collapsed back into the chair.

"Well, I never! How very, very kind!"

"It is unbelievably generous."

"We are rich!"

They looked at each other and smiled uneasily.

"I don't think anyone need know," said Jack, breaking a long silence. "It would feel awkward."

Rebecca thought about this. "Yes, people might treat us differently."

"Or expect us to treat them differently."

"We must continue as normal," said Rebecca.

"But you must choose a new Sunday dress and hat."

"And you must choose new boots and a much-needed greatcoat."

Opportunities to spend money are never in short supply. Only the following week a letter addressed to Mrs. Hayworth dropped onto the doormat. Jack recognised the neat, copperplate handwriting. He had never met Miss Miller, but the proper and precise lettering on the envelope seemed to sum her up: prim and business-like. Although Rebecca spoke warmly of her, Jack failed to warm up to her. He was grateful for Miss Miller's involvement in comforting Rebecca when her parents died, and for welcoming her to Broadstairs for a much-needed break a couple of years ago; but in his mind's eye, Miss Miller remained a formidable spinster of impeccable, unbending character, who viewed the best of men as a necessary evil. With unerring regularity, a letter from her arrived the third week of every month, and with the slightly reluctant air of a favourite pupil completing an assignment, and in her best handwriting, Rebecca faithfully replied.

Nothing in the solitary life of Miss Miller had changed since Rebecca's visit. She taught in the same small ragged school, she lived in the same spartan house. She probably wore the same plain dresses and ate the same bland food. She may become acquainted with a few more people, but none would become a friend. She neither needed nor sought friendship—not because she was selfish or uncaring, but simply because she was both self-sufficient and self-contained. This combination of attributes is admired in men, but when displayed by females, society either despises or pities them. *Maybe I'm just being mean to the old girl,* thought Jack.

Expecting no real news, Rebecca saved the letter to read during the evening. Jack lent her his pocketknife to open the envelope, then pulled out the Diocesan Gazette with equally low expectations.

"She's going at last!" exclaimed Rebecca jubilantly. "She's going to Africa."

Down went the Gazette, and down went Jack's jaw.

"How? When?"

Rebecca reread the letter.

"She has been accepted by the London Missionary Society as a tutor and companion for a missionary's family in Southern Africa. She and the missionary's wife are to start a work for women and abandoned girls. The family is there already, and she is to embark on her journey there as soon as is convenient. A replacement teacher has been found for the ragged school in Broadstairs. She will commence her language studies on the boat—and knowing her, she will be fluent by the time she disembarks. She has given the address of a guest-house in Southhampton for my next letter and—I quote—'all subsequent correspondence may be sent via the mission headquarters in London.'"

"And all this happened since her last letter to you?"

"Apparently, yes. She has never mentioned anything about it before."

"Well, I never."

"Good for her! It is just what she wanted. She has been praying about it for years and had almost given up hope."

"How will she get on living in with a family?"

Rebecca smiled. "I reckon she will insist on having her own mud-hut."

"I'm sure she will be very useful."

"She'll put her all into it," agreed Rebecca. "She may not be the most companionable companion—what a tongue twister!,—but she will master the local language, revel in the simplicity of life, be an excellent tutor, and do her very best for the local women."

Rebecca sipped her tea and gazed into the crackling fire.

"Why are you smiling at the fire, my dear?"

"Oh, Jack, I was just thinking about how, two and a half years ago, Miss Miller and I sat in her chilly sitting room talking about our unanswered prayers. She was longing to go to Africa, and I was longing for a godly husband. Now look at us both! God is very kind."

"Kind to me too."

"You know our newfound wealth?"

"Yes," replied Jack cautiously.

"Can we send Miss Miller a bit for her passage to Africa?"

"How much do you suggest?"

"What about ten pounds? It can be like a tithe—for the Lord's work."

"I think that is a wonderful idea."

Jack looked fondly at his wife, but her serious face was turning playful.

"Shame you'll have to forgo your greatcoat," she teased.

"Pity you'll have to have less frills and furbelows on your dress," Jack replied, springing up to make a grab at his wife.

CHAPTER 27

VIOLET WISHED MR. THORPE HAD twice as many ewes. By the end of April, all the lambing paraphernalia had been put away, the hurdle pens removed from the Orchard Meadow and Four Acres, and the sheep were allowed to graze undisturbed.

"That's not the end of it," Joe told Violet when she said something about the job being done. "Those lambs demand more than their share of my attention, right up until the day we send them to Tunbridge Market and they meet the mint sauce."

Violet knew from listening to her father of all that could go wrong with a sheep: wet, stodgy grass could cause foot rot, and dirty wool attracted flies, leading to maggots. Ewes got bad udders or the shudders. Lambs got sore mouths and runny eyes. They died if they ate wool or rhododendrons. In fact, they could die for little or no reason.

Lambing might not be the end of the sheep work, but it marked the end of Violet's visits to the lambing hut, and she wondered if Joe would miss her. Having nowhere to go now, she slowly and mindlessly washed up the dinner dishes. Her mother was trimming the lamps, ready to sit down to an evening of darning, and her father was peacefully snoring in an armchair, toasting his toes on the fire-fender. His steaming socks gave off a musty smell of old cheese and wet wool. *I'm in for an exciting evening,* sighed Violet as she hung her tea towel to dry by the stove.

Much to her annoyance, right from early on in lambing, her mother had put two and two together and made four. With a parent like Mrs. Brookes, one could not disappear from the house (especially if one is an unmarried daughter) without questions being asked. Violet had to smile at her mother's dilemma as to how to react—encouraging her daughter to fraternize unchaperoned in the dusk with a man was unthinkable. But the man happened to be Joe. Trustworthy, reliable Joe—the very man she had recommended (with no success) to her daughter for many years. So, Mrs. Brookes did something she was unaccustomed to doing: she turned a blind eye. Violet knew she was bursting to ask a barrage of questions about the friendship and, much to her own surprise, Violet was bursting to talk about Joe, but they both held their peace, as if Violet's evening visits were a thing of little or no consequence. And now Violet had to act as if the termination of the visits was also of little or no consequence.

Without an ounce of enthusiasm, Violet wandered upstairs to her room for her knitting bag. Instead of finding it and joining her mother in the warm kitchen, she flopped on her bed with a sigh. She lay, staring at the wooden beams, unwilling to move despite the chill penetrating through her clothes.

She looked at the pine-cones in her fireplace—what a ridiculous rule her mother insisted on! "No fires in bedrooms." When Violet was younger the excuse had been the fire hazard, but now it was the unsociability of sitting in her own room. "Fires in bedrooms break up family unity." Family unity!? When there is only you and your parents left in the family house, and the female parent is inclined to nag and criticize your every decision! Still, it was not really Ma Violet was fed up with today, just life in general and Canada in particular.

"Violet!" her mother called shrilly up the stairs.

"I'm just coming," she said a slight groan, sliding off the bed onto her feet.

"We've got a visitor!"

Probably only one of the snotty grandchildren, thought Violet, grabbing her knitting bag.

On entering the kitchen, she found it wasn't a niece or nephew wanting help with homework. It was Joe. And her parents were being embarrassingly attentive. Ma had captured his hat and coat to ensure he stayed a while, and Pa seemed to have forgotten that they had worked together all day and greeted him like a long-lost friend.

"Put on the kettle, Violet," instructed Mrs. Brookes, although her daughter was already doing so.

Without being asked, Violet also found the biscuits she had made the evening before. Then, acutely aware of her parents, she turned to the visitor.

"Good evening, Joe. So, you have an evening off."

"Not entirely. I've just put a few hurricane lanterns around the fields to deter foxes."

"Good lad!" praised Mr. Brookes, "Saves me a job."

As she hovered by the stove, waiting for the watched kettle to boil, Joe and her father talked shop. There seemed no end of observations that could be made about grass growth, the weather, ewe health, and Tunbridge auctioneers. It was not until Violet approached them with a tray of clattering cups that her father's attention turned to things nearer home.

"Why, haven't we got anything stronger to offer the lad?" he asked.

"The cellar and its contents are your business," Ma replied.

"How about a cider, Joe?"

"Your own brew?"

"Of course!"

"Then the answer is obvious."

"Good lad!" Mr. Brookes said with a wink before he headed for the cellar door.

Violet turned over two now-unneeded cups. She was pleased with her father's actions—he never offered his cider to anyone he disliked or to children. She had suspected him of considering Joe and her as children and almost expected him to offer them a glass of milk or a candy.

However, she was not pleased with her mother. Right there, in front of a visitor, Ma sat darning Violet's ancient stockings! Violet flushed with discomfort. How embarrassing to have her undergarments so on display—and holey ones at that! She hoped Joe wouldn't notice, or at least not realize they were hers. Knowing her mother, she would probably further humiliate Violet by saying something like, "There you are, Violet, nicely mended for you." Violet sipped her tea and wished she was drinking out of a tin mug in a shepherd's hut, far away from parents and holey stockings.

Once the cider had been suitably appreciated, the conversation continued to flow. Violet's contribution was minimal, and she was puzzled. Why had Joe come? Originally, she imagined it was for her, but now, seeing him comfortably ensconced in an armchair, laughing at her father's worn-out witticisms, she began to wonder. The evening ticked past, and she became none the wiser.

"Speaking of lamps . . . " (they hadn't been), "how much oil did you put in them fox lamps?" Mr. Brookes asked.

"Not as much as I would have liked. I ran out."

"Well, they don't 'alf burn it up."

"Should I top 'em up?"

"Best do, lad. I've got some paraffin oil from the farm in me lean-to."

Joe got up to take his leave, and Mr. Brookes turned to Violet.

"Vi, be a darling and show Joe where me cans are. The lean-to is a bit of a muddle."

"Careful with the lamps near the paraffin!" called out Mrs. Brookes as Violet ran to get her shawl.

The lean-to was indeed a muddle, and it took a while to identify the correct can.

"Does your father ever throw anything away?" asked Joe as he shone his lamp around the shed and inspected the contents.

"Not if he can help it because 'It might come in handy sometime.'"

On completing his inspection, Joe turned to Violet. "Come with me to top up the lamps."

"All right."

An hour later, Violet returned home.

"Why, Violet, what took you so long?" asked her mother.

"I helped Joe top up the lamps."

"There must have been an awful lot of lamps."

"Them lamps can't 'alf be troublesome," her father said, laughter in his voice and a wink in his eye.

Violet couldn't help the twinkle in her own eyes. "Terribly troublesome," she agreed.

It was late, and she had to work in the morning. After the family Bible reading, Violet kissed her parents goodnight.

"I assume I'm the only man you kissed tonight," teased Mr. Brookes, in a whisper so as not to be scolded by his wife. Violet playfully punched him on the arm and said nothing. How she wished he was wrong!

From that evening on, the lighting of the hurricane lamps was a task for two. Never in the history of sheep husbandry were fox lamps better trimmed or tended. Maybe it was the stillness of the meadows or the tranquility of the twilight. Maybe it was soft radiance of the lamp light itself, or the peaceful presence of the sheep. But whatever it was, Violet found the evenings almost magical—the company, the surroundings, and the conversation was just perfect. Perfect . . . except Canada. The thought of Joe leaving Capford was the fly in the ointment, the maggot in the apple. For evening after evening it was on the tip of her tongue to ask about his plans, but she was too scared of what she might hear.

Then one evening it seemed as if she would burst if she was left in suspense any longer. It was better to know the truth than live a dream. If she was going to lose him, it would be best to know.

"Joe, when are you going to Canada?" The question jumped out her mouth, and it was too late to take it back. Her mouth went dry, and her fingers shook as she waited for a reply. What a long wait it was. Unusually long. *He is probably figuring out how to break the news gently.*

Joe continued changing the wick with painstaking slowness. Violet felt a sudden urge to kick the lamp—glass and all—as far as possible. She resisted. Why be so ridiculously fastidious about the wick size right now?

"I don't know," Joe eventually replied. "It depends on a few things."

Violet impatiently waited for more enlightenment. He lit the new wick, but that was not the enlightenment she needed.

"I've got to save up for my passage across and the journey there. They are practically giving land away, but I want to take enough money to buy agricultural equipment, stock, and timber. Half my wages go to Mother, so I am not saving as fast as I would like to."

By now they were plodding across the muddy meadow to the next lamp.

"But also, I am not as enthusiastic about it as I used to be."

"Oh."

"Somehow, since us getting more friendly, a life alone doesn't appeal as much as it once did."

"Then don't leave."

"But I do want to go to Canada."

"Take me with you." Violet blurted out, desperation making her bold.

Joe swung around, and the light of his lamp blinded her eyes.

"What are you saying? Do you really mean that?"

"I really want to go with you, Joe."

"Because of Canada, or because of me?"

"Both."

"I can't expect such a big thing of you—to leave your family and friends and all that."

"I'll be with you."

Joe stepped closer. “Vi, I love you with all my heart. I’d give up Canada or anything else to be with you.”

An overwhelming wave of joy swept over Violet, weakening her knees and flushing her cheeks. “I love you too, Joe. I’d give up anything for you.”

Joe dropped his lantern in the mud and wrapped his arms around Violet. Her whole body tingled when he kissed her. Tearing himself away, Joe knelt down on one knee.

“Vi , will you marry me?”

“Joe!” cried Violet. “Don’t kneel there!”

Joe remained in position. “Violet Brookes, that is not an answer.”

“Joe Mason, I would be delighted to marry you, and for you to get up out of the mud and sheep-muck.”

CHAPTER 28

SOPHIA AND REBECCA SAT IN Biggenden Manor drawing room and giggled like naughty school girls.

"At first I couldn't make head nor tail of her explanations," said Sophia. "She was all breathlessness and apologies. 'Oh, Mrs. Thorpe, I am sorry to disturb you,' she said, 'but I can't find Mrs. Hayworth or Mrs. Brookes anywhere.' 'I am sure they are all right, Mrs. Grey,' I assured her. 'Oh, no, no, I don't mean that. I mean that sloping meadow is ploughed up, Mother has broken her arm, and I don't want soggy egg sandwiches.' 'Did your mother fall in the ploughed field?' I asked. 'Oh, no, no, no,' she said. 'She fell at home, and now she is with me.' I asked if her mother liked egg sandwiches, and she said, 'Oh, no, no, no, she only eats jam ones.' Well, by that time I was completely bewildered, so I sat her down, rang for a pot of tea, and tried to get to the bottom of the field, the arm, and the soggy sandwiches. It turns out she is most concerned about the Sunday school outing. The field of Lord Wilson's that it is normally held in has been ploughed up. Her mother is staying with her, so she feels unable to help, and she normally makes the egg sandwiches for the event. Anyone else tends to make them too soggy."

Sophia mimicked Mrs. Grey's flustered voice. "You must boil them, not scramble. They need to cool down well first. It needs to be old and dry—the bread, I mean. People these days don't understand bread. It's no good being too fresh. You can't cut it thin enough, and it doesn't absorb properly. The previous baker understood these things, but the new one does not. I knew his mother, dear old lady and not a tooth in her mouth."

Sophia paused and put a hand over her heart. "Forgive me, Rebecca, but I couldn't help asking how the old lady managed dry bread with no teeth."

"You didn't!"

"I'm afraid I did."

"And how did she manage?"

"Dunk it and suck it!"

The two women shrieked with laughter and were still wiping away their tears when a housemaid announced a visitor.

"Excuse me, ma'am, but Reverend Hayworth is here to see his wife."

All mirth drained from Rebecca. This was an unusual occurrence. Something must have happened.

Jack was shown into the room, and his face confirmed her suspicions. Forgetting his normal manners, he omitted any greeting to Sophia and addressed Rebecca.

"I have just received a telegram from Uncle Hector's housekeeper, Mrs. Hill. He has had a large stroke and is unconscious."

"Then I must go."

Hardly aware of what was happening, Rebecca donned her cloak and left. Had she even said good-bye to Sophia? In numb haste, she packed her case and changed into her best frock. Violet kindly offered to escort her, but Rebecca, knowing how hard it would be for her to leave Joe, declined. Meanwhile, Jack had scouted the village for a willing driver, only to find that Sophia had mobilised her coachman into action. Rebecca struggled to hold back her tears as Jack helped her into the carriage and climbed in beside her. She chided herself. She was not crying for Uncle Hector, but for herself: for leaving Capford, leaving her husband, and returning to the prison house.

The sight of poor Uncle Hector was truly alarming. Any self-pity drained away as Rebecca stared aghast at his ashen, unresponsive face. Rebecca bent down to kiss him and found that his skin was cold and clammy.

"'E's right bad," whispered Mrs. Hill, rather unnecessarily.

"What did his physician say?" Rebecca whispered back.

"'E said . . . only time will tell."

"Highly scientific."

Rebecca had wished for more detailed medical guidance. In the dim light of the darkened room, the two ladies stood silently assessing the situation. It was clear to both that Uncle Hector needed full nursing care, and it was equally clear that they needed assistance. But where can one find a good, reliable nurse? Mrs. Hill knew only tradesmen and housekeepers, and Rebecca knew absolutely no one. She offered up a silent prayer as they sighed despondently.

Over a much-needed cup of tea, Rebecca remembered the dear old nurse that had attended the Dowager Wilson so faithfully. Jack had spoken of her most warmly, and she seemed a woman of Christian convictions. Would her fees be too prohibitive? Judging from his largesse, surely Uncle Hector could afford to employ a good nurse. Yes, Rebecca convinced herself, as his nearest relatives, she and Jack were duty-bound to provide Uncle Hector with the best possible care and to act on his behalf in securing it.

Without delay, she sent a telegram to Jack asking him to make enquiries into the whereabouts of the nurse and request her assistance if available. Having done this, she mentally girded up her loins. Until help arrived, she and Mrs. Hill must stand in the breach.

The days and nights merged into one as Rebecca and Mrs. Hill attended the stricken man. With gentle care, they cleaned and turned him, held his limp hand, and stroked his clammy brow. They sought signs of consciousness but detected nothing. Once a day the physician arrived to apply leeches or give directions. At his instruction, they put small cubes of ice in Uncle Hector's mouth to give him fluid, but most of the melted water ran down his sagging chin onto his nightshirt.

The first night had been the worst, for Rebecca was unprepared for the long vigil ahead. The staff members were attentive and asked if she had everything necessary, but it was only after they had all retired to bed that she began to realise what was necessary. Unless she rationed the coal, the fire would die out before dawn. Her corset was not designed for slouching in an armchair and began to rub her back and pinch her armpits. As the darkness deepened and London sank into silence, a chill crept over her. How she longed for a couple of warm blankets and her outside shawl! She also wanted to relieve herself, but could she leave Uncle Hector? What if he slipped out of bed, suddenly awoke or—even worse—passed away when she was absent?

After a couple of slow, uncomfortable hours, she could bear it no longer. Steeling herself for decisive action, she took her lamp, crept to the water closet, and then went to her room. Hastily she wriggled out of her dress and corset. She found another woolen vest, her nighty, and a shawl and removed the blankets and counterpane from her bed. Thus equipped, she returned to her uncle, who seemed no worse for her absence.

Changing his position was almost impossible on her own, but Rebecca did her best by pushing pillows behind his back. The new position made him snore in such an awful gurgling manner that Rebecca, with strength produced by alarm, pulled out the pillows and flipped him on his side. She was still shaking when she threw a shovel load of coal on the fire and sank back into the chair.

Having wrapped herself up, she tried to relax. Her hairpins stuck into her head, so she removed them all and plaited her hair instead. She looked reproachfully at the ticking clock. The loudest object in the room, how slowly it moved its hands! Turning her gaze to Uncle Hector, she wondered what he was experiencing. And from the present, her thoughts moved to the future. Did Uncle Hector have an earthly future? And what of his eternal? She knew his opinion on many things but not his opinion on Christ. That was the only thing that mattered now.

Rebecca felt annoyed with Jack. He was a minister, after all. Why had he never steered the conversation to spiritual matters? That is what ministers are supposed to do, aren't they? She was annoyed with herself too. She had been too hesitant, too polite, too timid. She wanted to shake Uncle Hector out of his perilous slumber and ask him if he was ready for his journey from time to eternity. The bedroom was so still and peaceful, it seemed hardly possible that it could be the scene of such a momentous event. How awesome it was that one moment a person could be mindlessly drifting in sleep and the next instant standing, more awake than they had ever been, before their Judge.

Rebecca shivered and once again committed her soul to the Lord. She prayed for Uncle Hector, pleading that if he wasn't ready for eternity that he would wake up, realise his danger, and flee to Christ. In Christian magazines like *Sundays at Home,* she had frequently seen deathbed scenes portrayed—grieving relatives kneeling at the bedside and praying as they clutched their dying relative's hand. Moved by memories of these images, Rebecca flung off her blankets and did the same.

Returning to her chair afterwards, she reflected on her actions. Was it a bit melodramatic? Was God moved by such displays of emotion? She doubted it—not because she thought God uncaring, but because she knew, from bitter experience, that the heart could be near to breaking in silent prayer, despite everyone around being oblivious to the soul struggle. How often, on her low days, had she been secretly wrestling with God despite bustling about in a gathering of women? *We don't need to pretend to a God who sees our innermost being,* thought Rebecca, and the thought made her thankful.

She must have drifted off to sleep, for she dreamed strange dreams of physicians, leeches, and Mr. Gascoigne. It was almost a relief to be woken by Mrs. Hill. The cup of tea tasted strange in her dry mouth, and her head throbbed. It took very little persuading for her to hand over Uncle Hector's care to the housekeeper, take breakfast, and go to bed. It was blissfully relaxing to stretch out between the sheets, but the deep chill, unique to a sleepless night and exhaustion, took a long time to disappear, despite hot water bottles.

Very gradually Rebecca warmed up, and when she did eventually fall asleep, she slept for hours on end, only to wake with a muzzy head and a gnawing stomach.

Letters from Jack were always welcome, but Rebecca could have danced a jig after reading the next letter, for the Wilson's former nurse had been named and located. She was called Hester Haynes, and she lodged with her brother's widow in Bournemouth when unable to secure work. This much had been gleaned from the housekeeper at Kenwood Manor, who had forwarded her final wages to the address. Not only was Hester without work, but she was willing to nurse Uncle Hector and would be arriving within two days. A huge weight seemed to lift from Rebecca's tense shoulders, and her headache almost disappeared. Mrs. Hill was no less delighted and, despite her tiredness, organised the transforming of Uncle Hector's dressing room into a suitable bedroom for the nurse.

On arriving at 27 Milton Square, Hester Haynes was rewarded with a warm reception. Rebecca and Mrs. Hill already admired her, although they had not yet witnessed her in action. As soon as she had finished her cup of tea, Nurse Haynes unpacked her apron and went to inspect her charge. She was a formidable sight in her copious apron, which rendered her almost as wide as she was tall. Hands on hips, she silently studied the room, the bed, and its occupant. With calm authority, she organised the rearranging of the room to maximize the patient's comfort and her convenience. She wanted more light and air entering the room and, within an hour of her arrival, it seemed that hope and optimism had entered too.

CHAPTER 29

HAVING FUMBLED AROUND, TRYING TO get the key in the keyhole, Jack entered the pitch black hallway. Rebecca would have left a lit lamp for him on the hall table. He felt for the lamp, found it, then with frustration realised he had no idea where the matches were. The whole evening was just one long irritation! Grabbing the lamp, he moved down the hallway toward the kitchen. The location of matches was another item he could add to his mental list of "Things to ask your wife before she unexpectedly disappears."

Before he had taken more than three steps, he collided with the hat stand and fell flat on the floor. There was an ominous crash as the lamp chimney shattered on the hard stone surface. Jack groaned as he heaved himself onto his feet. The sharp stinging of his right hand and warm oozing of blood galvanized him into action. Feeling along the wall with his left hand, with the right one held close to his chest, Jack made his way into the kitchen. The stove was burning low but produced just enough glow to be located. His left hand ineptly opened the stove door so he could stir the embers and produce more light. Finding kindling wood in a basket nearby, he stoked the fire and looked around the room. A tea cloth on the back of a chair would serve as a bandage, and a butcher's receipt became a wick to light the kitchen lamp. With more illumination, he inspected the wound. It wasn't too deep, but it was in an awkward place—it started bleeding every time he opened his palm. Jack sank onto the wooden kitchen chair, cradling his head in his arms on the table top.

Technically speaking, the injury wasn't Lord Wilson's fault, but Jack put the blame firmly at his door. Why else would he still be up, at well past midnight, on such a wet and gloomy night? Jack's uninjured hand thumped the kitchen table in frustration. *That obnoxious man! Asks questions, but never listens to the reply! Deaf as a door nail when he chooses to be! Drinks too much. Eats too much! Born with more status than his intellect deserves.*

Having had a private and somewhat satisfying rant, Jack decided he should head for bed after bandaging his hand. Bandages!—another thing to add to the growing "wife list." Having unsuccessfully explored a few drawers, he opted for another tea cloth and bound up his still-oozing hand the best he could. As he lay in bed, fearing the pain would keep him awake, he made up his mind. Next time Lord Wilson sent for him, he would refuse to go. Having made that Queen Vashti-like decision, he fell into a fitful sleep.

The following morning, Violet was suitably impressed with the blood stains, shattered glass, and misused tea-cloths. She located the bandages and professionally applied one. The matches were, and had always been, right next to the lamp on the hall table. Jack wandered about the house feeling sore, fed up, and belligerent. He had only two more days to prepare his Sunday sermons. He scrapped his notes for the morning service. He had a new subject, and he was in just the right mood to give it his best shot.

His sermon notes looked like a schoolboy's first, clumsy attempt at writing, thanks to Violet's liberal bandaging, and everything seemed to take twice as long. Jack fumbled his way through the thin leaves of his Cruden's Concordance, Matthew Henry, and other commentaries. But his brain made up for the speed his fingers lacked. *Maybe the subject deserved a series, not just one sermon.*

Violet took her half day on Saturday. Once she had left, Jack was free to be a slovenly bachelor for the remainder of the day. He ate his dinner at his desk, mindlessly shoveling in the forkfuls as he continued his preparation. He hardly noticed the afternoon fading into evening until he was abruptly disturbed by the front door bell. Looking up at the study clock, he was surprised to see it was half past eight. His heart sank—Lord Wilson! Sure enough, the caller was Lord Wilson's groom. Jack steeled himself.

"Evening, parson. The big man be wanting ya again."

"Sorry, John, but I am not coming tonight."

"'E's sent me te fetch ya."

"Then please send my apologies and say I am too busy preparing tomorrow's sermons."

"'E won't like that."

"I know, but I am here to serve the parish, not just his lordship."

"'E don't think of no one but 'imself."

"Indeed."

"So ya ain't coming?"

"No John, I ain't . . . I mean I'm not."

"You're a brave man, parson."

"Maybe foolhardy, John."

"Maybe, maybe."

"Goodnight." Jack closed the door before he could waver and go. That was the end of his sermon preparation for the evening. Pacing about the house, he wondered if he had done the right thing.

The next morning, fortified by hot porridge he had ended up burning, Jack strode to church. In the chilly vestry he fell on his knees and begged for divine aid. During the first hymn, he looked around the church. It was pleasingly full. In the luxury pews to the side of him sat the stony-faced Wilson family. The readings were short—Psalm 14 and Luke 12 verses 16 to 21. Instead of announcing a text at the beginning of the sermon as was his normal custom, he launched straight into his theme.

"We all know what the atheist thinks about God," the Reverend Hayworth said. "We are left in no doubt: their voice is strong in the written press, in science, and in conversation. With loud and lofty words, they pour scorn on the faith of their forefathers. They mock the simple beliefs of the godly and puff themselves up in arrogance and conceit. Only a decade ago they would have been ashamed to utter their opinions in public, but now they shout them from the housetops. Instead of believing the God of the Bible, they prefer to believe that we are a random selection of atoms, the offspring of apes, and a product of chance.

"The atheist denounces the truths of the Bible—the very truths Tyndale so highly prized, that Ridley and Latimer died for. The truths that sustained the Protestant martyrs in Queen Mary's reign as they faced their deaths with assured hope of salvation in Christ. They denounce the faith of the saints of old, the cloud of witnesses we read of in Hebrews 11. And what do they give us instead? Will it be any comfort to you on your deathbed to believe you are a random group of atoms? Will you comfort your dear dying daughter with the theory of evolution? Will the idea that she is only different from animals because she has developed opposable thumbs bring her comfort? Why mourn for an ape's offspring? In adversity, is there any comfort in imagining no one is in control and life's events occur at random?

"Yes, we all know the increasingly vocal opinions of the atheists, but this morning I am going to tell you God's opinion of them. What does He say about them? In Psalm 14 verse 1 we have His opinion. How does God describe them? Does He praise their intellectual ability and free thinking? No—He calls them fools. 'The fool hath said in his heart, "There is no God."' A fool!

"It is not pleasant to be called a fool. No one wants to hear that said of himself or herself. But this is God's assessment of anyone here who says there is no God. A spiritual fool! To be foolish with money is bad: you may lose all your possessions. To be foolish with your health is awful: you may reap years of painful illness. To be foolish in your relationships is terrible: you may endure a life of domestic troubles and heartache. But to be a fool with your soul, your never-dying soul! You may endure an eternity of torment.

"In our New Testament reading, we heard about the rich fool and how God said, 'Thou fool, this night thy soul shall be required of thee.' This night! The very God you mock and loudly assert does not exist is the very God who lends you your every breath. He is the one who appoints the moment of your death. This night! Maybe it will not be literally 'this night,' but to God a thousand years are as one day. In eternity, won't your puny life on earth be like an evening that is past? A tale that is told? A drop in the bucket of eternity? Be sure of this: there are no atheists in hell. As J.C. Ryle says, 'Hell is truth known too late.' Too late, too late—what folly!"

Jack paused for effect. The church was silent. No fidgeting, no playing of noughts and crosses or reading of the marriage service as he sometimes saw from his lofty position in the pulpit.

"Angels and arch-angels cover their faces as they worship their King," he continued. "The devils believe and tremble. It is only man, foolish man, who dares to, as it were, spit in the face of his Creator and say, 'There is no God.' Is God alarmed by this? Is He scared that His rule may be overthrown? Does He quake as men come up with theories like Darwin's? No! We read His response in Psalm 37, see verse 13: 'The Lord shall laugh at him.' Why? 'For He seeth that his day is coming.' Do you want God to laugh at you? How dreadful to have the Maker of heaven and earth hold you in derision and laugh at you, just as you laughed at Him!"

Jack could no longer resist glancing at the Wilson pew. There was nothing wrong with Lord Wilson's hearing today. Sitting there with a red face and bulging eyes, he looked ready to blow a gasket. Unperturbed, Jack continued through a few more fools in the Bible, highlighting their folly and their end. Then he changed his tone and spoke to believers.

"In this modern age of science, you may be made to feel a fool for believing in Creation, in God, and in the life to come. Does God tremble when He sees the invention of the microscope, the telescope, and other scientific equipment? Not at all. With the right use of these things, we can explore more of God's amazing creation—the details of His designs and the vastness of His universe. We can learn more about how we are 'fearfully and wonderfully made.' These inventions do not disprove God. If anything, they prove the infinite wisdom and power of God. People may mock us and call us Luddites, as if we are hankering for the past and for old, antiquated ideas and theories. Let them call us what they will. We embrace any invention with the firm confidence that it will teach us more about our great Creator God.

"In conclusion, let us turn to Psalm 37 and briefly look at a huge contrast in the way the Lord deals with the evildoers (the fools) and the righteous (the wise). Over and over again the destruction of the evildoers is assured. They are likened to grass, to the burning fat of lambs, a green bay tree that is cut down and found no more. Their present hostility, hate, and venom are short-lived and futile. Contrast that with the loving encouragements to the righteous; they are promised spiritual sustenance, answers to their prayers, God's abundant peace, guidance for every footstep, and an eternal inheritance. Blessing upon blessing!

"And what is it to be righteous? To be wise? 'The fear of God is the beginning of wisdom'—fear that makes a soul flee to Christ for salvation. To make peace with your Judge and to be adopted into the Heavenly Father's family forever. Have you come to Christ, my friends? Or are you still a fool?"

Jack wearily sat down. As the congregation sang the final hymn, he begged the Lord to bless his words with divine power and application. Standing up to join in with the last verse, he noticed Lord Wilson stomping angrily down the aisle. By the time the benediction had been said, the Wilson carriage had departed, leaving the rest of the family to await its return or walk home.

With a pounding head, Jack retreated to the vicarage. He had stoked the kitchen stove prior to the service but forgotten to put in a jacket potato. Rummaging through the pantry, he found a loaf of bread, some cold beef, and a shriveled apple to make up a passable dinner.

CHAPTER 30

MEANWHILE AT BIGGENDEN MANOR, THE Thorpes sat down to Sunday lunch. Mrs. Harrington was gracing them with her presence, having regained her voice in sunny France and having a great desire to see her grandson once again.

"What a ranter your minister is!" she exclaimed, liberally helping herself to roast potatoes.

"No, he is not!" retorted Sophia.

"Well, you could hardly call him calm and collected. Such passion is hardly decent."

"It was highly appropriate, Mother," corrected Sophia. "He was talking about eternal issues. Surely one is able to show a bit of spirit when speaking of such important things?"

"I rather distrust any minister who discards the liturgy, makes up his own prayers, and inflicts on his congregation long sermons of his own devising."

"That is the whole point of ministry."

"Well, it isn't proper. It may be acceptable for your village rustics, but it makes people of finer sensibilities, like myself, rather uncomfortable."

"Being made to feel uncomfortable isn't a bad thing, Mother, if it helps us focus on eternal matters."

Edward looked up from his plate. He was pleasantly surprised at his wife's directness.

"Religion is too personal to be discussed," admonished Mrs. Harrington. "I am surprised how quickly you have forgotten the fundamentals of good manners!"

The remainder of the main course was eaten in silence. But by the time dessert was served, Mrs. Harrington was back in full flow, extolling the delights of the French Riviera. All seemed harmonious again until Edward mentioned the afternoon service.

"You attend twice?" asked Mrs. Harrington, all astonishment.

"That is our common practice," said Edward.

"It wasn't previously."

"Much to our shame," admitted Sophia.

"You are going too?" Mrs. Harrington's surprise increased.

"Yes, unless I stay to look after Bertie."

"Isn't that what you pay the nursemaid to do?"

"Indeed it is, Mother, but I like her to be able to get to at least one service a Sunday."

"Oh, how sweet of you," mocked her mother, "to care so much for the spiritual welfare of your staff."

"We do care."

"Well, in that case, would it please you religious fanatics if I stayed behind to look after Bertie so that your nursemaid can listen to your Reverend Hayworth?"

"Thank you, Mother, that would be most helpful," replied Sophia mildly, ignoring all provocation.

And so it was that both Mr. and Mrs. Thorpe attended church that evening. Sophia was very thankful she was present, for Reverend

Jack Hayworth was equally as powerful in his exposition as he had been that morning. His text was 'Unto you therefore which believe He is precious.' She already knew something of the preciousness of Christ, but as Jack described the various characteristics of Jesus, like a diamond cutter showing the perfection of each facet of a rare diamond, she was melted by her Saviour's beauty and loveliness. She was not the only one thus effected. On glancing across the aisle, she saw Violet sitting with Joe. They were both listening intently, and Violet's tear-stained face held a smile. Sophia felt a surge of love for her, and indeed for anyone who loved the Lord. She would never understand why Christ should love her, but now she had no doubt that He did.

After the service, Edward and Sophia lingered by their front door, unwilling to enter and face Mrs. Harrington. They shared their delight in the service and wished they could continue the discussion. Their mutual delight in Christ drew them together into a new depth of love.

Sophia's gaze dropped to the ground. "I don't want Mother spoiling my newfound joy."

"Then avoid her," Edward said. "Go straight to bed. I'll entertain her."

Her gaze flew to his face. "Really? Are you sure?"

"Yes, and if it gets too bad, I'll walk Rex or make some other laudable excuse to escape."

"Such sacrificial love deserves a kiss."

"Or two or three."

During her fortnight's visit, Mrs. Harrington was more than usually quarrelsome and outspoken. Edward and Sophia wondered if it was an after-effect of a wonderful time in France. Mr. Harrington had declined accompanying her to Kent; now they understood why and hoped he was benefiting from her absence.

In Mrs. Harrington's private opinion, which she freely voiced, Biggenden Manor and Estate was moving in the wrong direction. Sophia's involvement with the knitting group was an unnatural mixing of the social classes.

"There you are, serving tea for those who are in service or aspire to be in service themselves. It cannot be right. And tradesmen's wives!" She shuddered. "They come into your home, bringing with them all the strange germs that the working class carries. Just imagine! A butcher's wife who has been handling offal and pigs' eyes may have sat in this very chair! I can barely tolerate the thought! It is not good for Bertie's well-being. Anyway, are they honest? Do you hide your silver?"

"Mother, they are honourable women of the church!"

"Well, they may be tempted to covetousness."

But it was not only Sophia who came in for criticism. Edward received his fair share as well.

"Your visitor's book looks decidedly blank for last winter."

"Yes, we entertained very little. What with our village commitments and having Bertie, we had very little inclination to entertain as we used to."

"This is my fear. You both seem to be withdrawing from polished society and embracing the rustics. Let me warn you—you can never help them aspire to greater things, but they can drag you down."

Before either of them could draw a breath or muster an appropriate response, she was onto the next subject.

"And I understand you have given up raising pheasants."

"That is correct," Edward acknowledged.

"Just because some fool got shot."

"Not just because of poor Benny, but mainly because of all the monotonous business of shooting parties and the expense of employing a gamekeeper."

"I understand you sacked him."

"Then you understand wrongly. He decided to move off to an estate where his expertise would be more appreciated."

"And what are you planning to do with the woods?"

"The trees are mainly birch and hazel, so we will coppice them and sell the wood or use it on the estate. The villagers will be free to snare rabbits once again for their pot without fear of being apprehended by the gamekeeper. I think it is a shame on our country that some poor people are deported to Australia just for poaching a rabbit from their landlord's estate to keep the family fed."

"You exaggerate."

"No, I do not. Read the newspaper for yourself."

"I would not defile myself with such sensational reading."

CHAPTER 31

JOHN WAS EMPHATIC. "PARSON, YA really 'ave te come this time."

Jack agreed, since never before had Lord Wilson sent for him on a Thursday morning. This was unusual. Jogging along in the carriage, he wondered what the next hour would bring. He had half expected a summons from the big man on Sunday evening, but when nothing happened, he had hoped Lord Wilson had reflected on the sermon and slunk off in defeat. Maybe it was even used to awaken him spiritually. Miracles still happen! Ever since his heated sermon on Sunday morning, he had questioned himself. Was his anger righteous indignation, or was it just plain old, sinful anger? He still was not sure of the answer.

A footman opened the large door of the library and announced Jack's arrival. Lord Wilson ignored his salutations and thrust a letter in his hands.

"Read that, Hayworth!"

Jack stood and read. He immediately recognised the handwriting to be that of Reverend Sidney Brinkhill.

> My dear Lord Wilson,
>
> I do hope that you and your dear family are all in good health. I am sorry to hear that you are finding my curate's preaching unacceptable. Seeing as you undertake to pay for any expense in removing him and finding a more suitable

minister, I humbly take your advice and will dismiss him from my service. I am suffering from much pain and ill-health so am grateful to you for your kind condescension in arranging all the details and removing this burden from me.

Yours sincerely,

Sidney Brinkhill

Jack finished reading the letter, and on looking up saw Lord Wilson smiling smugly at him over his brandy glass. Not wanting him to see his shaking hands, Jack tossed back the letter and stuffed his hands in his coat pockets.

"No one beats me, Reverend Hayworth."

"'Vengeance is mine, I will repay,' says the Lord."

"Ha ha, you and your quotes."

"And when would you like the vicarage vacated?"

"Within the fortnight. But you have preached your last sermon already. As soon as you get the letter from Brinkhill, which will arrive before Sunday, you will be trespassing if you enter that pulpit."

"You bribed him!"

"Don't call it such a nasty name, but yes, I did use a bit of monetary persuasion. It usually works, even on men of the cloth."

"Does the Bishop of Maidstone know about this?"

"He will in due time; he has never been one to stand in my way."

"And what about the parishioners of Capford? Who will care for their souls?"

"How holy of you to care about the peasants! As it so happens, I have a nephew who has just finished his divinity training and is in need of a post."

"Is he a man of God?"

"Ho ho, I don't think he would aspire to that. No, he is a third son who needs an easy livelihood, does not have the wit to take up law or business, and is willing to be moulded by his dear uncle."

"This is despicable!"

"We are commanded to look after our own, Hayworth."

Fearing he would say something unadvisable, Jack turned on his heels and left the room without another word.

To add insult to injury, Lord Wilson had not ordered the carriage to wait, so there was no means of conveyance back to the vicarage. Jack kicked the gravel in annoyance, then decided that walking might be the best thing to do right now anyway. He walked briskly down the long drive and then took a path through the woods. *So what, if I am shot at by Wilson's gamekeeper? I don't have a job anyway.*

His mind was a heaving mass of thoughts, all vying for his attention. What of the Capford congregation? His preaching? His future? How would Rebecca react? And the parishioners? The church officers? What about Sunday? The Sunday school outing? His committees? He needed to get home and write to Rebecca. He needed to tell . . . to tell . . . there were so many people to tell. People who would be affected by the news.

As he strode through the undergrowth, getting splattered with mud, he wanted to pray, but a coherent prayer seemed impossible. All he could manage was "Lord, help me!"

As he emerged from Wilson's wood and crossed one of the Biggenden meadows, it started to rain. Jack trudged on, and his writhing thoughts were beginning to take shape. A letter would be a completely inadequate way of conveying the news to his wife—he would go to London himself and stay away for the Sunday. He needed to tell someone. Mr. Collins, his church warden, or Mr. Grey, the Sunday school superintendent, seemed the most appropriate choices, but he shrank back from visiting either. Mr. Collins would be at risk of a heart attack, and Mr. Grey would be with Mrs. Grey, who would flap and cluck around like a disturbed hen.

"Hello there, Reverend Hayworth," sang out a friendly voice.

Jack looked up to find he had nearly walked into Joe with the sheep dog.

"Hello, Joe. Rain has come on a bit."

"Has indeed. Caught you out, by the looks of things."

"Yes," agreed Jack looking at Joe's waxed galoshes, then at his own soaking trousers. "I'm not very suitably dressed."

"Well, good day to you, Vicar."

"Good day, Joe."

"Oh, sir, and by the way, Violet and I really enjoyed your Sunday sermons. They were top-notch. Thank you."

"I'm delighted to hear it. Thanks for telling me."

"We're both looking forward to next Sunday too!"

Jack smiled lamely and continued on his way.

Meeting Joe made him think of the Brookes family. They would be just the couple to speak to first. They were sensible, weathered folk with wisdom and wit in equal measure. Sanctified common sense, his mother would call it. They were also the kind of people who could cope with an unexpected visitor bringing in a trail of muddy puddles.

Just as he had hoped, Mr. Brookes was at home for his midday meal.

"Come in, my lad, come in and dry yourself out," came the warm, inviting welcome.

Mrs. Brookes hung Jack's dripping coat on the back of a chair near the stove, and her husband invited him to the kitchen table.

"Share a crust with us, boy."

They were all eating before more was said.

"I saw Wilson's carriage going to your place this morning. Is the man ill?"

Jack smiled within himself. Not much in the village went unnoticed by Mrs. Brookes. He swallowed a mouthful of bread and cheese and launched into his story.

CHAPTER 32

REBECCA LISTENED IN HORROR AS Jack told the story. Her delight in his surprise visit evaporated the moment he put his down his trunk and said, “We need to talk.” The tray of tea and biscuits went untouched as Jack described the situation, and Rebecca tried to grasp the implications. Apart from a few gasps and “Oh Jack’s,” she let him explain the unfolding situation uninterrupted. Now her inadequate response was an understatement.

“This is not good.”

Jack ignored the remark and fell silent.

“What did the Brookes’s say?”

“They were livid. Like me, they are horrified that church life can be over-ruled by a moneyed landlord and that the bishops are powerless to intervene. It seems so unscriptural. They encouraged me to come here straight away to tell you. Mr. Brookes wisely said that no Wilson employee should kick up a stink on my behalf, or they are sure to lose their jobs. I totally agree. I think we should go quietly and with dignity.”

“And let Lord Wilson win?”

“He’s not winning. God is.”

“Yes, but it is hard to see that.”

“We have to walk by faith.”

"Yes."

Rebecca squeezed Jack's unbandaged hand and was full of admiration for his mature and dignified manner of dealing with this huge blow. She needed to pull back her shoulders and stand united with him. He needed her to be strong and courageous. She begged the Lord to help.

Jack had more to tell. "The Brookes's suggest I do an unofficial leaving service in a field or barn somewhere. They will boycott the church and read a sermon at home—they think most of the Biggenden workforce may follow suit. It's up to the Wilson lot to do what they think best, but they have a lot more to consider. By the time I left Capford, the news was spreading like wild fire, and everyone I saw treated me like a hero. Again and again I heard people say 'If you're out, I'm out.'"

"Can't something more suitable be arranged for the boycotters? Reading at home is rather unsatisfactory, as I am learning myself."

"Joe took me to the station, and he said that Edward Thorpe is considering clearing out his big barn and inviting people there for services."

"Who will preach?"

"No one. It will be a prayer meeting and a reading service. I tell you what Rebecca—in those last few hours at Capford, I felt more valued by the folks there than I have ever felt. It was so touching to see how outraged everyone was, and how concerned they were for our well-being. Of course, there are some people who just like a sensational story to get indignant about."

"Yes, this is quite sensational for quiet, little Capford."

"Biggest excitement for years."

"I just wish we weren't at the centre of it."

The more Rebecca pondered their position, the more she realised how much she was set to lose. She was being brutally torn away from nearly every single one of her friends. Apart from Miss Miller, who was about to get on a boat for Africa, her in-laws, and Uncle Hector's household, she had not one acquaintance, let alone friend, outside Capford. With a heart overwhelmed with sadness, Rebecca escaped upstairs, laid on her bed, and cried. She cried for Mrs. Brookes's matter-of-fact advice. She cried for the untimely end of her growing friendship with Sophia. She cried for the loss of the best ever housemaid cum lady's maid—dear, outspoken Violet with her zest for life and interesting observations! She would miss every single committee member—even Mrs. Grey and her ramblings. There was so much to do at Capford. Who knew all the little details like she did? Which polish to use for the pews, what dishes the visiting ministers enjoyed, where to find various keys, altar cloths, and hymn sheets. What about the Sunday school and their treat? Normally crying had a therapeutic property, but when Rebecca eventually bestirred herself, she felt no better and no less burdened. How could she face the future with the calm confidence that befits a Christian? She remonstrated with herself: *"You need to pull yourself together, trust your God, support your husband, and help the household make wise decisions."*

Since Uncle Hector was in the capable hands of Nurse Haynes, Rebecca felt free to plan returning to Capford with Jack and help organise the packing up operation. However, the physician overturned the scheme.

"Mr. Stubbs is just beginning to show the early signs of recovery and alertness. To suddenly remove a person he is attached to, may result in a serious relapse." Jack and Rebecca were dismayed by the pronouncement, but Nurse Haynes calmly thanked the doctor for his advice and ushered him to the door.

"You must go to Capford," she quietly insisted as soon as the doctor's carriage had borne him away. "It is most important for you to go with your husband and say good-bye to all your friends there. It will help you to cope with your loss. The doctor is all very wise about the physical body, but just now we are dealing with the heart—and not the physical heart, or the heart of the patient in bed. A proper good-bye is not easy but will be most beneficial in the long run. Leave your uncle to me."

Rebecca looked at Nurse Haynes's lined and earnest face. She had known much loss personally and within the families she had helped. She knew what she was talking about. How wise and intuitive she was to liken the loss of Capford to a bereavement! Rebecca looked up at Jack, waiting for his response.

"Rebecca, I think the nurse is very wise, and we would do well to heed her sensible advice. We need not be long in Capford. Most of our possessions can be sold or given away. It would be nice if we could be there next Saturday for the Sunday School treat. It would also be better for all the children to see us there rather than to simply disappear out of their lives."

That evening as they sat at dinner they discussed the clearing of the vicarage. The housekeeper had already agreed that any furniture they wanted to keep could be stored in the second spare room. There was no doubt in anyone's mind that Uncle Hector's house would be the Hayworths' temporary home. Looking further ahead was like peering into the worst smog London's chimneys could produce. It was easier just to concentrate on the pressing matters of the here and now.

"Beside my personal bits and bobs, all I really want to keep is the beautiful wardrobe you made me before we married, our bedstead, and the things I have made, like the rag rugs and bedspread and tablecloths."

"All I want is my desk, my books, and my carpentry tools."

"What about the rest?"

"Let's ask the villagers if they want anything. Leave whatever was there from the Brinkhills and anything no one wants . . . that can be the dear nephew's problem."

"We will be traveling light."

"Like pilgrims and strangers."

"This palatial house is hardly a tent."

"I know which I would prefer."

CHAPTER 33

VIOLET THOUGHT IT MUST HAVE been the strangest Sunday in her life! Having no duties at the vicarage, she was free to help Joe look around the flock before the morning service. The lambs were stocky and playful and the grass was growing well, satisfying the ewes, so beyond a quick glance there was not a lot to do. But instead of heading home for a coffee, Joe and Violet made their way to Biggenden and helped set up the big barn for the service. The stone-walled and clay-tiled barn had no windows, so the huge wooden doors through which laden carts normally entered had to be flung wide to provide enough light for the proceedings. The warm beams of the May sun streamed in on the dancing dust and chaff particles. Empty bushel boxes were placed in rows on the straw-covered floor for pews. A wooden platform (formally a hen house roof) was set at the front for the reader. A small table covered with a white cloth would be the reading desk. Violet smiled as she surveyed the scene. It was not a genteel place of worship, but it seemed more authentic, maybe more biblical, than an ornate cathedral.

At the appointed time, Violet returned in her Sunday best and met Joe at the door. People had arrived early, and the barn was almost full. Violet guessed many had come in good time to check out who was and who was not there. *Is it foolish of us all to don our best frocks and bonnets, suits and waistcoats, to sit in a dusty barn?* Violet wondered as she took her place on a box. Joe bowed his head to pray, and immediately Violet knew the answer. *No, their clothing befitted the occasion—they had come to meet with the Lord of Lords and King of Kings, and the building was of no significance.*

None of the gallery band were at the barn service. The readiness of most of them to play folk music at village dances made the more serious members of the congregation wonder at the depth of their religious convictions, so their absence was discussed with much head shaking and murmurs of "Just as I had thought." Mr. Brookes started the singing with a loud nasal blast, which his wife turned into a tune. Violet enjoyed the a capella singing as the sopranos, altos, tenors, and basses weaved their notes together, unimpeded by the scratching of violins and cellos. Mr. Collins had remained "Church," so it fell to Mr. Grey to conduct the service and read the sermon. He was a fluent and expressive reader and had carefully chosen a good and suitable subject—standing firm for the truth. It was one of Spurgeon's Penny Pulpit sermons. Violet enjoyed it so much that she decided it would be well worth her and Joe subscribing to Spurgeon's weekly sermons and build up a stock to take to Canada. Maybe they would be worshiping in similar conditions over there. Sundays on the boat would also be a strange experience.

After the service, the congregation milled about for a long time. There was such a sense of unity and so much to discuss that everyone seemed reluctant to go home. The burning question was "Who attended church?" The answer only came by deduction but, looking at the barn gathering, it was obvious that the church would be very empty. Wilson's workers would feel obliged to go; everyone understood that. To go against such a powerful employer and landlord could see one jobless and evicted. The butcher was also in a quandary.

The Wilson household's meat consumption was well over half of his weekly income. If he removed from church to barn, would they remove their custom? In the butcher's absence, his dilemma was thoroughly chewed over and deliberated. Violet was pleased to see Mr. and Mrs. Thorpe mingling with the crowd. *Being the owner of the barn, Mr. Thorpe is almost church warden, or to be more precise, barn warden.*

Mrs. Harrington had been so incensed at the Thorpe's involvement in the "little squabble" that she had retreated to Hampshire and her local parish church where "the vicar knows his place, never oversteps the mark, and does not suffer from religious mania."

On Monday morning, Violet was at a loss to know what to do at the vicarage. There were so many rumours and counter-rumours. Were the Hayworths planning to stay until they were forcefully evicted, or should she start packing? Was a new vicar arriving next week, or would the house stand empty? There was very little washing in the clothes basket, no meals to prepare, and no tidying up required. Once the hens had been fed, the handful of washing dealt with, and a feather duster flicked about, she wandered around aimlessly.

Amid all the uncertainty, there was one thing she was sure about—if a new vicar did come, she would definitely not volunteer to be his maid. She would not stoop to working for Lord Wilson's yes-man and, besides, there were more exciting ways to earn money these days. She and Joe needed to save hard to pay for their passage to Canada, so she needed a position that offered more money. She would apply to be a shop girl in Tunbridge or Tunbridge Wells. She would probably have to lodge in town, but she would have more time off and could still see Joe on Sundays. The quicker they saved, the sooner they could marry.

The Hayworths returned to Capford on Tuesday. Violet thought they looked tense, drawn, and aged. All her unspoken questions were soon answered: they were going, and they must pack. After sobbing on each other's shoulders, Rebecca and Violet got down to some serious planning. Everything in the house needed to be sorted out into three categories—things going to London, things to sell or give away, and things to leave behind. Anything in the give or sell section could be got rid of as soon as possible unless needed in preparation for the Sunday school treat.

The two activities seemed so incompatible, but even worse was the inordinate number of visitors demanding the Hayworths' attention and time. Violet wished she could shield her employers from the steady flow of weeping women and angry men. Did they really think their displays of emotion would help the ejected (and dejected) couple? How she would love to bolt and bar the door and disconnect the bell! Failing that, she would like to establish some simple rules: only visit if you are in control of your emotions and are willing to pack boxes, dismantle book shelves, or find essential equipment packed by mistake.

Violet was rather alarmed by the somewhat reckless attitude the Hayworths displayed toward their property. Maybe it was due to haste, lack of space, or general glumness, but the result was a huge pile of perfectly good but unwanted household items gradually filling the dining room. Violet hated to see such waste and expressed her concern. With a dismissive wave, her employers told her she could deal with it if she wanted to. Joe's eyes glistened when he heard the challenge, and as soon as he could the next evening, he came around to inspect the motley array.

"Reverend Hayworth, this lot is worth a lot."

"I'm not so sure. Most of it is old junk."

"I could sell most of it in Tunbridge Market and make you a bit of cash. I'm not bad at selling things."

Rebecca laughed. "With your sparkling eyes and wit, you could sell shoes to a cobbler!"

"Okay, Joe," agreed her husband. "We'll make a deal. You sell or get rid of this lot, and you can have half the takings."

"You're on!" Joe grinned and shook Jack's hand.

Violet did not mind working late into the evenings helping the Hayworths, for now Joe was there too, loading up his stock and generally making himself useful. Soon the house was a maze of boxes, dismantled furniture, and packed trunks.

"It will be easier to say good-bye to this place now that everything is in such un-cosy disarray," said Rebecca.

"I thought you didn't like the vicarage anyway," said Violet as she tucked a tea towel around a boxed teapot.

"I didn't, but soon it became full of us, our life and memories. Now all the memories seem packed in boxes too."

"I hope you get another and a better vicarage soon, ma'am."

"Oh, so do I, Violet! Preferably one in the countryside, with roses in the garden."

"And a few children as well."

Violet wished she hadn't said that. Maybe knowing their time together was short, she was becoming too outspoken.

"Yes, that is my hope and dream, but the Lord knows best."

"Maybe it is just about timing."

"Maybe. Anyway, He knew what was best for you with Joe," said Rebecca, changing the subject.

Violet blushed. "He certainly did. Joe is just the man I need."

Rebecca gazed out of the dusty window. "Even if we stayed here, life would move on, you would leave and go to Canada, and I would never have found anyone to replace you."

"Plenty of girls would be pleased to take my place."

"That's not what I mean. I have enjoyed your company, not just your work output. I like you for who you are, not just for what you do."

"And you have been the best mistress ever. You're more like a friend than a boss."

"And you're more like a friend than a maid. Violet, I really mean it. Thank you for your support, your hard work, and all you have done for me." Rebecca fought back tears.

Violet put down her tea cloth and hugged her employer. "Thank you for all your help and wisdom. The chats with you were better than sermons to me."

"I hope all goes really well for you in Canada."

"I think it will. God is in Canada too."

"And you are trusting Him?"

"Yes, completely, for body and soul, in life and death."

"That is wonderful."

Violet volunteered to work all day Saturday as Joe would be at Tunbridge Market. She had toyed with the idea of accompanying him, but as they filled the farm cart, it soon became apparent there would be no space for her. The previous day Jack had organised the transportation of most of their wanted possessions by train. The vicarage was now looking bare, desolate, and uninviting. Violet was instructed to clean the emptiness, although she thought it was a bit of a waste of time. It was surprising how many cobwebs gathered behind furniture, but surely the next, unwanted occupant could deal with them—and any other grime that had gathered in the meantime. Still, she knew her cleaning job would be easier than the Hayworths' task of supervising the Sunday school treat with all those over-excited children and the ever-present cloud of their own imminent departure.

In all the bustle of getting ready, packing picnic baskets, and spreading bread, Rebecca and Violet were interrupted.

"Rebecca!" Jack shouted from the study. "Where is my skittle set?"

Violet froze.

"I've no idea. Maybe you've packed it."

"I haven't touched it."

"Sorry, but I am up to my ears in egg sandwiches. It's hardly a priority."

"I think it is." And he rummaged on.

Guilt flooded through Violet. After what seemed a long time, Jack entered the kitchen.

"I've found them, but they are in a bit of a state. I hadn't realised they were so chipped. They need repainting, but it's too late."

"I'm sure the children won't notice," Rebecca said dismissively, hardly looking up from her task.

"I know, it's just annoying," replied Jack, slamming the door.

Violet felt awful. The Hayworths were coping well with their present difficulty, but the slight irritability toward each other was a symptom of the strain they were under. It was unusual and unpleasant—and her stupidity had not helped.

CHAPTER 34

REBECCA HAD BEEN ON TENTERHOOKS all week. Keeping her emotions in check for the sake of her husband, her pride, and those around her was incredibly tiring. Her mother would say "What cannot be changed must be endured." What she really meant was "Stop moaning and get on with it." And that is what Rebecca had to do. Endure the Sunday school treat, then the emotional parting services on Sunday. On Monday, it would all be over, and they would be on a train back to London. *Things must be awful when one actually looks forward to escaping to Milton Square,* she thought ruefully.

She survived the Sunday school treat with a simple but effective tactic: she immersed herself in the games and chatter of the children, thus avoiding adult interaction as much as possible. Jack produced his leather football and had soon rounded up the boys for a match. This had become the expected routine for any Jack-related event. Before long he was down to shirtsleeves and in among the action. The girls were always more difficult to entertain, but Rebecca set up the skittles and organised a tournament. She had also brought along a lengthy skipping rope and helped swing one end as the girls skipped to all the songs and rhymes that generations of school girls had chanted before them. The girls pestered her to join in the skipping, but her long, voluminous skirt caught the rope and spoiled the rhythm. Realising that the activity had the potential for becoming rather undignified, Rebecca made her excuses and went back to being a rope swinger with the biggest girl.

The sun broke through the clouds, and soon everyone was hot and thirsty from their exertions. Just in the nick of time, Mrs. Brookes, Mrs. Grey, and Violet arrived in the meadow with jugs of milk and the picnic. With exaggerated demonstrations of exhaustion, the football players flopped down onto the mats, colliding with each other and prompting several wrestling matches. Calling order, Jack gave thanks and everyone tucked in. The food disappeared too rapidly for anyone, including Mrs. Grey, to notice whether the egg sandwiches were soggy or not.

Just as the cakes were being distributed, the Thorpe family came along to greet the picnickers and check that everything was satisfactory. Little Bertie could just about walk and, supported by a parent on either side, he toddled across the grass. Every few steps he lifted both his chubby legs and let his parents swing him along, which made him chuckle and cry, "'gen, 'gen!" Prompted by Mrs. Brookes, the children gave the family three cheers for the loan of the meadow and offered them food. Edward sat down near Jack and, once the children finished eating and dispersed, began discussing the barn situation. Sophia joined the ladies on a mat and left Bertie with an admiring crowd of motherly girls. Mrs. Brookes, Mrs. Grey, and Violet busied themselves in shaking the crumb strewn mats and collecting cups, while Rebecca and Sophia discussed the Hayworths' imminent departure.

"I'm going to miss you both terribly," confessed Sophia.

"We are already aching inside for Capford and all of you," Rebecca quietly responded.

"Jack's preaching has been such a blessing, and you are such a wonderful vicar's wife."

"Thank you."

The two women absentmindedly watched the children playing.

"By the way, what will Violet do now?" asked Sophia.

"I think she wants to get a shop assistant's post somewhere in Tunbridge."

"I wronged her, you know, with that unfortunate business with my cousin. I owe her an apology and would be pleased to offer her a job—if she would consider working for me again."

"She is a great lass, and I would heartily recommend her."

"Would she be interested?"

"One thing I have learned about Violet is that you can never second-guess her. You'll need to ask her yourself."

"Would she make a good lady's maid?"

"She'd be an excellent one—and a fun one too! What's wrong with your current maid?"

"She's got a better position in London."

"London? Poor girl."

"Do you hate London so very much?"

"Yes, but I shouldn't be like that. Please pray for me that I will be more submissive about my lot in life."

Sophia reached out and touched Rebecca's hand sympathetically. "You are having a really tough time."

"But I should be more trusting."

"Trusting doesn't mean we always enjoy our circumstances."

"But we are instructed to rejoice always, and that can be very difficult."

"You can rejoice in the good you have been able to do in the village over the years."

"But why has it been cut short?"

"Maybe the Lord has another task for you to do."

"Maybe."

Sunday passed in a haze of sadness and gloom. The barn was full in the morning and overflowing in the evening. Many of Lord Wilson's employees took advantage of the fact he attended only the morning service and joined their friends at Biggenden. Rebecca was amazed at Jack's composure and clarity as he spoke in the morning. Attending the evening service, she decided, was almost like being present at your own funeral. She sat in the front row (miscellaneous chairs and benches had replaced the boxes), armed on either side by Sophia and Mrs. Brookes. She knew they were holding her up in prayer like Joshua and Aaron. Various men took part in the service to read, pray, or to say a few words of thanks to the Hayworths. Then Jack preached from Jude:

> *Now unto him that is able to keep you from falling, and to present you faultless before the presence of his glory with exceeding joy,*
>
> *To the only wise God our Saviour, be glory and majesty, dominion and power, both now and ever. Amen.*

During his sermon, he expressed his sadness at having to leave those present and exhorted them to stay close to the Lord. As he spoke of the Lord's ongoing care for them, he seemed to remove a yoke of responsibility he had been carrying for the congregation and place it solely in Christ's hands. The final hymn was announced, and instead of using the normal tune *Dennis*, Mr. Brookes started the melancholic melody *Franconia.*

Blest be the tie that binds
Our hearts in Christian love;
The fellowship of kindred minds
Is like to that above.

Before our Father's throne
We pour our ardent prayers;
Our fears, our hopes, our alms, are one,
Our comforts and our cares.

We share our mutual woes,
Our mutual burdens bear,
And often for each other flows
The sympathizing tear.

When here our pathways part,
We suffer bitter pain;
Yet, one in Christ and one in heart,
We hope to meet again.

This glorious hope revives
Our courage by the way,
While each in expectation lives
And longs to see the day.

From sorrow, toil, and pain,
And sin we shall be free
And perfect love and friendship reign
Through all eternity.

The apt words of John Fawcett and the sad tune were more than Rebecca could bear. She wanted to sing, for the words held the sentiments of her heart, but before they had even reached "sympathising tear," her breath caught in her throat and her composure slipped. Mrs. Brookes's sonorous voice began to break, and Sophia stopped singing altogether. Looking up through her tear-blurred vision, she saw Jack, no longer singing, biting his bottom lip. The pent-up emotion broke free in an erupting snort of sadness, and she crumbled. Sophia wrapped her arms around her, but they were soon replaced by Jack's. He left the new preaching platform, enfolded her in his arms, then with a loud, firm voice pronounced the benediction.

"Did you know," asked Jack, once they were finally at their fireside for the last time, "about the writer of that last hymn, John Fawcett? He was a pastor of a congregation in Yorkshire, but after some years he accepted a new pastorate in London. He was packed and all ready to go, but he was so moved by the love and sorrow of his Yorkshire congregation at his leaving service that he changed his mind and stayed. I like the man."

"So do I!" said Rebecca. "I wish we had the option to stay. I've never loved Capford and its people as much as I do today."

"Me neither. Why do they only tell you how much they appreciate you and how helpful your ministry has been when you are about to leave?"

They would have preferred slinking out of Capford under the cover of darkness, but even in this their wishes were over-ruled. Edward Thorpe insisted on the loan of his best carriage to convey them to Tunbridge Station. They could easily have filled the cab with their luggage, but instead of being collected by an empty carriage, they found that Edward and Sophia had decided to accompany them to the station. The groom strapped the trunks and boxes to the back of the carriage, and the bags were squeezed in between and on the passengers. No one knew what to say. Normal pleasantries seemed inappropriate, and no one had the wit or will to construct a wise or meaningful sentence. However fond she was of the Thorpes, Rebecca wished they had not burdened themselves the task of waving them off. It just prolonged the pain.

But finally, the last good-byes were said, along with the last firm handshake and the last tearful kiss. Having deposited the luggage into the guard's van, Jack and Rebecca found an empty carriage and sank into the springy seats. As the train pulled out of Tunbridge Station and into the Surrey countryside, the burden of sharing other people's emotions slowly rolled off Rebecca's shoulders. For once, a delay in the journey would have been welcome, but the train did not run out of steam, and there were no sheep on the line, so the engine progressed at relentless speed. As the train puffed past the smoking factories and terraced houses of London and into Victoria Station, the burden of Uncle Hector returned.

CHAPTER 35

JACK HAD BEEN AMAZINGLY GRACIOUS and calm while packing up at Capford, but now, two weeks after their eviction, his mood had deteriorated. Pacing like a caged lion, he prowled around Uncle Hector's house, bored and grumpy. He had no study, no workshop, no income, and no job. Rebecca wished she could help, but her sympathy was wearing thin. She was in the same predicament. She missed her friends, responsibilities, chores, and kitchen and was having to invent things to do. Never had time dragged so frightfully!

Uncle Hector received the very best of care from Hester. Hester seemed to require no time off, and the housekeeper was extremely efficient at running the household. In short, there was very little to occupy Rebecca. Of course, she frequently spent time with Uncle Hector, reading to him or telling him about the day's events, but there was so little to tell.

The physician seemed pleased with Uncle Hector's progress, but Rebecca could not share his optimism. It was true that he could now eat slops and understand speech, but he was unable to move his left side and was still bed-bound. His awareness only increased his frustration with his own limitations. He had become highly emotional and uninhibited, roaring with exasperation or weeping with despair at the most trifling problems or news. Hester knew how to handle his moods and humour him, for she had seen this fragile emotional state in many a stroke victim, but Rebecca felt at a loss to know what to do or say for the best. His lack of conformity to normal social graces was so out of character that she hardly knew how to treat him, or indeed, who he was. His frustration at not having his slurred speech understood made conversation painful for all involved. Jack, particularly, had problems in deciphering his words so began avoiding conversations, limiting his interaction with him to twice daily reading and prayer.

Nurse Hester Haynes, though, was worth her weight in gold. Not only was she a kind and devoted nurse, but she was also a good companion. In a quiet, unobtrusive way, she mothered the Hayworths as well as nursing Uncle Hector. Despite initial protests, Hessie, as she encouraged them to call her, agreed to eat dinner with them every evening. During the many hours they spent together, Rebecca gradually heard her story. Hessie was born and brought up in Bournemouth, enjoying a happy childhood by the sea. She met a handsome merchant sailor when still young, and they soon married. To avoid painful periods of separation, her husband, David, gave up life at sea and took a job at Poole Harbour. One day while unloading cargo, David was knocked onto the stone quay by a tumbling bale of cotton, and falling awkwardly, he broke his spine. David was carried home to die. Hessie lovingly nursed him for three painful months as his life slowly ebbed away like the receding tide. Alone and bereft, Hessie had to find her own way in the world. She had no extraordinary skill or experience other than caring for her husband. The relentless regularity of industrial accidents meant that experienced caregivers were in frequent demand.

At first Hessie helped families who were unable to offer more than board and lodging, but as her skill and experience increased, so did her modest fees.

Whereas Hessie's care of the patient was superb, Rebecca felt that Jack was not persevering enough in trying to understand Uncle Hector or his slurred speech. He seemed to blame him for the semi-captive state they were living in and to resent Uncle Hector's emotional reliance on his niece.

"It is hardly living," grumbled Jack. "It is just waiting without knowing what we are waiting for. It seems ironic that just when we are in a house with gas lamps, so can work late into the evening, we have no work to do, let alone to stay up late for."

"The lamps make reading easier."

"But what is the point of studying?"

"I'm not studying. I'm just reading a bit of Brönte, a bit of Austen, and dipping into Dickens."

"I wasn't talking about you." Jack's tone sent Rebecca's eyebrows upward. "Anyway, those books aren't my taste. I want to be preparing sermons."

"Why not prepare one?"

"What's the point? I may never preach again."

"Oh Jack, don't say that. I expect you will get another parish soon."

"Do I really want one? Do I want to stay in the Church of England, with all its unbiblical associations with the crown and the aristocracy?"

"Not everyone in authority is as bad as Lord Wilson."

"But why should they be in authority when they have no Christian convictions? They shouldn't be meddling with the church at all."

Rebecca changed the subject. She had heard his views on church government many times in the past fortnight.

"Why not do some carpentry? You enjoy that."

"What's the point?" asked Jack, throwing a log into the fire with unnecessary force.

"To do something pleasurable."

"I wouldn't know what to make."

"Something for us."

"We haven't even got a home to put anything in."

"Make something to sell."

"No one around here would want stuff from me. They want elegant and expensive furniture. Anyway, there is nowhere here to set up my work bench."

Jack picked up the newspaper, flicked through it for a few minutes, and then chucked it on the floor.

"I'm quite jealous of Joe and Violet."

"Have they got into the news?" asked Rebecca jokingly.

Jack ignored this attempt at wit.

"The way they are going to leave everything behind and emigrate."

"You're not fed up with your nation as well as the national church, are you?"

"No, but a new start sounds nice. As does the luxury of actually having a plan."

"God has a plan for us."

Jack sighed and drew a hand over his face as if to wipe away his disgruntled mood. "You are right, my darling. I just wish we had some clue as to what it is." He stretched out in the chair and studied the ceiling. "Maybe we should be joining your nun-like friend and be missionaries in Africa."

Rebecca stopped knitting. "I have often wondered if we are childless so we can do something like that."

"I've wondered too, but I'm not convinced it is what we are supposed to do next."

Rebecca nodded and returned to her knitting. "We will just have to keep on praying for guidance."

"And patience as we sit here idly and wait."

Waiting! That word perfectly described their present existence. Waiting for what? For Uncle Hector to recover, or (they dare not say it) to die? Waiting for a child, for guidance, for work? Back at the vicarage, Rebecca had longed for more time with Jack; now she had his undivided attention but not his cheerfulness. On busy committee days, she had longed for leisure; now she had so much it hung heavy. She had longed for relief from domestic tasks; now she longed for a morning in the kitchen. In Capford her walks around the parish had been purposeful. Now the afternoon walks with Jack were only a means of exercise and a change of scenery.

As the weeks dragged on, Rebecca looked for new ways of filling the time. *Is this how unmarried daughters of the upper-class feel? Filling their days with the latest craze of paper folding, fern collecting (which magazines mockingly called pteridomania), or tatting, petit point tapestry and painting shells, in a pointless endeavour of keeping occupied and looking fulfilled?* The fashionable periodicals were full of these laborious—and often bizarre—time-wasters and useless things women could make or give away but never lower themselves to sell. How many pairs of embroidered slippers or decorated tobacco jars did a man really need? Was this really the best way for women to use their skills and demonstrate their accomplishments? Rebecca despised them all and longed for some honest, hard work. Meanwhile, Uncle Hector got no better and Jack got worse. In his view the local church was rubbish, the house was too hot, the gas lamps caused headaches, and the food was too rich.

After weeks of inertia, something strange happened: Jack started going out. With no explanation, he would leave Milton Square early in the morning and return late at night, totally exhausted from walking but unwilling to share his impressions. At first Rebecca was glad that he had started exploring London, but as his return became later and later, she started to worry. Was her marriage, the one thing she thought was rock-solid, also going to crumble under her feet?

CHAPTER 36

WANDERING AROUND THE MUSEUMS AND galleries of London, Jack could not escape a sense of deep dissatisfaction with himself. Was his godliness merely a cloak he put on when other people were watching, only to be worn when he had a congregation looking up to him? He was thankful to God for the strength given during those last few, traumatic days in Capford, but now! Now he was in a melancholy state of self-pity. He recognised the symptoms and knew the cure, but one ingredient of the remedy eluded him—namely, hard work. He also needed childlike faith in his Heavenly Father. He was not being childlike in the biblical sense—but childish. Like a stubborn boy, he was sulking and asking why, why, why? God is not moved by such irritability, and Jack knew it.

Unable to work himself into a better frame of mind, Jack had decided to explore more of London. Had he been feeling more positive, the museums and art galleries might have been immensely interesting, but he walked around them in a detached haze of indifference. The world's best paintings and artifacts were before his eyes, but they all seemed futile—vanity of vanities. Indeed, he felt he could have enjoyed the despondent company of King Solomon when he discovered that everything was fleeting and empty, and wrote the book Ecclesiastes. As Jack visited music halls and listened to amazing recitals of Bach and Mozart, the music transported him from his cares but proved to provide only temporary solace. The music was beautiful, but looking around him at the affluent audience, being forced to listen to their petty, superficial conversation caused Jack's enjoyment to evaporate. Their whole aim in life was to see and be seen, cultivating their coveting and seeking to produce covetousness in others.

Despairing of ever finding godliness in London, Jack visited church after church. They were full of saints and worthy men—all buried six feet underground with a brass plaque identifying their resting place. But Jack was not seeking human companionship; he preferred an empty pew hidden behind pillars where he could read and pray quietly. Whenever possible, he attended services of Choral Evensong and enjoyed the simple plain-song or chants of the psalmody, the various settings of the Canticles, and the richness of the anthems as the choir and pipe organ filled the ancient buildings to the rafters with full-bodied harmony. He delighted in the collects (set prayers) of the Book of Common Prayer. As the evening approached, remembering the long walk home ahead of him, he particularly liked the prayer for safety:

LIGHTEN our darkness, we beseech thee, O Lord; and by thy great mercy defend us from all perils and dangers of this night; for the love of thy only Son, our Saviour, Jesus Christ. Amen.

Jack could have invited Rebecca on his excursions—she would have enjoyed them and he would have enjoyed her company, but he did not. He was not sure of his reasons for this omission, for they were complex. There was a certain freedom in being alone and not having to consult anyone on choice of destination, route, pace, or timing.

His negativity had produced a sense of recklessness that almost scared him. He disregarded his own comfort and even safety, ignoring meal times or distance, but he could not have behaved that way with Rebecca by his side. Anyway, she seemed content with her shrunken horizons within the four walls of 27 Milton Square. At least she had a purpose—helping the nurse, approving the menu, supporting Uncle Hector. What an under-valued blessing a purpose was! In that aspect, Jack felt that Rebecca had lost less than he had. She was still doing what good wives do—organising, supporting, and caring. He, on the other hand, was not doing what good husbands do—working, providing, and leading. The inability to perform his role had knocked his self-esteem—or was it pride? How long would it be before Rebecca's esteem of him also faltered?

Entering the house late in the evening, Jack found that Rebecca had already retired to bed. Throwing another log on the living room fire, Jack poured himself a sherry and sank into a chair. His mind was still far too busy to contemplate sleep, so he flicked through a novel from the table. The book was entitled, "Oliver Twist, or, The Parish Boy's Progress" by Charles Dickens.

Jack knew of the book but had never read it. Idly he flicked through the pages. He was interested, for Charles Dickens was not only a novelist but also a vocal social critic who campaigned tirelessly for social reform, children's rights, and education. He had also funded a home for fallen women. His own father had been incarcerated in a debtor's prison, forcing Charles to leave school early and earn money by working a ten-hour day in a boot blacking factory. Jack knew Dickens' fictional narratives were based on the true conditions of the underbelly of society.

Despite the late hour and the dark storyline, Jack was soon gripped. The terrible childhood of Oliver, the orphan, descended from bad to worse, from baby farm to orphanage, and from orphanage to child labour. Jack desperately wanted to lift poor Oliver out of the pages and offer him love, food, and security: things the tragic lad knew little of. Sometime in the small hours, Jack's eyes became too dry to continue reading, so he went to bed. But, despite the comfort of his London bed, he was unable to sleep. Oliver Twist was a fictional character, but the conditions he faced were not.

Thousands of people, from the countryside and abroad, had flooded into London over the past couple of decades. Jews came to escape persecution, the Irish to escape hunger, and the unemployed to find work. London seemed promising, with its ambitious building projects like the underground railway, Joseph Bazalgette's amazing sewage system, and numerous new industrial buildings. Big factories were smothering the cottage industry, leaving countless workers unemployed and making many traditional skills and trades obsolete. Agricultural workers were replaced by machinery, driving rural families off the land and into overcrowded towns and cities. Jack had read all about these upheavals, but now he was determined to find out more—but the burning question that kept him awake was "What are churches doing for the poor?"

Despite a bad night, the next morning found Jack leaving the house with a new, budding sense of purpose. What he saw and heard during the next few weeks made his heart bleed for suffering humanity. After extensive searching and enquiring, Jack discovered many small charities were trying to help the destitute, and some churches were running soup kitchens and overnight shelters in deprived areas. Warned not to enter the dangerous slums alone, Jack eagerly accepted the invitation to help in a soup kitchen run by the members of a non-conformist church near Whitechapel who worked alongside London City Mission staff.

At first the mission's good intentions had been met with skepticism—the slum dwellers suspected them of being undercover police spies, but their regular, compassionate visits gradually had won them trust and admiration. During a cholera epidemic in the 1840s, the London City Mission staff had continued their work among the sick and dying, resulting in two missionaries even sacrificing their own lives in their determination to continue the work. This noble commitment had forged even stronger bonds of respect with the community, and London City Mission staff were able to operate freely in the dangerous alleys and crowded tenements where they served. The small non-conformist church, recognising the mission's unique standing in the community, now worked with them to provide further relief.

Jack would never forget the first evening he spent in the soup kitchen. Hurrying through narrow streets and filthy alleys, the small team made their way to an unused old workshop that served as their base. Making soup was normally deemed the work of women, but here, the men and women worked together (for the women's safety), cutting up and boiling mountains of root vegetables, offal, and pearl barley. As the darkness gathered, so did a mass of hungry humanity. At first filling soup bowls kept Jack too busy to notice much else, but once the long queue had finally been served and the last drop of soup distributed, he looked around. Every square inch of the workshop floor was occupied by a motley crowd of diners from whom a stuffy air rose up, reeking of the stench of unwashed bodies and soiled rags. As the rabble sipped their hot soup, the minister climbed onto a table and read a portion of Scripture. Over the hubbub of babies' cries, clattering bowls, and family arguments, his voice rang out loud and clear. With warmth and simplicity, he explained the good news of salvation through the finished work of Christ, assuring the listeners of God's forgiveness and love for repentant sinners.

Deeply moved by all he had witnessed that night, Jack began the long journey back to Milton Square. London became dangerous after dark, so he hurried through the shadowy streets, praying as he went. Despite the shocking poverty he had witnessed and his hazardous walk home, Jack felt more energized than he had felt since leaving Capford. At last he had found somewhere to be useful, and he couldn't wait to tell Rebecca.

CHAPTER 37

REBECCA WAS DOZING IN FRONT of the living room fire when Jack burst in. She awoke with a start and listened agog as Jack recounted his day.

As he described the pitiful state of the half-starved families and babies too weak to even cry, Rebecca was moved to exclaim, "We must help!"

"I am going back tomorrow, and a man from the London City Mission agreed to let me accompany him on his rounds."

"Is he a clergyman?"

"No, the LCM prefer to employ lay people, preferably ones with a similar background to those they are ministering to. This particular man, Mr. Smith, worked in the docks before his conversion. He speaks their speech and looks as rough and ready as a tough dock man should."

"You better wear your old gardening clothes."

"And a cap. You can put moth balls around my clerical garb and bowler hat."

"Will you go to the soup kitchen?"

"I'd like to, but I'm not sure that it operates every evening. I'll find out. There's an awful lot I need to find out."

"Can I come?"

Jack paused. "Rebecca, I would like to take you, but it takes me two hours to walk there. We could get a carriage some of the way, but not into the slum—it wouldn't look right. I'm not sure if I want you exposed to all the misery . . . or the danger."

Rebecca straightened her shoulders. "I'm tough enough."

"Let me explore the situation more myself, before involving you," Jack replied cautiously.

Accompanying the wise and experienced Mr. Smith, Jack entered the unexplored world of the grim East End slum area. It was a world of dashed hopes and bleak prospects, a world of filth, destitution, disease, and the struggle for survival. Many of its population had been born into abject poverty, and the mere fact that they had got through childhood alive testified to their toughness. Many babies never reached their first birthday. Others in the overcrowded slums had journeyed to the capital looking for work, employment, or safety from persecution. As their aspirations, hopes, and finances sank lower and lower, they were driven into the crowded tenements in search of cheap accommodation and local work. Greedy landlords packed as many people as possible into one house, even renting out damp, dark cellars to families who were desperate for shelter.

Sanitation seemed an unknown concept, and sewage ran freely down the gutters where filthy children played. Wet, grey washing hung on lines across dark alleys, damp corridors, or mouldy one-room dwellings in the vain hope of drying. Communal wells were pumped dry as women tried to provide enough water for their family's needs. Children collected anything that could burn to keep the stoves smouldering. Skeletal women, who knew the importance of keeping the working men and boys fed, eked out meals, using foodstuffs normally considered fit only for animals.

As well as seeing to the daily grind of housekeeping with inadequate resources, many women also worked themselves. With children in tow, they took in washing or sewing, or ran market stalls. Others made matches or manufactured products that the local factories outsourced as piecework.

Men and boys worked or sought work. Joining the heaving crowd by the dockyard gates, men, hopeful of a day's work and wage, jostled together until the huge doors were opened. The mass of men swept through the gates, sometimes crushing someone on the way to the area where foremen would pick their teams for the day. Only the strongest were chosen, for it was strength alone the bosses were after.

During long hours at the docks or in the many warehouses around, men would act as beasts of burden, carrying cargo and commodities for owners who disregarded safety and thought only of profit. The small wages scarcely secured money for the day and rent for the night, meaning that life was a relentless grind of hard labour and aching, prematurely aging bodies. Any dreams of betterment or aspirations for the future were smothered by the unremitting slog of daily life. Upright, honest men were ground down by poverty until a life of crime seemed an inescapable, even legitimate option. It was an area of utter physical, moral, and spiritual corruption. Fear of illness and injury dogged the existence of every adult and child. No employer would give work to a person incapable of fulfilling the task, and if there was no work, there would be no pay. Illness in the crowded, filthy slums was common, and so were work-place injuries. Infant deaths were sad but meant there was one less mouth to feed.

Jack was shocked at the stoic, matter-of-fact attitude of families to such bereavements. But the death or serious injury of the breadwinner could, within days, lead to homelessness and starvation.

One step down from living in damp, dark cellars were the Common Lodging Houses, locally known as doss houses. For a small fee, one could sleep in a coffin size bed for the night. Some doss houses were run by charities and provided food, but others were run by unscrupulous businessmen and were vile. If the fee for a bed was still too much, a bench against a wall was provided. A string ran in front of the wooden bench to flop one's arms over, making it possible to sleep sitting up. Jack was horrified to see the swollen feet of men who had been forced to sleep in such a position all night. Others avoided these grim places by sleeping rough, thus exposing themselves to theft, attacks, and the harsh elements.

Down even lower on the ladder of existence were the dreaded debtors' prisons and work houses. Their grim high walls threw a dark metaphoric shadow over the slum dwellers' lives. Here families were torn apart, probably forever, and the inmates were treated harshly, as if criminals, with poverty as their only crime. Stripped of their own clothes and shaved of their hair, anyone entering a workhouse was stripped of their identity too and treated as an inconvenience. Men were put to hard labour, while the women and children were put to mindless, repetitive tasks, all of which numbed the brain and extinguished hope. Without warning, children could be removed from their mothers and sent to orphanages or to work, never to be seen again. To avoid admission to the workhouse or debtor's prison, many, in desperation and despair, took their own lives in the murky waters of the River Thames.

It was in this hard-pressed and diverse community that Mr. Smith and his brethren worked, bringing the good news of the Lord Jesus. Jack was almost overwhelmed by the suffering he witnessed. These desperate people needed hope for this life and for the life to come. Jack was pleased he had found faithful believers who gave out food for both body and soul, bread and the Bible, soup and Scripture, earthly sustenance and heavenly promises. Both were needed, and one seemed futile without the other. Day after day he laboured with Mr. Smith, visiting the needy and dying, serving food at the soup kitchen, and speaking of Christ. Soon he began to recognise individuals in the crowd of diners and to remember their life stories. Gradually he built up friendships, winning over trust and confidence. Within a week, he was also asked to join the rota for giving the evangelistic address at the soup kitchen.

The friendly, weathered faces of a few widows became familiar as they welcomed him with toothless grins and ready wit. Despite their poverty and homelessness, they always managed a wheezy laugh and a cheeky wink. Some young mothers secretly sneaked their children into the soup kitchen while their husbands drank their day's wages in the nearby public house. Other families came only on days when the father could not find any work, or when the rent was due and money was tight. Many people disappeared, and it was hard to know if their situation had improved or dramatically worsened. Mr. Smith made it his job to peruse all lines of enquiry and keep track of his contacts.

One family Jack got to know well was the Roberts family. Mr. Benjamin Roberts had been a skilled tailor in Yorkshire, but his business failed due to the increase of large, mechanised factories producing standardised, cheaper garments. With his wife and young daughter, he left the north to travel south and seek work. While still looking for employment with a tailor, he accepted work at a brick making kiln, working long hours in scorching conditions to provide for his family. Too exhausted after each shift, he was unable to better himself in the way he had hoped or to search for more skilled work. Things took a further turn for the worse when his now-pregnant wife became ill and required expensive medical attention. Impoverished and barely making ends meet, the Roberts became regular attendees of the soup kitchen. On hearing about the gospel and love of Christ for the first time, they gladly turned to Him and through grace found peace and safety. Exploring every contact they knew, Jack and Mr. Smith finally helped Mr. Roberts secure a position with a Christian tailor who attended Mr. Spurgeon's Metropolitan Tabernacle in the Elephant and Castle district.

Not every encounter was so rewarding. Some regulars showed signs of promise, but as soon as money came their way, they reverted to old habits of gambling, drinking, or immorality. Jack had to learn to be sympathetic but not gullible, cautious but not cold-hearted.

One responsibility led to another, and Jack soon found himself with a regular preaching engagement. Mr. Smith had tried unsuccessfully to gain access to the Whitechapel and Spitalfields Union Workhouse to conduct Sunday services. The warden was not averse to the idea, but the powerful board of guardians decreed that only ordained ministers should be granted entry. Jack's Sunday morning congregation now comprised of a depressed crowd of hollow-eyed humanity who were forced to attend his meetings. Sitting on rows of hard, backless benches in the dingy dining hall, they gazed vacantly at him before falling asleep on each other's scrawny shoulders. They seemed like the living dead, having given up hope and faith in anyone or anything. Without an opportunity to show practical Christian charity, Jack's words seemed as sounding brass or a tinkling cymbal. Jack felt desperate for them and prayed to the God of Ezekiel to breathe on the congregation of near corpses and make the dry bones live.

On entering the workhouse, having successfully proved the severity of one's plight to the relieving officer and the board of guardians, one was stripped of clothing, shaved, and de-loused. From then on everything was standardized, from the coarse, ill-fitting uniform, the rough blankets on the bed, to the daily labour. The day was ruled by bells and strict time-tables, and behaviour was controlled by rules, which, much to Jack's discomfort, were read aloud at the commencement of every service for the benefit of the illiterate and forgetful. There was no place in the system for the colourful, warm shawls or knitted blankets that Rebecca and the Capford women had been busy knitting for the soup-kitchen attendees.

CHAPTER 38

VIOLET ENJOYED EVERY MOMENT OF that summer. After the upheaval of the awful spring, it was reassuring to find that life could be wonderful again. Mrs. Hayworth had urged her to take up Mrs. Thorpe's job offer, and Violet was pleased she had complied, for working with the team at Biggenden Manor was most agreeable. Mrs. Thorpe was good to work for—she was stunningly pretty, and it was a pleasure to style her beautiful hair. She was gentle and witty, easy-going, yet firm and fair in maintaining high standards. Violet enjoyed being responsible for her extensive wardrobe of exquisite dresses and finery. With the experience gained from working for Mrs. Hayworth, the advice she received during staff meals, and from fashion magazines, she learned how to mend, clean, and store each delicate material, maintaining its pristine condition.

Instead of living under her parents' roof and gaze, Violet now had a pretty, little attic room at Biggenden Manor. Because she was now a lady's maid and needed somewhere to mend and modify delicate garments, Violet had the whole room to herself. It was her little kingdom, and she loved the privacy. Equally as enjoyable was life in the kitchen—the lively conversations during staff meals and lazy companionship at the end of a busy day. Molly was now head cook, and thanks to an absorbing interest in the wheel-wright's new apprentice, could wholeheartedly congratulate Violet on her engagement to Joe. Clara had recently been promoted to housekeeper, and she was finding her new role challenging and lonely.

"Now I know 'ow ol' Stubbs felt when we were giggling li'le girls an' she were responsible."

"I'm not a giggly li'le girl."

"No, Violet, ya're a mature engaged woman, but ya'll always be giggly, I bet."

"Dyeing these ridiculous feathers for me lady's new hat wipes any smile off me face."

"I'd raver be messing about wiv feathers than doing me weekly accounts."

"This isn't messing about. It's science."

"I'll 'elp ya, if ya 'elp me wiv me number work."

"Deal!"

Clara and Violet felt mature and experienced as they oversaw the training of the young housemaids who were keen and dutiful but tryingly uninitiated.

"They're still wet behind the ears, Clara," moaned Violet, having had to remake her lady's bed yet again after the maids had done a poor job.

"Were we as 'opeless once?"

"No. It's these youngsters—all slapdash and slipshod."

"So says the ancient lady's maid at the great age of seventeen!" the twenty-year-old housekeeper said with a smile.

"Nearly eighteen, I'll have you know."

"And don't 'it me wiv the pilla, t'would be a bad example!" Clara laughed as she retreated out the bedroom.

Violet had thought that the vicarage had been the hub of parish activity, but now it seemed that Biggenden Manor and farm were the centre of action. The threshing barn was soon to be required for its original use, so many evening meetings were held to discuss the future of the break-away congregation. The easiest option would be for them to go their separate ways and join existing non-conformist churches in the area—the Strict Baptists or the Methodists. But the sense of unity was so strong that no one felt inclined to affiliate themselves with another group.

Mr. Thorpe generously offered to give the congregation a couple of acres of land so that a new building could be erected. The proposal was pounced on with alacrity, and soon plans were being drawn up. The premises would be a plain, multi-purpose hall with no ecclesiastical trimmings and be as suitable as a general meeting venue as for a divine service. As in Nehemiah's day, the faithful folks of Capford *strengthened their hands for this good work* and started to build. Like Sanballat, Lord Wilson *was wroth and took great indignation* but found he was unable to interfere.

The building project was not the only thing to provoke Lord Wilson to wrath. During his brief absence from Capford to take the sea air in Ramsgate, his eldest daughter had redirected the carriage taking her to church and attended the barn service instead. Such blatant flouting of his authority and display of independent willfulness was intolerable. Miss Wilson was whisked off to London the very next week and frog-marched to the most fashionable ballrooms and theatres. Lord Wilson knew only one cure for headstrong daughters, and that was marriage.

Violet was pleased to hear via the servant grapevine that Lord Wilson was also annoyed with his nephew, Reverend Mervin Wilson. Instead of being grateful to his uncle for finding such a suitable place for him to cut his teeth as a vicar, he seemed nonchalant and downright lazy. Lord Wilson hadn't expected him to pastor the parish, but he did expect a different sermon every week, and not just a different text. After a month, Lord Wilson realised what the parishioners had concluded within days—his relative was devoid of both personal charm and intellectual flare. Purposely forgetting the trifling details of Jack Hayworth's dismissal, Lord Wilson bemoaned all the trouble he had taken to secure this post for his nephew. There was certainly no prospect of diverting evening debates with this oaf of a parson, and Lord Wilson felt his loss.

All these interesting topics and many more were thoroughly discussed over meals with the other servants in the Biggenden kitchen and in the dressing room with Mrs. Thorpe as she was having her hair styled. Each fact and theory was neatly recorded in beautiful copperplate handwriting by Sophia and sent off to Rebecca. From the letters she received back, Sophia and Violet suspected that Rebecca was bored and homesick for Capford, for she wrote in length of Jack's interesting exploits but mentioned precious little of her own doings.

Having risen up the ranks, Violet's work was no longer as strenuous or tiring as before, but her hours were still long. She had to be available from the moment Mrs. Thorpe awoke to the moment she was gowned, groomed, and ready for bed. On a normal day, Violet knew she was unlikely to be called between the duties of dressing her mistress for dinner and bedtime, so she often sneaked out to meet Joe. They stayed within earshot of the kitchen door, and if Violet was unexpectedly needed, a coded whistle from Clara would send her running back to attend to Mrs. Thorpe. As much as she liked her duties, Violet was always pleased when the Thorpes went out for the evening and left her knowing exactly how much time she had for courting. Parting from Joe without a proper good-bye was never satisfactory.

One warm evening in July, Joe was impatiently waiting at the washing line when Violet appeared.

"I thought you would never come. Did she want to try a new hair-do?"

"I'm no later than usual. Anyway, I thought you would still be busy harvesting."

"We finished one field, and the next isn't quite ready. If you didn't expect me, why are you here?" Joe teased.

Ducking under the clothes line, they headed toward the kitchen garden, through the gate, and toward the big, wooden wheelbarrow.

"We need to talk, Vi," said Joe as he brushed away the soil and gestured to Violet to take a seat.

"This sounds serious," said Violet, puzzled by his tone as she sat herself in the barrow and let him squeeze in beside her.

"Mr. Thorpe spoke to me today, offering us the use of the vacant rooms above the stable."

"Oh," said Violet, none the wiser.

"He said that they were built to board male servants, but as they don't have any, we could have it as a little house if we wanted."

"Do we want it? I thought we were going to wait."

"I don't find waiting easy, Vi," Joe said carefully with a sideways glance. "And I keep wondering why we should wait, especially as we made a good few bob for the Hayworths' stuff we sold."

"I thought we had talked all about it. We are waiting so we save money, so we don't set up home, and so . . . " Violet's voice petered out as she stared at the radish row.

"So we don't have babies?"

"Yes."

"Well, I've been thinking. Babies travel. Maybe even travel better than expecting mothers."

Violet smiled to herself. Only medical men or farmers would talk about reproducing in such a matter-of-fact way.

"But if we get married, I would have to give up work."

"No. I sorted that one out with the boss too. He said you could continue for a while, 'cos you would be easily reachable from our rooms. They even have a bell so you can be summoned."

Violet silently digested the information. Joe caught her nearest hand and looked at her intently.

"So, darling, what do you think?"

"It's a nice idea."

Joe heaved Violet onto her feet and whirled her around between the vegetable rows.

"Mind me hair, Joe. I'm still on duty." She laughed then and planted a big kiss on his stubbly cheek.

"You'll soon be my wife."

"Only if I approve of the stable loft."

"I'd live in a pig-sty, so long as you were with me."

"The stable loft sounds romantic, doesn't it."

"It certainly does."

The unwelcome sound of a shrill whistle interrupted their embrace.

"How inconsiderate!" Joe said and reluctantly released her with a sigh. Violet blew a raspberry in the direction of the summons, but after pecking Joe's cheek, she dashed toward the back door.

"We'll explore the rooms tomorrow!" called Joe as she retreated.

Sticking up a thumb as she ran, Violet showed her approval of the plan.

Even in her excitement, Violet realised that the stable rooms were decidedly inconvenient. Joe joked that the only thing to recommend them was their potential and water-tightness, but he worried about the disadvantages. The two rooms were of a decent size and were highly suitable for their current job of storing horse food, but not for living in. They were not adjoined but both came off the same corridor. Violet teased him that they could have one room each. Using their imaginations, they tried to visualise the dingy rooms with clean windows, curtains, and furniture.

Any spare time the couple had between the wheat and apple harvests was spent cleaning up the rooms and making them habitable. Generations of spiders were driven out, and the grimy walls were washed and whitewashed. With Violet's elbow grease, the windows became transparent again and the floorboards shone. Joe and his father constructed a bed-frame, and his mother got together enough feathers to make a mattress.

One Saturday when Violet had a half day, she and Joe went to Tunbridge Market and returned with a second-hand cooking stove, a few ill-matching chairs, and a table. Their families dug deep into their kitchen cupboards and supplied them with a strange assortment of cooking utensils and crockery. Joe and Violet were delighted with their treasures. After a good sanding and polish, the chairs looked fairly respectable, and a gingham tablecloth hid the stained surface of the old table.

Violet and her married sisters got busy making cheerful curtains and rag mats for the attic rooms, and her mother presented her with a beautiful patchwork quilt for the bed. All in all, everything was hodgepodge and perfect! Now all they needed was a day off together to tie the knot, but a day off in harvest was unthinkable, so they and their lovenest would have to wait until at least October.

CHAPTER 39

THROUGH THE WARM SUMMER, UNCLE Hector slowly but steadily improved. He could now take a few steps, but his left hand was still useless. His speech had become more understandable, but his emotions were still uncontrolled. His pathetic reliance on Rebecca's presence for reassurance was a heavy ball and chain that kept her captive.

Hessie cared for Uncle Hector's physical needs and did her utmost to protect Rebecca from exhaustion, although she must have been exhausted herself. Rebecca purchased a wicker bath chair that she had seen advertised in a magazine. It opened up her and Uncle Hector's world. Any day that Uncle Hector was feeling well enough, Jack and the footman would carry him down the stairs and into his new chair. Being only a shadow of the man he used to be, moving him around was not difficult now. On wet days, he would sit in the parlour listening to Rebecca playing the piano or reading to him. On sunny days, she would take him outside, even venturing as far as Kensington Gardens and the rose garden in particular. Protected in warm tartan blankets against the mild summer breeze, Uncle Hector was as passive as an infant. His sunken, watery eyes gazed in silence as Rebecca pointed out the beauty of the flower beds, the statues, and the water features. She always wanted to tarry longer, but her patient's tiredness, chilliness, or incontinence always brought their trips to an abrupt end.

Rebecca wished that Jack would sometimes have an evening at home, for she longed for interesting company and to hear stories of life beyond the walls of 27 Milton Square. She knew he was doing important work and realised the soup-kitchen attendees' needs were greater than her own, but she couldn't help wishing. Even better would be the opportunity to accompany Jack!

"Please let me come with you tonight," Rebecca asked again over dinner.

"You have enough cares at the moment, without my loading you with more."

"I want to see it for myself."

"You'll be shattered with tiredness."

"So what?" snapped Rebecca. "Being stuck in this prison is shattering too. I need to escape just for a little while and see who else is out there in the world beside Uncle Hector and Hessie."

Much to her surprise, Rebecca had thumped the dining room table and set the crockery clattering. But she wasn't done. "I am fed up with being cooped up here. I do need to get out!"

Rebecca felt guilty, embarrassed, but desperate. She was angry with Jack. *Why are men so stupid and don't see things until you spell it out in ugly words?* She looked at Jack through her tears.

"I see," said Jack.

"And what?" retorted Rebecca. "Are you going to let me come along, or am I going to stay here until I go mad and need admission to Mr. Gascoigne's recommended asylum?"

"I didn't realise things were so difficult for you."

"Well, they are!"

"I thought they were getting easier now that you have the chariot chair."

"Bath chair," corrected Rebecca pedantically. "It only lengthens my chain."

Jack put his hand sympathetically over Rebecca's, but she pulled hers away. She didn't want useless "there, there"-ing. She wanted him to do something.

"Come along tonight then," said Jack.

"Thank you, darling." Rebecca smiled through her tears and grabbed his retreating hand.

Walking out the front door with Jack to catch a horse-drawn omnibus felt like a guilty escape. Hessie was all for it, but Rebecca felt awful when she kissed her uncle goodnight. Her victory felt hollow. She wasn't sure if Jack wanted her company and wondered if she had let everyone down.

Squeezing themselves into the overcrowded omnibus, Jack and Rebecca were parted. There was a strange medley of people in the carriage, and grand buildings outside were interesting, but despite all this, Rebecca kept finding herself watching Jack. He looked so distant, stern, and cold. A chilliness radiating from one's husband can cast a gloomy cloud over any adventure, however diverting.

There was no direct omnibus route from opulent South Kensington to dingy Whitechapel, so Jack and Rebecca changed carriages several times. Each omnibus they entered seemed to contain a scruffier and smellier clientele. Rebecca was wearing her oldest summer frock, but she still felt ridiculously over-dressed. It was a relief to alight from the swaying carriage and trot next to Jack through the dirty side-streets and hidden back alleys.

On reaching the warehouse soup kitchen, Jack and Rebecca received a warm, hearty welcome. Jack acted as if they were the most harmonious of couples, and Rebecca tried to follow suit. Many of Rebecca's misgivings melted away as she donned her apron and helped chop up sack loads of vegetables. The friendly kitchen team welcomed any help, especially if offered by Jack's wife. Time and time again Rebecca heard how much they appreciated his input and ministry. Rebecca felt proud of him, but she wanted to prove her own worth too. She felt a bit nervous when the big doors opened and the heaving mass of hungry humanity flooded into the warehouse. Safely behind the trestle table, Rebecca concentrated on serving the hot soup, ladle by ladle, into the proffered receptacles—jam jars, bowls, chipped cups, and jugs—the bigger, the better. After the staid existence of life at 27 Milton Square, the chaos and commotion of the warehouse was almost overwhelming, so Rebecca focused on her given task and tried to ignore the bigger scene until later.

Once the soup had been served and the noise levels were somewhat reduced, Rebecca saw Jack and Mr. Smith climbing onto a large table to start the worship. Seeing them, jackets discarded, in their rolled-up shirtsleeves and braces, Rebecca thought they looked more like boxers entering the ring than preachers. Indeed, Mr. Smith's general bearing and crooked nose made him look like a rugged champion boxer. Jack would not have stood a chance! Mr. Smith read a portion from the Bible and prayed, then Jack took over. Rebecca could not catch every word, but she was struck by his commanding presence and engaging manner. Within a few minutes, he had covered the essentials of the gospel and urged each hearer to flee to Christ. Without sounding condescending, he had spoken simply and clearly. Without sounding condemning, he had described how deeply fallen mankind is and set forth God's remedy for sin and guilt in Christ Jesus.

Rebecca would have been pleased to hide at the sinks with the washing up, but a bunch of toothless old ladies approached her, wanting to meet the "parson's missus." Soon she was in among the crowd, chatting to this one and that, holding a baby or helping a toddler with their soup cup. With a beaming face, Jack called her over to meet several of his acquaintances.

The sun was sinking, and there was a chill in the air when the Hayworths finally extracted themselves from the now-stuffy warehouse and headed for home. Too late to catch an omnibus, they walked through the slums toward a more respectable district where hansom cabs ventured. Jack held Rebecca's hand tightly as they weaved their way through a maze of dark alleys.

After the scenes she had witnessed, it seemed an extravagant luxury to sink into the padded seat of a hansom cab. Rebecca wondered how many poor, aching bodies would lie on the hard ground or thin straw mattresses that night. She imagined the discomfort, smells, noises, and vermin in a typical bunkhouse—and shuddered.

Her musings were interrupted by Jack putting his arm around her shoulder. "So, what do you think of my equivalent to a gentlemen's club?" he said with a smile.

"I found it very interesting."

"You looked as if you enjoyed yourself."

"I did!" said Rebecca. "It was so interesting seeing all the goings-on, and the people you have talked about. And it all seems so . . . " She paused to find the right word. "So very useful."

"It certainly is."

"I hope it wasn't too bad having me there."

Jack squeezed her shoulder. "It was lovely."

"You didn't look enthusiastic about my presence on the journey there."

"Didn't I?"

"No, you looked positively sullen and sulky."

"That wasn't a sullen and sulky face," Jack confessed with a laugh. "That was me suddenly realising I was doing the address today and not Smith!"

"So you prepared it on the journey?"

"Yes, I suppose you could say that. With a volley of arrow prayers."

"Well, I believe they were fully answered."

"Thank you—and thank God!"

"Yes."

"And when will her ladyship next see fit to accompany me again?" asked Jack as he helped his wife alight from the carriage.

"As soon as his lordship sees fit to invite her."

Hessie was very interested to hear about the soup kitchen and encouraged Rebecca's involvement, but not everyone was quite so enthusiastic. Mrs. Hill disapproved of the project. Giving out food encouraged idleness. She had to work for every meal and penny she received, and so should others.

Rebecca understood her disappointment. For years Mrs. Hill had longed for a lady of the house to bring an air of gentility to the establishment; but instead of Rebecca organising at-home afternoons with cucumber sandwiches and bone china tea cups, she was now organising bags of pearl barley to be delivered to the Whitechapel slums. Instead of welcoming elegant ladies and gentlemen to 27 Milton Square and watching them admire the furniture and flowers, Mrs. Hill now lived in fear of smelly beggars knocking on the door and being invited inside—no doubt, they wouldn't even have the decency to go to the servants' entrance! How could one run a house like a well-oiled machine if those in charge were cranky Christian enthusiasts? She wondered how poor Mr. Stubbs really felt about the couple's choices.

CHAPTER 40

SOMETIME DURING THE SMALL HOURS of the third of September, Hector Stubbs drew his final breath and departed to his eternal destination. Rebecca was distraught that she had been fast asleep and not by his side for the fateful moment. The physician's conjecture was that his patient had suffered a massive stroke in his sleep and had died instantly. This was somewhat reassuring to Rebecca.

While Hessie and Rebecca laid Uncle Hector out, Mrs. Hill draped the whole house in mourning. Black crepe was tied to the front door knocker, curtains were drawn, and all mirrors were veiled. She even stopped all the clocks and put them to the time she suspected her master had died. Jack thought most of her actions were superstitious hocus-pocus, but as they were harmless, he let her continue in her self-appointed task. Meanwhile, he ordered black-edged stationery and routed through Uncle Hector's desk for addresses of those he should inform.

The arranging of the funeral, the hearse, and carriages for the mourners occupied Jack's time; Rebecca was busy making black mourning clothes from cloth secretly ordered in spring in readiness.

On the appointed day, Jack led the small group of mourners out through the front door and into the funeral coaches. Rebecca ushered the female servants and Hessie into the dark, draped mourning room. The servant girls looked ill at ease as they perched on chairs in respectful silence. Rebecca, dressed in black and with a veiled hat, felt equally as uncomfortable. Was anything expected of her? They could not just sit in silence for an hour. As the church bell tolled, Rebecca picked up a Bible and read Psalm 90. She knew she was adding to Mrs. Hill's discomfort, but felt she had to pray, so pray she did. After a reverential pause in which everyone studied the carpet, Rebecca broke the heavy silence.

"Now we need to ensure that all is ready when the guests return. We do not know how many will come back here for refreshment, so please ensure some food is kept back for latecomers."

With relief, the staff fled the room and returned to their work. Rebecca and Hessie remained seated. Rebecca felt numb: the magnitude of eternity and the uncertainty of Uncle Hector's fate hung so heavily upon her that a detached benumbing was welcome. How she longed to throw herself into the activities of the kitchen! Instead, she would have to formulate appropriate responses to the polite and wooden condolences of Uncle Hector's acquaintances, who had long ago stopped visiting him.

Having quenched their thirst with tea, the mourners drowned their professed sorrow with Uncle Hector's liquor. Once the atmosphere had degenerated to that of a men's club, Rebecca silently withdrew. She headed upstairs and aimlessly entered her uncle's now-empty bedroom. At least, for the first few seconds, Rebecca believed it was empty, but on turning herself away from the striped bed, she was surprised to discover Hessie weeping in a chair next to the unlit fireplace. Hessie seemed embarrassed at being caught and tried to hide her tears when Rebecca approached her.

"Hessie, you must be freezing. I'll fetch your shawl and ring for the fire to be lit."

"Don't worry about me."

Ignoring this, Rebecca hurried away, returning with a shawl that she draped over her dear friend's shoulders.

"It has been a sad day," she observed, not knowing quite what to say.

"That is how my job always ends." Hessie sniffed pitifully.

"It must be very hard," said Rebecca, wishing she could offer something less bland and more encouraging.

A maid entered the room to light the fire. Rebecca asked for a tray of food to be sent up for the neglected nurse. Once this had been arranged, Hessie observed, "Some bereavements are harder than others. Sometimes it is a relief to leave a house, but other times, it is a huge wrench. And this will be the hardest. When would you like me to leave?"

Hessie leaving? This was an aspect of the passing of Uncle Hector that Rebecca had not anticipated. The prospect of her faithful companion leaving the house and having to embark on a new, lonely situation seemed unthinkable.

"Please don't leave yet!" urged Rebecca. "Stay for a while as a houseguest. You deserve a break—a month at least."

Hessie looked at her through tear-filled eyes. "I could not impose on you like that. Reverend Hayworth would not like me tarrying here aimlessly."

"He would be delighted, I'm sure. Why, you could also come and see the soup kitchen!" Rebecca made it sound as if she were suggesting a visit to Buckingham Palace.

"That would indeed be fascinating," admitted Hessie.

"Well, that's it then!" said Rebecca. "You stay on and be our guest. And don't you dare suggest packing your cases until you are utterly fed up with us."

Hessie smiled. "If you really, genuinely insist, I will gladly accept the offer and make myself as useful as possible."

"Hessie, you don't have to earn our hospitality—you have more than done that already. Please have some leisure and please yourself for once."

And so it was decided to the mutual satisfaction of both women.

Even without the responsibility of caring for Uncle Hector, life at 27 Milton Square remained busy. In fact, the business seemed to gain momentum. Jack, Mr. Smith, and another worker from the London City Mission decided to venture into a small slum nearer South Kensington. As its name suggested, The Devil's Acre was a notoriously vile and depraved area. Almost in the shadow of Westminster Abbey, the squalid slum was an embarrassment to be ignored and avoided. It was renowned for its wretchedness, filth, and disease. The Catholics had been unable to penetrate its spiritual and moral darkness, and this was enough of a challenge to provoke Mr. Smith's interest in the area.

Also closer to home, Jack now had access to St. Mary Abbots, the Kensington workhouse in Marloes Road. Not only was Jack able to conduct Sunday services, but he was also allowed to visit those in the infirmary during the week. Whether this ruling was a sign of the board members' concern for the souls of the sick or merely their realisation that the ill were not working anyway and thus a ministerial visit would not impair productivity, nobody could say, but Jack took advantage of it.

As well as these new ventures, the Whitechapel visits and soup-kitchen work continued as usual. The team and attendees welcomed Hessie into their midst, and she soon found a useful role treating various ulcers, boils, and sores. Back at Milton Square, she and Rebecca were not only ordering ingredients for the soup but also finding stockists for bandages and herbal remedies. Much to Mrs. Hill's disgust, they used the kitchen to experiment with honey, charcoal, bran, and bread for absorbent poultice mixtures.

When Jack offered the use of the dining room for a weekly prayer meeting for local London City Mission workers and supporters, Mrs. Hill decided that enough was enough and handed in her notice. The cook and footman followed suit. They were all given a generous gift from Uncle Hector's estate and a good, clean reference, and so left with little ill feeling.

Though busy, Jack and Rebecca still wondered about the Lord's purpose for their lives. Was London to be their permanent sphere of labour? How were they to use Milton Square? In bed, late into the night, they proposed and rejected various possibilities. Should they open a hostel for fallen women? Or maybe an orphanage? Although with what Rebecca had inherited they could continue to live in London, should they sell the property and use the money elsewhere? They prayed much for guidance and clarity in these decisions.

Their prayer for children remained unchanged. They had been able to see wisdom in being childless during Uncle Hector's illness, but now, surely a child could fit in with their work and life. Even in all her activities and duties, Rebecca knew there was an aching void in her heart that nothing but a child could fill. Despite her prayers, the ache did not disappear, and the gap remained unfilled.

CHAPTER 41

REBECCA SAT DOWN AT UNCLE Hector's desk in the front room to write a long-overdue letter to Sophia. The kind ladies of Capford had sent a large parcel of blankets and clothing for the Whitechapel families, and this needed acknowledging. For the time being, Hessie had appointed herself as cook and was busy in the kitchen. Rebecca hoped she would not confuse the pie and poultice recipes.

Rebecca was just signing off her letter when a bedraggled Jack charged into the room. His wet outerwear and muddy shoes would have caused Mrs. Hill to expire.

"Rebecca, you must come quickly! Something must be done!"

Rebecca leapt up. "Whatever has happened? Is someone ill?"

"Just get your bonnet and shawl. I will explain on the way."

Instead of waiting for a servant, Rebecca rushed upstairs to grab her things.

Trotting after Jack along the wet pavement, Rebecca could hardly make out his breathless explanation. Gathering together fragments, she understood they were going to St. Mary Abbot's workhouse, where there were three orphan infants almost dying.

Jack knocked loudly on the imposing workhouse door and was admitted by the warden.

"Back already, parson?"

"Yes, Mr. Brocklehurst. I want my wife to see those poor infants."

"Them of the dead woman?"

"Yes."

The warden shuffled his way along a dark corridor to the infirmary.

"It were a strange thing," he explained as he went. "She were almost dead at t' door last night. Like she used 'er last bit o' strength to bring 'er bairns 'ere."

Opening a door, he let the Hayworths into the gloomy infirmary ward.

"Here they be."

The infirmary looked more like a mortuary. Situated in the cellars, the only thing likely to flourish in such a chilly, damp environment was the mildew. Rebecca shuddered as she entered.

Jack hurried her along to a little cot. There, huddled in a corner sat the most pathetic sight Rebecca had ever seen. A tiny tot of two or three years old was hugging her two scrawny brothers close as they cried for milk. The little family was dressed in clothing that had long ago turned to rags. The girl's brown curls hung matted around her grimy face. Tears had created clean streaks down her hollow cheeks. The boys were of an undeterminable age, probably somewhere around a year old, and their careworn faces testified that they had experienced much hardship in their short lifetime. Their rags were wet and their thin, underdressed bodies shivered with cold, hunger, and misery. The cot was wet with tears, urine, and spilt milk.

Putting her thumb in her brother's mouth and temporarily silencing his cries, the girl looked up to the adults with her brown trusting eyes and said, "Baba, gink."

"She wants a drink for 'em," Mr. Brocklehurst said. "Me wife tried 'em with weak tea earlier but got nowhere."

"What will happen to them?" asked Rebecca. "Could anyone try and trace their father?"

"The muver were in widow's weeds, so there ain't a farver. We'll feed them a bit, but I reckon them boys'll join their poor muver within two days. They never survive. I'll keep 'em quiet on laudanum till they slip away."

"And her?"

"She may be okay. Bit young really. Too young to put to a trade. Could send 'er to an orphanage, then she'll go into service. Mind you, me wife reckons she'll die of a broken 'eart, and I reckon she's right."

Jack's eyes were full of tenderness as he gently picked up the most distressed twin. Nothing could have been clearer.

"Jack, we need to take them home."

"Immediately!" agreed Jack as he tucked the baby inside his coat.

"They'll die within a week," the warden warned them.

"Then they can have a week of love," said Rebecca.

She picked up the girl, who kicked and screamed until the other baby was removed too.

"She don't 'arf fight for 'em," said the warden. "I fort me 'eart were 'ardened wiv me work and that, till I saw them li'le uns."

Jack and Rebecca headed toward the door.

"But 'ang on. No one is allowed to leave the workhouse without the board members' permission."

"And do the board members know about these children?" asked Jack.

"Not yet. I 'aven't 'ad time te inform 'em."

"Then they need never know. It'll save you a job."

Rebecca imagined an officious board member paying an unexpected visit and catching them baby-stealing. She wanted to smuggle them out of the building as quickly as possible. But Jack wanted to see the poor dead mother first. With great reluctance, Rebecca had to leave the sobbing children in their stinking cot and face the stark scene of the mortuary.

In a small, cold cell, forsaken and neglected by all, the young woman lay, unreachable to either love or help. Her bare, ashen arms were crossed over her rough workhouse shroud. Her only personal possession was a curtain ring as a wedding band. Her pallid face was peaceful in repose and might once have been beautiful, but now only her hair remained stunning. Rebecca almost wanted to comfort the corpse with a warm blanket.

"We'll sell 'er 'air te cover any cost," said Mr. Brocklehurst.

Rebecca was aghast. *The poor girl has lost everything, surely she can take her own hair to the grave!*

"Jack, we can't let that happen!"

Routing in his pocket for loose change, Jack paid the warden the going rate for long hair and extracted a promise that her tresses would remain on her. Just before leaving the room, Rebecca approached the body.

"We will do all we can for your lovely children, I promise," she said through her tears.

Persuading a hansom cab driver to allow them a ride with three dirty, squawking infants was not easy, but finally a horseman obliged. As they neared Milton Square, the enormity of what they were attempting hit Rebecca. How could they provide for these vulnerable, defenseless little people whose reliance on them was absolute? Just keeping them safe in a jolting carriage seemed a big enough task! To engage in conversation with Jack over the cries of the perplexed infants was impossible, so Rebecca addressed her Heavenly Father instead. As she clung onto the seat and her wet, wriggling charges, she sent up a quick prayer for divine assistance.

Surprised by the bedraggled group that met her eyes when opening the door, Kitty, the housemaid, did what any rational creature would do in these circumstances: she called for Hessie. Emerging with floury hands from the kitchen, Hessie took stock of the situation. In a few short sentences, Rebecca explained the salient details, and Hessie took control. Water was heated for bathing; the charity boxes were raided for clothing, and the kitchen maid was sent out to find goat's milk.

"Now, take note, child," Hessie said firmly, "we don't want cow's milk—goat's is best for little tots. Use your extensive family contacts and find someone who has a goat. We need a regular supply and will pay beyond the normal price if a reliable source can be found."

Meanwhile, the little girl was offered bread spread with butter and honey and then dipped into milk. She pointed to her brothers. "One a baba," she insisted.

Rebecca understood. "She wants the boys to have some."

The lads were less keen, spitting out spoonful after spoonful, then totally refusing to cooperate. The girl finished her bowlful and her brothers' as well. Now content, the girl submitted unprotestingly to a warm bath and fresh set of clothes. Thumb in mouth, she sat full square and serious on the sofa before flopping to one side and falling asleep.

The boys were less easy to please. Still hungry and irritable, they cried and splashed their way through a bath, soaking Rebecca for a second time. Every cup in the kitchen must have been used in trying to encourage them to drink. Some made them splutter, and some they just flatly refused to try. Rebecca could have wept in desperation. Finally Hessie suggested dipping fingers in honey and letting the boys suck them. Using their little fingers, Hessie and Rebecca did this with success.

Supper was totally forgotten that evening as the household's actions revolved around the orphans. Goat's milk was eventually procured and, with Uncle Hector's old feeding cup, a small amount of fluid was reluctantly swallowed by the boys, though most of it was absorbed by their new clothes.

That evening, in a rare moment of tranquility, Jack wondered aloud what their names might be. "The girl has said very little but calls both boys 'baba,' and when wanting something herself says 'Gas gink' or 'Gas more.'"

"Gas? However useful the discovery, who would call their daughter Gas?" asked Rebecca. "Maybe her name is Gladys? Grace? G—"

"Grace!" exclaimed Jack. "It must be Grace."

"Hush!" protested Rebecca. "You'll wake her up, Grace or no Grace. But we'll try it on her later."

"And the lads? We can't call them Baba One and Baba Two."

"David and Jonathan?"

"Peter and Andrew?"

"John and James?"

They looked at the gaunt pair, lying together in fitful sleep.

"As thin as they are, maybe one should be called Jeremiah," said Jack.

"They won't always be so skinny," Rebecca protested, gazing at them fondly. "Wait until they have a week's worth of goat's milk inside them."

"What was your father's name?" asked Jack.

"Thomas. And yours?"

"Daniel."

"Tom and Dan. Perfect."

"And Thomas and Daniel on official occasions or when in serious trouble."

Rebecca couldn't stop gazing at their innocent, tranquil faces, and she voiced her musings. "Do you know what is so amazing?"

"What?"

"There were just the right size clothes in the charity box. God was caring for these children long before we were."

A blanket chest was emptied out and transformed into a cot for Tom and Dan, and a little bed was made on the floor for Grace. These sleeping arrangements lasted all of two hours. Just as Jack and Rebecca were getting tired and ready for bed, the infants decided something was amiss and made their discontentment known loudly. The long night was punctuated with trips to the kitchen to warm up the milk and the honey jar; the changing of cloth rags (a more absorbent nappy arrangement was a priority the following day); and wandering around the bedroom singing lullabies that failed to lull. As the pale morning sun shone through the curtains, the exhausted new family lay sprawled on the bed together, finally fast asleep.

CHAPTER 42

FEELING EXHAUSTED AND DESPONDENT, REBECCA helped Hessie write a long shopping list of baby items. In the back of her mind, she wondered if Mr. Brocklehurst's prediction of a week would prove to be correct. Maybe the shopping spree would be a waste of money.

After another fraught day, Rebecca was pleased to welcome back Kitty with her big basket of shopping. A box of thick nappy squares had been delivered earlier. The basket seemed bottomless as more and more paper bags were pulled out. Safety pins, glass feeding bottles, rubber teats, calf teats, and feeding spoons. With renewed hope, Rebecca warmed yet more milk, praying that it would be ingested rather than soaked into clothing.

Rebecca woke the next morning, bleary-eyed but bushy-tailed. At five o'clock in the morning, Dan had realised that sucking a calf's teat was manageable and that goat's milk was palatable. Having guzzled a whole bottle-full, the resulting hiccoughs had kept him and her awake for another half an hour, but that was a price worth paying. Tom was ahead of his brother in the discovery, but preferred the rubber teat; now their futures seemed more hopeful. The warning of "only a week" rang in her ears, but now she saw it as a challenge rather than a prediction. Mr. Brocklehurst had not calculated in the fact that God works miracles.

The days and nights ran into each other as Rebecca and Hessie cared for the three needy children. Jack flitted in and out of the domestic scene. He continued his Whitechapel commitments as usual, but also spent much of his scarce free time in the garden shed with his carpentry tools making a cot and wooden bricks. Sometimes Rebecca became exasperated—surely feeding the hungry trio was of more importance than making building blocks! On pondering the situation, Rebecca concluded that, while the arrival of children changes a woman's daily life completely, a man's life can continue relatively untouched. Did she envy or pity men for this? Her answer changed on a daily, even hourly, basis.

Rather against Hessie's wishes, Rebecca requested a visit from the local physician to perform a medical examination of the children. His pronouncements were a mixed blessing. On one hand, he was helpful in trying to ascertain the age of the infants. As Dan and Tom were pulling themselves up to a standing position and shuffling about on their bottoms, he suggested they were about eight months old. Grace, he imagined, was about two and a half years.

"Her lack of speech could indicate backwardness," he added grimly. Packing his bag to leave, he concluded, "At present they look reasonably healthy—underweight, of course, but nothing too alarming or extreme. The trouble is, they may be harbouring diseases. Being from a presumably lower-class family, they are susceptible to a whole host of illnesses. It is not inconceivable that their mother died of consumption. They may be harbouring that, for instance. Only time will tell. I would strongly advise against close, prolonged contact with them, for your own safety. And, whatever else you choose to do, boil their soiled nappies and clean their bottles with boiling water."

Having thanked him for his advice, Rebecca ushered him out, then picked up each of the children and kissed them fondly.

Rebecca marveled how three little children could create such chaos. Every day, more and more baby-related items were purchased, transforming the house from a bachelor pad into a family home. As the boys gained more energy (and they did every day), so did their thirst for exploration. Using anything to heave themselves up on their feet, they either pulled the object over, ending up in a heap on the floor, or succeeded in standing and headed for the next pull-able item. Anything breakable was either removed from the room or elevated to a higher position, away from little hands. Uncle Hector had collected very few china ornaments, but his numerous books were in danger of having pages ripped out or eaten. None would have felt the loss of these learned but boring tomes if they were ingested, but it did not feel quite right to let them come to such a sad end, so Jack moved the ones within reach to the trunk room.

Dan rewarded anyone who spoke to him with wide, toothless smiles, and Tom chuckled uncontrollably at endless rounds of peek-a-boo. Whether it be day or night, appropriate or inappropriate, the boys' thirst for fun was unquenchable. They loved being dandled, tickled, and flown through the air. Their faces beamed every time Jack entered the room as they anticipated a good-old rough-and-tumble. Pulling themselves onto their feet on his trouser legs, they vied for his attention. Rebecca couldn't stop herself from smiling every time she looked at them. She smiled appreciatively at Jack too. When he played with the lads, he looked ten years younger.

Grace, on the other hand, was most cautious. Perpetually on guard, she seldom allowed herself to play. Sitting solemnly on a chair, thumb in mouth, she sat watching the antics of her brothers. She rarely cried for herself but became acutely distressed if Dan or Tom was removed from the room. In fact, she was inconsolable until they were returned. Her care and concern was in no way reciprocated, for her brothers were too busy exploring their world to notice their sister's unease.

The boys were happy to be held, but Grace resisted. The only way to coax her onto one's knee was to read a picture book. Almost against her better judgment, Grace would gradually come nearer, allow herself to be picked up, and sit—but only for the duration of the story. Rebecca longed to get through to Grace's tiny, broken heart and lavish it with healing love.

After a thorough cleaning operation and airing, Uncle Hector's bedroom became the nursery. In the place of pride stood three beautiful wooden cots lovingly created by Jack. The children were not as keen on the idea of the cots and the nursery as the adults, but after a week of protests and bedtime tantrums, a reasonable bedtime routine was established and the Hayworths regained the privacy of their bedroom. Auntie Hessie, having become a light sleeper in the course of her work, monitored the nursery during the night.

Life developed a new kind of normality. Rebecca was unable to attend the soup kitchen, but Hessie continued to accompany Jack twice a week to apply her remedies and potions, which were always much in demand.

Every evening before bed, Jack and Rebecca crept into the nursery to gaze at the sleeping infants. The boys' innocent, angelic faces in sleep belied their mischievous daytime characters. In sleep, Grace enjoyed all the peace and tranquility that waking hours denied her.

"So," whispered Jack, "is this the start of the Hector Stubbs Memorial Orphanage?"

He spoke in jest, but Rebecca recognised a serious element to the question. They were still trying to discern God's will for their lives, and an orphanage now seemed a useful option.

Rebecca did not reply until they had kissed the sleepers and returned to their own room.

"I am getting less keen on the orphanage idea," she said slowly.

"It would be awfully hard work," agreed Jack.

"It isn't just that." Rebecca struggled to find the right words. "Orphanages do a good job. Some children thrive in them—the boys might. But Grace, she would grow physically, but she would never open up and flourish. She is like a closed little bud that needs tender nurturing if she is ever to open into a flower."

"Will she blossom?" asked Jack sadly.

"I just hope and pray she will," said Rebecca. "My heart bleeds for her sometimes. She is such a beautiful little bud that she will make a wonderful flower someday—I hope."

"I don't think an orphanage is the thing for us, either," Jack confessed as he undressed. "It would be a noble thing to do, and I admire anyone who undertakes such a project, but I just am not convinced that it is something we should be doing. I still think it is my calling to preach, and a house overflowing with children is hardly conducive to sermon preparation."

Rebecca's breath was caught in her throat. "You're not fed up with these children, are you?"

"Of course not! I reckon I would fight to the death for them now, they have got me so much."

"Exactly." Rebecca felt the same.

"An orphanage seems too institutional for us—and for our three."

"I want them to be a family with us. A normal little family."

"Hear, hear! In fact, while I was at the South Kensington Workhouse today, I bumped into Mrs. Brocklehurst and asked her if she had heard any more about the poor mother's history or if anyone had come enquiring after the children."

Rebecca trembled. "And?"

"Nothing. No information. No enquiries. She seemed surprised that the children were still alive and kicking. I think she was pleased for us. I then went to the town hall to see the clerk who issues birth certificates and explained our situation."

"Oh."

"He said there is no more paperwork for taking on children than for taking in a stray dog."

Rebecca frowned. "How odd."

"He said that some countries like America have adoption laws and whatnot, but there is nothing official over here. He also said that birth certificates aren't compulsory, so it doesn't matter that the children don't have one." Jack met Rebecca's frown with one of his own. "I got the distinct impression that the government doesn't care a ha'penny for orphans, and people can do what they like with them. They are totally surplus to requirements in the world's eyes."

Lifting her chin, Rebecca said, "Then we will keep ours."

"Yes, and call them little Hayworths, and no one will be any the wiser."

"But, I would feel a bit safer if we were out of London and untraceable to anyone who might claim them."

"If their poor mother had had anywhere else to go to or anyone else to help her, she would not have gone to the workhouse. The workhouse is everyone's last resort. I don't think we need worry."

"I probably will, though." Rebecca sighed as she climbed into bed.

"I know God has given them to us, Rebecca, so we shouldn't worry."

Rebecca did not reply. She wanted to agree, but she could not help thinking of poor Job in the Old Testament and his great losses. He said, "The Lord gave and the Lord hath taken away; Blessed be the name of the Lord." God had given her children only a few weeks ago, but her love for them was already rooted so deeply in her heart that she could not imagine being able to emulate Job if they were taken away.

Jack blew out the candle and rolled toward her to say goodnight.

"Do you think our many prayers for children have been answered?" asked Rebecca as she snuggled into his arms.

"I certainly do." Jack kissed her forehead. "Abundantly answered."

"I once heard a good minister say that God answers prayer by either giving you what you ask for or giving something better, and I now think he was actually right."

"Of course, he was right. Aren't I always?" teased Jack.

"Good thing you're so humble." Rebecca tickled his ribs and laughed as he yelped.

CHAPTER 43

EVEN THOUGH HIS MOTHER-IN-LAW WAS staying, Edward was pleased to be heading indoors. The chilly northeasterly wind and icy rain were even more biting than Mrs. Harrington's ridiculous comments—but she was not quite so relentless . . .

Edward was amazed at the uncomplaining toughness of his workforce who were exposed to the raw elements all day, fencing or tree planting. With hay stuffed in their boots and wearing waxed trousers for warmth, as well as multiple layers of clothing, they moved awkwardly, like living scarecrows.

Who would choose to be a farm labourer? Maybe no one did choose—fourteen-year-old boys did what their fathers told them and followed in their laborious footsteps. Once a man had been given a tied cottage to live in, he was bound to the farm as long as he wanted a roof over his head. Tied cottage, tied worker. Edward admired Joe's decision to break loose and risk all for independence. He smiled as he thought of Joe's shrewdness. He was far too savvy to stay a farmhand all his life. With his practical wit, he would battle his way through any challenges of the new frontier. If he didn't succeed in farming, Edward imagined him selling superior totem poles to the Red Indians.

Leaving his dripping outerwear in the hall, Edward headed toward the parlour. Before entering he ran his fingers through his damp hair in a vain attempt to look groomed. As he sat by the warm fire, his wet trousers began to steam.

"I hardly think your trousers are suitable attire for the parlour," Mrs. Harrington said with a sniff, wrinkling up her delicate nose. "And if I am not mistaken, they are giving off a distinctly pig-sty odour."

"Shall I remove them, then?" asked Edward, standing up and reaching for his buttons.

"Edward, don't provoke," said Sophia, unsuccessfully stifling a laugh.

"*Pecunia non olet*," Edward muttered as he sat down again and waited for his coffee. Money does not stink.

The coffee pot and its aroma distracted Mrs. Harrington's attention nicely. But as soon as her mouth was not otherwise engaged, Edward's mother-in-law recommenced talking.

"As I was saying, I'm rather shocked at the Hayworths." She piously nibbled at a biscuit before continuing. "It almost seems to be going against providence. If nature has decreed a woman to be childless, what right does she have to take the matter into her own hands?"

"They would argue the exact opposite, mother," said Sophia. "They believe the Lord has brought the children directly onto their path. Maybe they were unable to have children so that these ones would be provided with a loving home. I think it is lovely, and actually—" she turned to face Edward, "I was wondering if we could invite them down for Christmas and New Year? Little Dan is suffering with the smoggy London weather."

"What a good idea!" agreed Edward. "Then Jack could preach at the services."

"Invite them to stay *here*?" Mrs. Harrington put down her cup and saucer in disgust. "Here—at Biggenden Manor?"

"Yes indeed."

"I think that is most unwise. Potentially subjecting yourself, in your expectant condition, and dear little Bertie, to workhouse germs would be folly. Gross folly!"

"I am sure they have been thoroughly fumigated," Edward said wryly.

"This is a serious matter, young man!" snapped the matriarch. "To put your son and unborn child at risk of paupers' illnesses is not amusing."

Edward raised his brow. "Are upper-class illnesses more desirable?"

"I will not be diverted into an argument of metaphysical speculation," she said, wagging her finger pointedly. "Once again, I am forced to sit and watch you ignore the long-held and beneficial principles of clear class divides and come up with some madcap plan. If it isn't your tin chapel or your women's meetings, you invite any old riff-raff to stay."

"Jack and Rebecca aren't riff-raff, Mother."

"Well, all I will say is that if you go ahead with your ridiculous idea, I will not stay. Your brother has invited us to celebrate Christmas with them, and I am minded to accept the offer."

"That is a loss that we will bravely bear," Edward observed under his breath.

On Sunday while speaking to Mr. Brookes and Mr. Grey, Edward discussed the idea of inviting Reverend Jack Hayworth to preach over the festive season. Both men were delighted by the idea, since the church had survived on a diet of prayer meetings and reading sermons for a number of months. To have an actual preacher to conduct the service would be a luxury—and far less work. And for said preacher to be Jack seemed a dream.

"But what would the Bishop of Maidstone say?" asked the ever-cautious Mr. Grey.

"We are an independent church, Hayworth is an independent individual, and we and he can do as we please. Anyway, according to my wife, Hayworth received a letter from his bishop in which he more or less apologised for the unfortunate situation in Capford, but also saying that his hands are tied as Wilson holds the purse-strings."

"What a tangled business!" Mr. Brookes nodded his head. "Let's invite the lad down, and his response is his responsibility, but I for one will be right glad to hear him again."

The following Sunday, Edward was able to announce that Reverend Jack Hayworth had agreed to conduct the Christmas morning service, the New Year's Day service, and preach twice on the Sunday in between. A ripple of approval flowed through the congregation as they silently showed their satisfaction by smiles and nods while they found the next hymn. Edward never found public speaking easy and dreaded it when it was his turn to read the sermon. His voice became unnaturally high-pitched and breathless. He had to force himself to slow down instead of galloping through the paragraphs as if the final *amen* was the finishing post of a race. In the privacy of their home, Sophia aided him as his critic and tutor in the art of expressive and engaging public speaking. After each service, Edward received such warm expressions of appreciation from the congregation that the dreaded duty of choosing and reading the sermon seemed a privilege. In his weakness, he also felt the Lord's strength and support.

Locking up the new chapel after the afternoon service and wandering back to Biggenden, Edward's heart swelled with gratitude to his Saviour and King. He had read a sermon on the longsuffering and steadfast love of God, and the phrase aptly described the Lord's kind dealings with him personally: in spite of his own faltering faith and half-hearted commitment, the Lord had been boundless in mercy and grace. Everything he had to give to the Lord was tainted with sin and mixed motives. Yet even these filthy rags of his own good works were completely covered with the perfect righteousness of Christ.

Although his life was now busier than ever with estate responsibilities, church duties, household concerns, and financial worries, Edward was at peace. As he walked down the Biggenden drive, he found himself humming the last hymn, which expressed his thoughts exactly.

Oh, bless the Lord, my soul!
Let all within me join
And aid my tongue to bless His name
Whose favours are divine.

Oh, bless the Lord, my soul,
Nor let His mercies lie
Forgotten in unthankfulness
And without praises die!

CHAPTER 44

VIOLET STARED AT JOE IN delight and amazement.

"Jack Hayworth to marry us?"

"Yes. When I heard he was coming for Christmas, I thought I might as well drop him a line and ask if he could squeeze that in during his trip to the country."

"Wonderful! That sorts out the problem then."

"Exactly. He wrote back saying he would be delighted. But he wasn't sure if it would be against some sort of rule for him to conduct the service in the old church or new chapel, so he would prefer to do it in your parents' front room."

Violet beamed with joy. "Home weddings are so cosy."

Although they had a license to marry, the couple had postponed their wedding for months due to a lack of available and suitably licensed men to carry out the formalities. Reverend Wilson was out of the question, as was his fee. It was unseemly for them to meet alone in their stable rooms, and the cold, wet weather made a wheelbarrow rendezvous impossible. Joe and Violet longed to be lawfully wedded, able to be together in comfort and warmth, in the privacy of their own home.

"He will do it next Thursday, if we can get the day off."

"Next week?"

"It means we will be married before Christmas."

"I can't take Christmas off! Mrs. Thorpe will still need dressing. Even more so for Christmas!"

"You make her sound like a Christmas goose! You dress 'er and Molly can stuff 'er." Joe clearly thought his remarks were clever. "Anyway, she won't take all day to dress. And you can cook me my breakfast before you go."

Violet rested her head on Joe's shoulder. Nothing could be more wonderful than waking up next to Joe on Christmas Day and making his breakfast porridge on their little stove. Her heart glowed as she imagined the scene—for her and her very own husband!

"Come on," she said, jumping up and pulling him to his feet. "We had better tell Ma and then watch her become a whirling flurry of action and ideas."

Within half an hour, Mrs. Brookes was busy organising the details of the day. The well-laced Christmas cake would be metamorphosed into a wedding cake and with a little extra lace, Violet's new Sunday frock would become a wedding dress. Mr. Brookes talked through which furniture could be removed and where extra chairs could be placed to allow for the maximum number of guests. Mrs. Brookes found a suitable coffee table and lace cloth on which Jack's Bible and service book could be placed.

Violet felt butterflies of excitement as she imagined the ceremony taking place among the sagging old armchairs, on the worn and faded carpet, with the non-descript paintings on the wall, all of which had been reassuringly present all her life. She thought of traveling to Canada in April, of trekking through unknown valleys and of setting up home in some remote spot; and all the while the old front room of her parents' cottage would remain exactly the same—and rightly so.

One's family home should be immune to all change, especially when one has moved out.

"A penny for your thoughts," whispered Joe, breaking into her contemplations.

"I was just thinking how this room has always been the same throughout my lifetime and how hopefully it will always stay the same. The sameness will be reassuring when we are so far away."

"Are you getting cold feet?"

"Not at all! I am ready for an adventure—as long as I am with you."

Joe wrapped his arm around her waist.

"And now that the voyage is only seven to ten days with the new steamers, we can dream of coming back to visit. With the penny-post, a network of railroads, and steamers, the world seems to be shrinking."

Joe escorted his bride-to-be back to Biggenden Manor for her evening duties. The rain clouds had dispersed, leaving the night sky clear. Tarrying along the path, they gazed up to the heavens.

"Remember stargazing back in lambing season?" asked Joe.

"How could I forget?"

"Stars always seem to preach a sermon, don't they?"

"Yes, of our smallness."

"And God's greatness."

"And His faithfulness."

"I am pleased we will see the same sermon in the Canadian sky."

To Violet, the following six days felt all topsy-turvy and surreal. She wanted to be with her bridegroom-to-be, but hardly had a moment to spare for meeting him. The manor house was occupied by two women, both of whom she had served and one of whom used to be the housekeeper in the building where she was now an honoured guest.

It was a relief to all that Mrs. Harrington had carried out her threat and made a haughty departure. The Hayworths were by no means demanding guests, but all visitors produce more work, especially if there are six of them. No one had yet explained the maxim "Children should be seen and not heard" to the three young Hayworths who, unsettled by the change of scenery, frequently and loudly voiced their displeasure. Hessie Haynes spent most of her time in the nursery or in the farmyard with the twin boys. Grace, being even more perplexed by the move, clung to her new mother. Violet thought her clinginess must be a burden to Mrs. Hayworth, but apparently it was seen as a great step forward in Grace's bonding process.

One activity that brought smiles to little Grace's otherwise solemn face was feeding the ducks and hens in the backyard. Any mention of feeding time made her clap for joy, wriggle off her mother's knee, and toddle after the one responsible for feeding the poultry —usually Clara. Mrs. Thorpe had presented her with a pretty, pink-cheeked rag doll, and ever since Grace had carried it with her wherever she went. Her brown eyes looked deeply into its French knot eyes as she kissed and caressed its smiley (and increasingly grimy) face. By playing with and talking to the dolly, Rebecca had been able to engage Grace in play and conversation, previously impossible. Everyone was delighted.

When Violet was not involved in the activities at Biggenden Manor, she popped in and out of the stable attic to clean out the cobwebs, sweep the floor, and air the rooms. Once it was all to her satisfaction, she lit the small stove to dispel the dampness. It gave her a strange thrill to see Joe's clothes neatly stacked in the wardrobe and to put hers alongside. It felt even stranger making up the marital bed. Carrying jugs of water from the stable yard pump up to the kettle made her realise how impractical the arrangements really were. Hopefully the novelty of keeping house would not wear off once they moved on—at the end of the lambing season. Anyway, with a little womanly guile, Violet reckoned she could persuade Joe that the hauling of logs and drawing of water was men's work.

Violet had hoped to assist her mother with the baking and other preparations for the wedding ceremony, but duty did not allow for such things. She had no doubt that her capable mother and married sisters would manage without her, but Violet wished she could be there to give her opinion on various arrangements. Not that they would listen to her anyway, if her wishes went against the general consensus. Violet had seen her female relatives in wedding-mode before and knew that their combined force was well able to steamroll over something as trifling as the bride's opinion. The Brookes family had a certain way of doing weddings, and that was that. Maybe, she decided, it was for the best that she was absent. It would save arguments. Let them do things their own sweet way— she would be the one walking off on the arm of Joe by the end of the day.

With great generosity of spirit, Mrs. Thorpe insisted that Violet have two nights off from her normal duties. Whether she wanted to or not, Violet was to spend her last night as a single woman under her parents' roof. This was something Violet very much wanted, so she failed to put up even polite resistance to her mistress's instructions. Neither woman thought it was at all unreasonable that Violet was expected back the morning after her wedding night to serve her mistress's customary cup of tea in bed.

The mixed aromas of baked bread and furniture polish hit Violet as she entered her parents' cottage that Wednesday evening. Joe was expected anytime, so before she had even been offered a bite to eat, Violet was rushed upstairs to try on her prettied-up dress. Looking at herself in the mirror, Violet was satisfied that the following day, with her hair properly dressed by Clara and with her new bonnet, she would look stunning.

Her mother merely said, "You'll do,"—but her eyes told a more generous and tender story.

Violet always imagined that one's wedding eve would be a uniquely special occasion, filled with nostalgic reminiscing and sound parental advice. She was rather annoyed that Joe and her father were treating it like a normal humdrum evening. Sitting in front of the fire, warming their stockinged feet on the rug mat, and drinking cider, they were discussing, instead of matrimonial matters, the likelihood of the Hayworths returning to Capford.

"Everyone wants 'im back," her father observed.

"With their new wealth, they can do what they want."

"Country life would be better for the children," said Mrs. Brookes with a knowing nod.

"I thought 'e were wedded to the work for the poor Londoners, but I had a chat with 'im in the lane today, and 'e said te work was nice, but that Londoners respond better to their own kind."

"Reverend Hayworth is our kind," put in Joe.

"That be true," agreed Mr. Brookes. "Seeing 'im today, wandering down the muddy lanes, 'e looked as 'appy as a sand-boy."

"And with those three children, Mrs. Hayworth looks so content now," said Violet. "She is a lovely mother."

"Of course she is," replied Mrs. Brookes. "We all knew she would be a great mother."

The conversation wandered from the Hayworths to Christmas, from Christmas to the weather, and from the bland to the mundane. Violet wanted her parents to retire to bed, but the more she wished them gone, the longer they talked.

Finally, Joe stood up. "I'd better be off—I've got an important job on t'morrow."

"That you 'ave, my lad. That you 'ave," said Mr. Brookes with a twinkle in his eye.

Violet followed him out, and they embraced on the doorstep.

"That is the last kiss I will give to Violet Brookes," said Joe.

Violet smiled up at her man. "I hope you will have plenty for Mrs. Joe Mason." A serious thought came to her, and she asked, "Do you think Reverend Hayworth will say 'You may now kiss the bride'?"

"I don't know. Somehow I doubt it—but I will anyway. I won't need anyone's permission to kiss my own wife."

"You wouldn't dare—not during the service."

"See if I don't!" And with a wink, he was gone.

CHAPTER 45

HER LITTLE BEDROOM FELT CROWDED when Molly and Clara arrived. With nervous giggles and some warmhearted teasing, they helped Violet prepare.

"Don't tug the strings so hard!" Violet gasped as Clara yanked her corset tighter. "I need enough breath to say my vows."

"Tie the strings up in knots what'll take Joe all night to undo," suggested Molly.

"Don't you dare!" Violet blushed. "He'd probably take his penknife to it. And corset ties are expensive; we can't be having that sort of expense."

"*That sort of expense*—Don't she talk like an old married woman already?"

Once Violet was arrayed in her beautiful wedding dress, Clara set to work on her golden locks. Various elaborate styles were attempted, but none were suitable for accommodating a bonnet.

"I can't have my bonnet perching on my head like a ridiculous after-thought," Violet moaned, beginning to feel anxious. "Hurry up, time's running out!"

"Let's have a nice, demure roll at the nape of your neck."

"Joe likes that," Violet said.

"Now, ya tell us!"

From downstairs, the clinking of cups and saucers and the hubbub of her sisters' excited voices could be heard. In the marital bedroom, Mr. Brookes grumbled about his top button and stiff collar.

"Leave it to me," ordered his wife. "And I suppose you want me to knot your tie too?"

"Of course. Why else did I marry you?"

Violet smiled wryly. How many times had she heard that one? It was all very well for her parents, but she hoped Joe would never become quite so predictable.

Molly and Clara pulled back the curtains and peered out the tiny bedroom window to watch the guests arrive. Their warm breath fogged up the cold glass as they elbowed each other for a better view.

"Here comes ponderous Mr. Grey, his wife on his arm, talking ten to the dozen."

"Why were they invited?" asked Violet, feeling put out.

Molly glanced back at Violet. "I suppose they had to be, seeing as Mrs. Grey volunteered to make some of the sandwiches."

Violet wanted to get a good view too, but it seemed undignified for a bride to show her face out of a bedroom window, and anyway, her outfit might get crushed.

"And here comes a gaggle of your nephews and nieces, almost colliding with the Greys," Clara said.

"Runny noses?"

"Can't see from here."

"There are your in-laws-to-be, trying to hide their disapproval behind friendly smiles," Molly teased.

"Here comes the minister, the man responsible for pronouncing you man and wife. His missus is looking very nice, with little Grace in a sweet little lace bonnet and dragging her dolly."

"Now Mr. and Mrs. Thorpe are opening the garden gate. She looks as stunning as ever." Molly quickly turned to Violet. "Nowhere near as stunning as you, I hasten to add."

"And here is the handsome bridegroom himself!" announced Clara, dramatically drawing the curtains together. "No peeping, Vi!"

"He's just turned on his heels and fled," teased Molly from behind the curtains.

The three girls giggled.

"Keep quiet," Violet said anxiously. "The guests are coming inside. You had better go down too."

Violet was pleased to be alone. She perched on the side of her bed and prayed. Her heart was full of gratitude to the Lord for His abundant mercy to her, and she beseeched Him for His presence to continue with her in the new phase of life she was about to begin.

After a while the hum of quiet conversation turned to silence. The creaking of the wooden stairs indicated that her father was coming up to escort her down. Violet stood up and straightened her skirts. Her composure almost faltered when she opened her door and saw the tender look in her father's eyes. He must have realised, for he gave her hand a gentle squeeze and said, "Let's show 'em, gal," before leading her down the narrow staircase.

Squeezing their way between the large, hooped skirts of their guests, Violet and her father reached the fireplace. There, waiting on each side of the coffee table were two smartly dressed men. Reverend Jack Hayworth looked formal and dignified, and Joe appeared abnormally official in his stiff new suit and shiny boots. As handsome as he looked, Violet preferred him in work clothes and an open-necked shirt. This fleeting thought vanished completely when he stepped forward to meet her and shot her a reassuringly cheeky grin. Joe would always be Joe, however trussed up in a formal suit!

Standing on the worn, faded hearth rug, surrounded by friends and family and in the sight of God, Joe and Violet exchanged their marriage vows. As predicted, after pronouncing them man and wife, Jack, being of an older generation, omitted the permission to kiss. But as promised, Joe took the matter into his own hands, pulled his bride to him, and landed a kiss on her lips. There was a moment of awkward silence when the gathered party did not know whether to clap or tut. Mr. Brookes saved the day by striking up the Doxology.

They nearly lifted the roof off the shepherd's cottage as, with one heart, the rustic voices sang out—

Praise God from whom all blessings flow,

Praise Him all people here below.

Praise Him above, ye heavenly host.

Praise Father, Son, and Holy Ghost.

CHAPTER 46

AFTER A RESPECTFUL PAUSE AT the end of the wedding ceremony, Mrs. Brookes scurried off to the kitchen to make tea for the guests. Her daughters duly followed. All except Violet, that is, for today and today only, she didn't have to lift a finger. All she had to do was stand by her husband's side and graciously receive the best wishes and congratulations their guests would bestow upon them.

"And my dear," Mrs. Grey burbled on, "always iron the sleeves of the shirt first."

Violet had failed to catch the first gem of advice, for she had been receiving the congratulations of Mrs. Thorpe.

"Thank you, Mrs. Grey, I will remember that," she replied.

"But not today!" Mrs. Thorpe said with grin. "No ironing today, Violet."

"I will try to resist the temptation," giggled Violet in return. But one look at Mrs. Grey's crestfallen face stopped her laughter. Mrs. Grey was aware she had been ridiculed, and Violet felt awful. On this happy day, she should be sharing her joy with everyone, even the Mrs. Greys of this world.

She flashed the older woman a reassuring smile. "I will remember your advice. Shirts can be tricky. I know from doing Pa's."

"Do them damp" was Mrs. Grey's parting advice as she headed toward the tea tray.

The rich fruit cake, which had been made in October and intended as a Christmas cake, was served on the Brookes' best china plates.

"I laced it with brandy once a week," explained Mrs. Brookes to those who were singing its praises.

"But, so did I!" exclaimed Mr. Brookes.

Everyone laughed and declared it the richest and most more-ish fruit cake ever tasted. Then, after a second cup of tea, the guests, knowing what was expected of them, congratulated the couple once again, complimented the cook, and took their leave one by one. The biting north wind had brought snow clouds to the sky and a few flakes starting to fall silently.

Violet could not let the Hayworths slip away without a special thank you. Pushing her way through the visitors, she caught up with Rebecca at the front door. The two women hugged each other warmly.

"Thank you for all your friendship and advice, Mrs. Hayworth."

"No," replied Rebecca, looking earnestly into her eyes, "thank you. You have been and always will be a dear friend. I really hope we can stay in touch, even when you emigrate."

"We must!"

"And it is wonderful to see you so happy, Violet," continued Rebecca as Violet picked up Grace, who had toddled to her.

Violet kissed the little girl's rosy cheeks.

"And you—so happy too. You're a lovely mother."

"We have both been greatly blessed." Rebecca smiled as she took Grace in her arms, her eyes brimming with joy and tears.

"Indeed, we have."

Once only the immediate family was left, the spare chairs were removed, and the atmosphere became less formal. The young Brookes and Mason children—who had sat still for too long—grabbed their coats and hats and ran excitedly into the garden to catch the steadily falling snowflakes. Violet and Joe retired to the parlour with the menfolk, while the ladies prepared the dinner. Mrs. Mason, who had been longing to help in the kitchen ever since the Doxology, grabbed the apron she had smuggled in and went to help. Mr. Mason gave his son a hearty slap on the back by way of congratulating him before making himself at home by the fire.

Soon the subject under discussion was logs and how long each type of wood should be seasoned. But Violet wasn't listening: her gaze turned from the roaring fire to the holly branches that decorated the room. They would be withered by Christmas, but young nephews could be relied on to gather more. Dried hydrangea heads decorated the mantelpiece. But in prize place on the dresser was a beautiful bunch of pink forced roses from Biggenden Manor's glass house, adding fresh colour to the rather sober floral arrangements. Their heady scent wafted toward Violet, mingling with the aroma of beef casserole and fresh bread from the kitchen. How wonderful everything was today!

Sitting at the table beside her husband, Violet found that the beef was succulent and the gravy rich. The company was agreeable and the cottage cosy. But try as she might to appreciate these things, she couldn't stop fiddling with her wedding band under the tablecloth, wondering how quickly she and Joe could make their escape without seeming rude. After all, people had said all they needed to say. Her brothers-in-law had teased her quite enough, and she had given them all the witty replies they had grown to expect. Glancing down at her left hand, she smiled. How mature and capable it looked! Joe noticed her action, captured her hand, and kissed it.

As soon as the Bible reading and prayer were over, Joe pushed back his chair. Violet's sigh of relief was almost audible.

"Well, I'd best get my wife home before it gets dark."

"Sundown isn't for a couple of hours," teased Agnes' husband as Violet quickly rose from her chair to stand by Joe.

"You can't be too careful when a woman is in finery like my beautiful bride is wearing today," replied Joe, smiling appreciatively at his wife.

Violet's heart sang as Joe put his arm around her waist and guided her to the door. Extracting themselves from the hugs and kisses of their families, and loaded up with a dish of hot casserole, a cottage loaf, and a package of wedding cake, they set off along the lane, now beautifully transformed with a light dusting of snow, to their snug stable attic and the life they would share together, no matter where it took them.

HISTORIC NOTES

To my Tonbridge readers who are appalled at my constant misspelling of their home town: Tonbridge was spelled with a *u* until, in the 1870s, it was considered confusing to have a Tunbridge and Tunbridge Wells in close proximity, and the name was changed to the present-day spelling. Of course, this was very controversial, and it was not totally accepted until the 1890s.

The story in Chapter 4 of the mother who lost so many children to diphtheria is true. The woman was my paternal great-grandmother. It was I, not Rebecca, who rubbed the lichen off the graves to read the inscriptions.

All other characters in this novel are purely fictional.

For more information about

Hannah Buckland

and

Dusters and Dreams

please contact:

hannahebuckland@gmail.com

For more information about
AMBASSADOR INTERNATIONAL
please visit:

www.ambassador-international.com
@AmbassadorIntl
www.facebook.com/AmbassadorIntl

If you enjoyed this book, please consider leaving us a review on Amazon, Goodreads, or our website.

Printed in Poland
by Amazon Fulfillment
Poland Sp. z o.o., Wrocław